In Other Words...
Murder

Mystery author and sometimes amateur sleuth
Christopher Holmes is now happily
(all things being relative)
engaged to be married
and toying with starting a new career
as a true-crime writer when he learns
a body has been discovered in the backyard
of his former home.

Then, to complicate matters,
Christopher's ex turns up out of the blue,
suggesting the body just may belong to
Christopher's former personal assistant.

It's life as usual at Chez Holmes.
In other words... Murder.

To David Warner and Marc Wittlif. Here's to having the courage to turn the page and go for your Happy Ever After.

IN OTHER WORDS...
MURDER

HOLMES & MORIARITY IV

JOSH LANYON

JUST JOSHIN'
PUBLISHING INC.

In Other Words... Murder
(Holmes & Moriarity 4)
July 2018
Copyright (c) 2018 by Josh Lanyon

Cover by L.C. Chase
Book design by Kevin Burton Smith
Editing by Keren "You Are My Hero" Reed
All rights reserved

ISBN: 978-1945802270
ISBN-10: 1945802278
Published in the United States of America

JustJoshin Publishing, Inc.
3053 Rancho Vista Blvd.Suite 116
Palmdale, CA 93551
www.joshlanyon.comT

This is a work of fiction. Any resemblance to persons living or dead is entirely coincidental.

CHAPTER ONE

"**M**urder."

"That's one word," J.X. objected.

"Hm?" I was studying the colorful travel brochures littering my lap and the raw-silk ivory comforter. *Walk in the footsteps of the Colosseum's ancient gladiators! Cruise canals in a golden gondola! Live La Dolce Vita!* read the cover of the brochure I held. I could practically feel the venerable blue of the Roman sky beneath my fingertips.

There was a bewildering array of options. Everything from private guided tours with personally tailored itineraries to culturally themed coach tours. We could do an eight-day Adriatic cruise or a fourteen-day grand tour by rail.

The only option not available to me was staying home.

"Kill. Slang. *Three* words," J.X. said. "First word starts with *D*."

It was eleven o'clock on a Friday night in late October, and we were cozily tucked up in our master bedroom at 321 Cherry Lane. J.X. was doing the *San Francisco Examiner* crossword, and I was figuring out our spring vacation plans. It really doesn't get much more domesticated than that.

"Oh. Do away with."

He was silent as his pencil scratched on paper. He made a disgusted sound. "Elementary, my dear Holmes."

I glanced at him. "Bad clues, my dear Moriarity. Do away with isn't slang. It's a phrasal verb."

"Right?" He regarded me for a moment, then nodded at the scattered brochures. "What do you think? What looks good to you?"

"I don't know. They're all pretty expensive."

"Money is no object."

I snorted. "It might not be the object, but it should be a consideration."

He got that dark-eyed, earnest look he always wore when applying the thumbscrews. "I *want* to do this for you, Kit. I don't care about the money. I want us to have this. We've never gone away on vacation together."

"Yeah, I know. Possibly averting an international incident."

His mouth quirked, but he said coaxingly, "Think about it. You and me. Hot, naked sex in a gondola."

I gave him a look of horror. "They have gondoliers, you know!"

He laughed. "Okay, then how about a gondola ride at sunset and candlelight dinner on the terrace of our private villa—and *then* hot, naked sex. Beneath the stars?"

I cleared my throat.

Spotting weakness in his prey, J.X. moved in for the kill. "I'm serious, though. Just you and me. Together. Doing whatever we want. No conference, no convention, no meetings with agents or editors, no deadlines. We could explore Rome's catacombs—or just visit a few museums and galleries. We could see the Pantheon and the Colosseum. We could go to Florence and see the Ponte Vecchio. Or spend a couple of days swimming with dolphins off the Isle of Capri. *Or* we could do nothing but sleep and eat and fu—"

"I get the picture," I said.

Despite the fact that I don't like to travel—*hate* to travel—a lot of that did sound appealing. I said, "Private villa, huh?"

"Whatever you want, Kit." He was suddenly serious, gaze solemn, the line of his mouth soft. Such a romantic guy. Especially for an ex-cop. Well, really, for anyone.

"It sounds...nice," I admitted. It sounded better than nice. Maybe even kind of lovely.

His smile was very white in the lamplight. He tossed the newspaper and pencil aside and drew me into his arms. We fell back against the mattress. The brochures whispered and crackled beneath us as his mouth found mine. He kissed me deeply, sweetly, whispered, "Maybe we could make it a honeymoon..."

My eyes popped open.

Before I could reply—not that I had a reply ready—the bedroom door pushed wide, and a small voice said, "Uncle Julie?"

J.X. sat up. "*Hey*, honey." He only sounded the tiniest bit flustered, plus got bonus points for not flinging me aside and springing completely off the bed as I had done to him the first few times this happened. "You're supposed to knock, remember?"

"I forgot." Gage said huskily, "I had a bad dream."

Gage was J.X.'s five-year-old nephew. Actually, it was more complicated than that, but the point was the kid was spending the weekend with us, as he did a couple of times a month.

"A bad dream, huh?" J.X. opened his arms, and Gage climbed into bed between us, snuggling against him. "We don't have bad dreams in this house."

I threw him a look of disbelief. He meant well, but come on. Everybody has nightmares. Him included.

"What did you dream?" I asked.

Gage rolled me a sideways look. Over the past four months we'd forged a truce, but he still largely took me on sufferance. Which was okay because frankly, I'm an acquired taste: best consumed with cream, sugar, and, yeah, a generous heaping of sufferance.

"Monsters," he said tersely.

"Hm."

"Monsters?" J.X. repeated thoughtfully. "There are no monsters here. This is a monster-free zone." He gave Gage a comforting squeeze. "You know what we do to monsters in this house?"

Gage shook his head, his gaze wary.

He was right to be wary because J.X. pretend-growled, "We *tickle* them," and pounced.

Gage squealed, and the two of them rolled around on the travel brochures, Gage wriggling and kicking—managing to land a few well-aimed blows at me in passing—before finally sitting up and resettling themselves against the pillows bulwarking the headboard.

J.X. winked at me. I shook my head resignedly.

"What you want to think about is all the fun we're going to have tomorrow when you and me and Uncle Kit—"

"Christopher," I interjected.

"—Uncle Christopher go to the Halloween Hootenanny."

Gage and I eyed each other in complete understanding. He knew I did not want to attend this Halloween Horrorama any more than he wanted me there. He knew, as did I, we neither of us had any choice. It was in these moments that we could actually walk a mile or two in the other's moccasins—though I admit fuzzy bunny slippers were a tight fit for my ethos.

J.X. continued to extol the ordeals—er, delights—of the day ahead, which was scheduled to conclude with the movie *Smallfoot* and dinner at Rosario's Pizzeria.

"So, no more bad dreams, okay?" he concluded.

"Okay," Gage said doubtfully. And then, "Can I sleep in here?"

J.X. wavered but stayed strong. "No, honey. You're getting too big to bunk in here. There's not enough room for all three of us. Uncle Christopher and I would fall right out onto the floor!"

And then the monster that lives under the bed would get us.

But see, I was getting fond of the little cheese mite because I didn't say it. Gage, however, had no doubt who the villain of the piece was. His bleak and beady gaze fell on me.

"What about a night-light?" I suggested.

His face brightened.

"Nnn." J.X. grimaced. "I don't think we want to get into that habit, do we?"

He seemed to be asking Gage, who looked to me like a kid who very much hoped they could maybe get into that habit.

"As habits go," I began. I remembered I was technically only an honorary uncle and should not be debating Gage's real uncle's child-rearing decisions in front of him. I shrugged, but couldn't help adding, "It's a big house, and it's still strange to him. I had a night-light when I was his age."

J.X. frowned. "Did you?"

"Sure."

"Night-lights can disrupt sleep patterns. Maybe that's why you have these bouts of insomnia."

"You know what disrupts sleep patterns? Being scared there's a monster watching you from the closet—or waiting under your bed for you to step onto the floor."

Gage gulped. J.X. exclaimed, *"Kit."*

I said hastily, "Not that monsters do that because monsters aren't real, and anyway, this is a monster-free zone. Like J.X., er, your uncle Julie said. *He's* the monster expert of the family."

Gage was still goggling at me, and J.X. was giving me the full-frontal unibrow in silent censure. Oh please. Like I hadn't voiced exactly what the kid was already thinking?

"Okay, I know what you need." I threw the bedclothes back and swung my legs over the side of the mattress, thereby demonstrating there were no monsters under *this* bed. "How about a nice warm cup of cocoa?"

Gage considered his options and nodded grudging approval. J.X. smiled, pleased that I was taking an avuncular interest, and suggested, "Make it three?"

"Sure. You want brandy in yours?"

"I want brandy," Gage offered.

"It won't mix with the sleeping pills," I said, and J.X. inhaled sharply. "Kidding," I told him.

He shook his head, though fondly. "Are you doing that Nutella thing again?"

"I can if you like."

"I like Nutella," Gage volunteered.

"That's a little rich before bed," Uncle Ebenezer Balfour objected.

I said, "Okay, a round of cocoa, one virgin and two nuts."

Gage giggled, J.X. looked undecided, and I departed posthaste.

I was thinking about the weirdness of my life, absently stirring the milk, Nutella, and four tablespoons of cream in a small saucepan, when the kitchen phone rang.

I tore my gaze from Gage's latest artistic efforts pinned to the refrigerator door—a frantic-looking stick figure was racing away from two other stick figures wearing Jack-o'-lantern heads. The Jack-o'-lantern people were brandishing what appeared to be very pointy knives.

Yikes. No wonder he didn't want to sleep alone.

Back when I lived on my own, I always used the answering machine to screen my calls. But J.X. was different. He liked to answer the phone and did so regularly. He looked forward to hearing from people. He enjoyed chatting. I don't think he even truly disliked telemarketers. I, on the other hand, agreed with Ambrose Bierce when he said the telephone was "an invention of the devil which abrogates some of the advantages of making a disagreeable person keep his distance."

It had taken a couple of months to teach him—J.X., not Ambrose—that I was rarely at home to random callers, even when I *was* at home, but eventually he got the message. Or at least permitted my callers to leave theirs.

But phone calls around the witching hour are never good news, and after the first startled-sounding ring, I picked up the handset.

"Hello?"

There was a hesitation—like someone had to pause to catch their breath. As slight as that sound was, I felt my heart drop through the cage of my rib bones and land with a *thump* on the black-and-white parquet floor. I too had to stop to catch my breath, as though picking up the phone had required monumental, heroic effort, and had I known who was on the other end, it would have. In fact, I *wouldn't* have answered.

"Christopher?" That deep baritone had once been as familiar as… Well, choose your favorite domestic simile. That voice had once been as familiar as J.X.'s because that was the role in my life the owner of the voice had played.

"David." My own voice was surprisingly flat, given the way emotions were zinging up and down my nervous system, emergency flares sparking into life—and promptly shorting out.

"I had a visit from the police a few hours ago." His voice was shaking. "They told me they found a body in our backyard. Our old backyard. *Your* backyard. You killed him, didn't you? *You killed Dicky!*"

CHAPTER TWO

I'm not often at a loss for words.

David's bizarre accusation, however, had me stumbling and stammering like an adolescent at a freshman dance. Did schools still organize events like dances? Or was it all about small-arms training and target practice these days?

"Are you— Have you— What are you— How can you— *What the hell do you mean*?" I finally got out.

"I *knew* Dicky didn't change his mind. You killed him, didn't you? Your ego couldn't take it. It wasn't love because the only person you've ever loved is Miss Butterwith. Oh, and maybe Inspector Appleby."

"*Me* kill Dicky? *Me?*"

"It sure as hell wasn't me!"

"Have you gone *crazy*?" I demanded. "I haven't seen Dicky since you and he slithered off into the sunset together a year ago."

"Don't pretend you don't—" I could practically hear the brakes squealing as he skidded to a stop. "Are you telling me you haven't talked to the police yet?"

"The *police*? Hell no, I haven't talked to the police. This is the first I've heard of any of this! You're saying you haven't seen Dicky for *how* long? And you're only now wondering what happened to him?"

"Of course I wondered before now. I thought he changed his mind!"

"I wouldn't blame him!"

Wow. Just like old times. We'd fallen right back into stride—or, more precisely, strident—without missing a beat. And all the while my gums were beating, I was trying to make sense of David's accusation. *A body in my old backyard?* Not just any body. Dicky's body? Impossible. Insane. It *couldn't* be true.

Except…if it wasn't true, why would David be calling me? I hadn't realized he even had my current contact info. I didn't have his. Could not imagine any circumstances where I'd want to talk to him. Including the current one.

I made an effort to sound less…well, to sound *less*, and asked, "You didn't think to phone him or drop by his place?"

My effort to take things down a few notches went unnoticed. David was still shouting as he replied, "Of *course* I did. He didn't answer his phone, and he'd already moved out of his place. He was supposed to stay with me while we house-hunted."

Impossible. This was *impossible*.

Was I dreaming? Had Gage kicked me in the head while he and J.X. were wrestling on the bed and I was now lying unconscious with X's for eyes? If so, this was a really weird dream. I hadn't thought of David, let alone Dicky, in months.

"Stop," I commanded. "Start at the beginning. When did the police contact you? What exactly did they say?"

"They showed up at my house this afternoon—" The rest of his words were interrupted as the receiver beeped a couple of times in my ear. I thought for a second the phone was dying, then realized it was our call-waiting service.

"Damn. Hang on." I pressed the Flash button.

I braced myself, expecting to hear the official tones of LAPD or SFPD, but instead got an earful of all-too-familiar semi-British accents. "Christopher! Bloody hell! David rang a few minutes ago to say they've discovered a body in the garden of your old house."

Rachel Ving was my long-time agent and partner in crime—sometimes literally my partner in crime. I now understood how David had hunted me down. Considering Rachel's opinion of him, the fact that she'd handed over my number meant she was taking this situation seriously.

"Talking to him now," I said tersely. "Hold, please." I pressed the Flash button again.

David was still speaking, so either he hadn't heard me ask him to hang on or, as ever, he was ignoring me.

"I missed all that," I said. "What exactly did the police say?"

"The people who bought the house from you were taking out some kind of gazebo you installed *after I left*—"

"A gazebo? There was no gazebo. I put in the pergola I'd been talking about building for the last ten years."

"It wasn't ten years! We only lived together ten years. You didn't even start talking about redoing the backyard until that last year."

"You're off the subject," I said. Unfairly, I admit. "The new owners took out the pergola and...what? Found a body?"

"Yes. They dug up the cement slab you put in—and found a man's body wrapped in a red blanket with a pillow."

A pillow? Was that so he could take a nap in the afterlife?

"I never owned a red blanket. Are they *sure* they got the right house?"

"Of course they got the right house. They found me, didn't they?"

"That doesn't mean anything if they got the wrong house."

"It's not the wrong house. How many houses on our street had a gazebo?"

"It wasn't a *gazebo*! If they're digging up a gazebo, they've got the wrong house."

"It's our street address!"

Oh. That. Okay. There was no arguing with street addresses. Even so.

"This can't be happening…" I didn't think I'd said it aloud, but David said accusingly, "Why not? It sounds exactly like the kind of thing you'd write."

Yes, it did.

"No it doesn't!" I protested. The smell of burning milk reached me. "Hell. Hold on." I pressed the Flash button and heard Rachel saying, "The timing could not be more fortuitous."

"The word is calamitous. Hold on, Rachel." I dropped the handset, grabbed the sizzling pan off the stovetop, and dropped it into the sink. I turned on the taps. The water hissed, and a small mushroom cloud of milk and Nutella formed over the basin.

"Everything okay?" J.X.'s voice inquired from behind me.

I spun guiltily. "Uh…well…no. Hang on a sec."

His eyebrows rose as I leaped back to the counter and picked up the phone. I pressed—well, I thought I pressed the Flash button again, but maybe not because the loud buzz of a dial tone met my ears.

Had David hung up on me? Or had I hung up on David?

"Shit!" Had that even been David? Maybe it was Rachel? I hit the Flash button a second time and got another loud dial tone.

What the hell? I began to thumb the Flash button in a manic tattoo, like a gamer in the final minutes of Crackdown 3.

"Oh, for God's sake!" I slammed the phone into the receiver. Then reslammed it—twice—to make sure it was resting properly.

"Ohhhh*kay.*" J.X. is pretty much unflappable. Which is both admirable and annoying. "What's going on, Kit?"

I turned to face him. His dark eyes were warm with concern. I opened my mouth, remembered We Are Not Alone, and glanced past him at the empty hallway. "Where's the...er, you know?"

"The...*er, you know*? You mean my nephew Gage?"

"Yes. The kid. Gage."

"He's watching TV in our room."

"Good. Hopefully it's a miniseries. That was David."

"David?" J.X.'s face changed. "Your David?"

"My former David. Yes."

J.X. scowled. "What does David want now?"

The *now* made it sound like David was constantly phoning up with lame excuses to see me, and nothing could have been further from the truth. If David had spared me a thought over the past year, it would have been only to gnash his teeth and curse my name for having gotten rid of his precious player piano in a yard sale. That had occurred in the first bitter stages of what more civilized persons refer to as "uncoupling." I preferred to refer to it as "utter fucking betrayal" and had planned accordingly.

I sucked in a deep breath—anticipating the need for extra oxygen—and the phone rang. I jumped as though I'd been holding the business end of a live wire, and J.X.'s scowl burgeoned into what Victorian novelists referred to as A Black Look.

"Let me get this," I said.

J.X. protested, "Kit, what the hell is going *on*?"

"One sec." I grabbed the phone and snapped, "Speak!"

"Speak?" Rachel snapped back. "Do you imagine I'm a poodle?"

"I picture you more as a miniature Pinscher, since you ask. What's going on, Rachel? I only got part of the story from David."

"I'm sure he only has part of the story. In any case, the gods are smiling on you, Christopher. You've been talking about turning to true crime, and a true crime has turned up in your very own garden."

Only Ving the Merciless could see my involvement in a possible homicide as an opportunity for career advancement, but I guess that's part of what makes her one of the best agents in the biz.

"First of all, that's not my garden. That's now the Kaynors' garden. Secondly, I haven't been talking about writing true crime. I told you I was *watching* a lot of true crime, and *you* suggested I try writing it."

"What's the difference?"

"The difference is I write fiction."

Rachel replied tartly, "Not lately you don't!"

Ouch. She was right, of course. I said shortly, "Possibly this is not the moment to discuss my career."

"*Do* inform me should that moment arrive," Rachel retorted.

Double ouch. "Can we get back to what David told you?"

"He was trying to locate you. He couldn't reach either of your parents, and your realtor is on holiday. He phoned me, explained the situation—in rather hysterical terms, I might add—and insisted he had to speak to you. What could I do? I *tried* to warn you, but he was too fast. I suppose there isn't any mistake about it?"

"I suppose there are *a lot* of mistakes about it," I said. "But since David and I got cut off midway through his call—"

"*Is* it possible it's Dicky?" Rachel sounded just a tad—uncharacteristically—worried.

"Are you asking me if I killed Dicky?"

J.X. made a sound unique to our acquaintanceship. My gaze veered to his, and I tried to silently communicate apology along with a request for more phone credits.

"Kit," he said in a warning tone.

"Not that I'd blame you if you *had* murdered the little sod," Rachel said, demonstrating one of the qualities that made her such a good agent.

"Yeah, but I didn't. And I don't believe it's Dicky buried in my old backyard."

"But then who could it be?"

"*Kit!*"

I threw my better half a guilty look and said hastily, "Rachel, we'll have to continue this later. J.X. wants a word."

"I'm going to need more than *a* word," J.X. said.

"Of course," Rachel said. "Just remember to take notes."

"No worries there. He usually repeats himself several times."

J.X. began to mutter darkly—with his sensual Spanish good looks, it's something he does quite well. Before J.X., I'd never known anyone who could make the three Rs—reproach, recrimination, and remonstrance—sound so sexy.

"I mean on the investigation! This is a godsend, Christopher. We mustn't waste it."

"Uh, righteo. I'll keep you posted," I said and clicked off. I turned to face J.X. "Hey, before you say anything—"

"Your former PA is buried in your backyard?"

"So again, before you say anything, I don't have the full story yet. What I do know is that when the new homeowners dug up the pergola in the backyard—which is annoying as hell because that structure was *beautiful, especially with the honeysuckle vines growing over it*—they discovered a body. It—he—is male, and he was wrapped in a red blanket. For the record, I never owned a red blanket."

"You owned the house, though."

"Well, yes."

"And the body has been identified as your former PA Dicky Dickison? The twink who ran off with David?"

"I don't know if the body has been formally identified, because I spoke to David, not the police. David thinks it's Dicky."

J.X. said in a protesting kind of tone, "How would that be possible?"

I shook my head. "I don't see how it could be. Unless David killed him and buried him in our backyard—and why would he?"

J.X. was gazing at me in what seemed to be wordless alarm. Like me, he is not often without words, and I recoiled as I realized what he must be thinking.

"You don't believe *I*—"

His eyes widened. His grim expression changed into one of affectionate exasperation. "What? Of course not. Is that a serious question? *Honey.*" He put his arms around me. "I'm sorry. I realize this has got to be a shock."

Funny thing. Until J.X. pulled me into that hug and started murmuring sympathy, I hadn't felt particularly shocked—I'd been too busy with the fight-or-flight response David always triggered in me. But yeah, come to think of it, this *was* kind of a shocking thing. A dead body discovered in my old backyard? David accusing me of murder?

I said, "My God. I guess the police are going to want to talk to me."

"Yes," J.X. said. "I'm surprised they haven't already. When did all this happen? When was the body discovered?"

"I don't know." I swallowed. "Do you think they're really going to view me as a suspect?"

J.X. bit his lip. As mannerisms go, not terribly reassuring. He said, "How soon after David left did you build the pergola?"

"I don't remember. Not long." I added defensively, "I was trying to keep busy. Anyway, it's not like I built the pergola myself. I wasn't out there laying concrete and raising timbers. I hired a landscaping company to do the actual construction."

"Good point." J.X. looked thoughtful. "When was the last time you saw Dicky?"

Remembering that period of my life was more painful than I expected. I freed myself from J.X.'s arms and went to clean the burned chocolate from the pan in the sink. With my back turned to him, I was able to say briskly, "The week after David left. He came to ask for his final paycheck."

"Wow. That guy had nerve."

"Yep. He did." I grabbed a Brillo pad and ferociously scoured the blackened bits at the bottom of the pan.

"What happened?" At the look I threw him, J.X. added quickly, "I know what *didn't* happen. You didn't kill him. But what occurred during that meeting? What was said?"

I made myself think back. "I paid Dicky and told him not to expect a reference letter." That was the *Reader's Digest* version. I'd also told him he was an ungrateful little bastard, that cheaters never prospered, and that he was going to get exactly what he deserved. But maybe it was better to keep that to myself. It had not been a pleasant encounter.

Dicky had been defensive and self-righteous. He'd told me I was a pain in the ass to work for and that by neglecting David, I had brought their twin defections on myself.

Even so, I hadn't wished Dicky dead. In fact, as time had passed, I'd pretty much sort-of-almost-though-not-entirely forgiven him. Partly— maybe mostly—that was due to J.X. resurfacing in my life. But partly… Dicky had been young and inexperienced, and I knew firsthand how charming and persuasive David could be. I had *not* forgiven David, but I had never wanted him dead either.

If I *had* wanted either of them dead, I wouldn't have bungled it by burying their bodies in my own backyard. You didn't have to be a fan of Hitchcock—or true-crime shows—to know that never worked out well.

"You never saw him again?" J.X.'s voice recalled me to the present.

"No."

"Did he cash the check?"

I looked up in surprised relief. "He did, yeah. I do remember that. He cashed the check right away. I think he was afraid I'd change my mind."

"There's a point in your favor right there."

"I guess so, yes. Unless someone can prove he returned to the house a second time—but why would he? He got what he wanted."

J.X. suddenly smiled, his teeth very white in the silky frame of his Van Dyke beard. He moved to take me into his arms once more, and I didn't resist.

"I'll tell you what I think, Kit. Whoever that is under your old pergola, it's not Dicky. I think Dicky wised up and passed on David."

"Yeah, but then whose body *is* it?"

"I'm guessing no one known to you. It's more likely one of your neighbors took advantage of your landscaping project and dumped their own problem into that hole in the ground. We had a case like this when I was on the force. I think you'll talk to the detectives and clear up any concerns they might have, and that will be that."

I said doubtfully, "You think?"

"I do, yeah." He winked, kissed me lightly. "Now why don't we fix a new batch of your special spiked hot chocolate, return my *er, you know* Gage to his own bed, and get back to practicing for our vacation."

"Practicing what?" I asked blankly.

J.X. offered a slow, sexy grin.

CHAPTER THREE

Cops. Before Breakfast. Before coffee even.

Now why did that sound so familiar?

Anyway, it wasn't before coffee. It was during coffee, which I was having while J.X. and Gage fixed blueberry-chocolate-chip pancakes. A process which entailed a lot of "testing" chocolate chips, giggling—on Gage's part—and singing loudly—and badly—with the Black Keys.

"'Strange times are here,'" warbled Gage.

J.X. echoed energetically and tunelessly, "'Strange times are here.'"

And so they were. But it had been a pleasant morning, following a pleasant—despite the odds—evening, until LAPD Detectives Dean and Quigley turned up on our doorstep promptly at nine o'clock.

Dean was a tall, willowy brunette, who looked more like a TV star than an actual cop. Granted, J.X. looked more like a TV star than an actual writer, and he was both a writer and an ex-cop. Appearances are often deceptive.

Quigley also looked like a cop on television, but starring in a very different kind of show. A show with less budget and lower ratings. Possibly straight to cable. He was shorter, squatter, redder, and a lot older than his partner. He had a mustache like Friedrich Nietzsche near the end, and, even before he opened his mouth, conveyed a similar aura of unpredictability.

"Is there somewhere we can speak privately, Mr. Holmes?" Dean inquired after badges had been flashed and the initial introductions were out of the way.

J.X. threw me a lopsided but encouraging smile, and ushered Gage back to the kitchen. I led the way to the living room.

I noticed Dean and Quigley exchanged looks as they glanced around the long room with cheerful, creamy-yellow walls and ivory decorative crown molding and corner pieces. The muted, rich tones of the Persian rug, elegant marble fireplace, and intricate etched glass and brass chandeliers were just a few of the house's beautiful little touches. But the silent communication between LA's finest was not admiration for our home decor. *Money,* Dean observed. *Used to getting away with murder,* concluded Quigley.

"You have a lovely home," Dean commented. Somehow, it didn't sound like a compliment.

"Thank you," I said. "Can I offer you coffee?"

Dean refused the offer of coffee with the air of one rejecting a bribe. Quigley accepted with a grin reminiscent of Foxy Loxy receiving an invitation from Chicken Little, and requested cream and sugar.

When I returned to the living room with the coffee, I found them in whispering conference in front of the built-in case that shelved my vintage collection of books on primitive criminology and obsolete investigative procedures.

"*How to Read Character: A New Illustrated Hand-Book of Phrenology and Physiognomy,*" Dean said to me. "Interesting choice of reading material."

"That? It's a little out-of-date," I said. The book had been published in 1869.

Quigley scanned the shelf, read aloud, "*Criminal Anthropology, Criminal Sociology, How to Read Faces: Nature's Danger Signals. Here's a good one: Evidence of Insanity in the Brains of Criminals.* Ever read that one, Dean?"

"No," Dean said.

"I guess you consider yourself an expert in criminal investigation, Mr. Holmes?"

I handed him his cup of coffee. "I guess you're being ironic, Detective Quigley?"

He looked wary. Fair enough, but did they really think I had some peculiar fixation on crime à la Hannibal Lecter, as revealed by my quirky reading habits?

Dean returned to the beige chesterfield sofa and said briskly, "Let's get down to it, shall we?"

Quigley slurped his coffee in apparent agreement and sauntered over to join her.

I've been interviewed by the police a few times, and these encounters always follow a certain pattern. They start with the easy questions and then move on to the more awkward topics such as...*why didn't you call us sooner?*

It doesn't matter how fast you call them, the cops always want to know why it wasn't sooner. As though prescience is one's civic duty.

"We had some trouble tracking you down, Mr. Holmes," Dean said crisply when the three of us were seated again. "Can I ask why you neglected to update your DMV records with your new address?"

I stared at her in surprise. "I...meant to. I don't drive much up here, and...I don't know. I just keep forgetting. It's not like it's expired or I moved to a different state."

Her perfectly shaped brows rose in open skepticism. "You weren't attempting to go off the grid?"

"What? Me? No. Why would I? I had my mail forwarded here. I've changed most of my credit cards. That's not exactly going to ground."

"Maybe you didn't want to get called for jury duty?" Quigley suggested. He winked at his partner and took another noisy mouthful of coffee.

Well, who wanted to be called for jury duty? But that wasn't the reason. The reason was maybe slightly more complicated and something I hadn't explored until that moment. Changing the address on my license somehow felt final, irrevocable, in a way forwarding my mail or even updating my credit cards had not.

To-have-and-to-hold final. From-this-day-forward irrevocable.

I mean, J.X. and I were living together, and we talked about making it official, but practicing energetically for a possible honeymoon aside, neither of us had actually popped the question. That first of many inevitable questions.

Regathering my thoughts, I said, "No. It wasn't a conscious thing. I intended to update my license. We've been…busy getting settled in."

Dean pounced on this. "You've been busy, all right. We understand four months ago you found a body in one of your moving crates."

I sat up straighter. "You've been busy yourselves. Yes, I did find a body. And that matter has been resolved to the satisfaction of SFPD and everybody else. That was nothing to do with…"

This.

She arched her brows politely.

But of course it had nothing to do with this, and not because I knew what *this* was. I *hadn't* had anything more to do with this than I had with that. And if trying to formulate that response in my head was complicated, I couldn't even imagine putting it into words.

Luckily, I didn't have to. Quigley said, "Nothing is ever resolved to the satisfaction of everyone. Your ex believes you knocked off your formal personal assistant and buried him in your backyard. He didn't come right out and say it, but it's obvious that's what he thinks."

So much for the easy questions. I gaped at them. "Why would he? Why would I?"

Dean said, "Deflection—answering a question with another question—is a common tactic."

This was not like any police interview I'd ever experienced. But then I'd never been interviewed as a serious suspect before. Or even as a flippant suspect.

I said, "A common tactic for whom? I realize your attitude is jaundiced by your line of work, but most people don't kill their cheating spouses or romantic rivals. Most people just divvy up the CDs and change the locks, which is what I did. And why the hell would I kill Dicky of all people? Wouldn't it be more likely I'd kill David?"

Dean said, "Maybe you hoped with your romantic rival out of the way, David would return to you."

I spluttered, "I wouldn't have had David back on a silver serving platter with an apple stuffed in his maw—or elsewhere." I could see by their expressions that was perhaps more frank than wise, but there's something really insulting about being suspected of murder. Okay, no. Not being suspected of murder. Being suspected of being so insecure, you'd commit murder in hopes of winning back the lame-ass boyfriend who dumped you. *That's* insulting.

I added more reasonably, "Anyway, even if I were nuts enough to commit murder, I'd have to be an idiot to bury someone in my own backyard."

From the kitchen I could hear the homey sounds of J.X. and Gage still busy with their breakfast preparations. The scent of coffee and sausages and buttermilk pancakes spreading across a hot griddle drifted into the living room. Quigley's stomach growled. He shrugged at Dean's look. My own stomach was in knots.

Dean said, "According to your ex, you write mysteries for a living. In the mysteries I've read, murderers always do completely illogical and idiotic things in an effort to throw law enforcement off the track. Perhaps you believed you were being clever in doing something completely reckless."

Great. An embittered mystery reader. Like I hadn't had enough of those in my life.

Quigley said, "It wouldn't be something you necessarily planned, but let's say an argument broke out, you wacked your former employee with something like, oh, maybe a bookend, and then you noticed the nice, deep hole in your backyard where the new pergola was being built."

I didn't think he'd accidentally lit on the idea of using a bookend as a weapon, and my unease—and hostility—grew.

"I don't know for a fact construction on the pergola had started yet."

"How convenient."

I spluttered and then said coldly, "Do you actually do this for a living?"

Coldly works better when you don't begin by spluttering.

"Do you own a firearm, Mr. Holmes?" Dean inquired right back at me.

"No. I don't." That was interesting news. I studied them. "So the victim was shot?"

"We'll know more once we have the ME's report."

Uh…sure. But, thanks to sixteen years of writing Miss Butterwith and Mr. Pinkerton's adventures, even I knew enough to recognize a bullet hole when I saw one. Don't tell me these two didn't know for sure.

I'm sure my skepticism showed because Dean changed the subject. "When was the last time you saw Mr. Dickison?"

Or maybe that was still the same subject. In either case, I was ready. I slid the copy of Dicky's final check—front and back—across the coffee table. I'd printed it out that morning in preparation for their visit.

Detective Dean picked the paper up and examined it. She handed it without comment to Quigley.

I said, "Dicky showed up the Monday after David moved out. He asked for his final paycheck, and I gave it to him. You can see that he cashed it the same day."

"You never saw him again?" Quigley squinted at the printout.

"I never saw him again. For the record, I don't believe that body belongs to Dicky."

Dean looked interested. "Who do you think was buried in your backyard?"

"I have no idea."

"If Dickison is not buried in your backyard, what's your theory as to what happened to him?"

"Again, no idea. Maybe he got cold feet. Maybe he got a better offer. As I recall, he had an active social life." I added, "Maybe David killed him."

I didn't really think David had killed Dicky; that was simply payback for accusing me. Old habits die hard.

Dean and Quigley exchanged looks again. Quigley said, "What's his motive?"

I shrugged. "David wasn't used to rejection."

Dean jumped on this angle. "Was your ex violent? Did he ever assault you? Did he ever threaten you?"

"He was loud. We both were. As I'm sure the neighbors can testify." I sighed. "I don't really think David killed Dicky. Like I said, I don't believe that body belongs to Dicky. It could have been there for years. Originally there was a gardening shed in that part of the yard. So…"

"You were the legal homeowner for fourteen years, correct?"

"Yes."

"So that would be going back quite a way."

"Yes. It would."

"Meanwhile, no one has heard from Mr. Dickison for nearly a year."

"Well, I haven't heard from him. David apparently hasn't heard from him. That doesn't mean no one has. Hasn't."

"Do you have contact information for Mr. Dickison?"

"I used to. If I do, it's lost in a box somewhere. It sounds like it would be out-of-date anyway."

"We would appreciate it if you could make an effort to locate that information."

"I can try."

She smiled, but it didn't reach her eyes. "Within the next day or so."

"Okay."

I didn't think they were out of questions, but they chose to end the interview there. They thanked me for my cooperation and departed with a promise to be in touch.

As I bolted the front door behind them, J.X. appeared in the hallway. There was a smudge of flour on his cheekbone. On him it was almost dashing.

He asked quietly, "You okay?"

"Splendid."

He grimaced at my tone and nodded toward the kitchen, where Gage and the Black Keys continued to dominate the airwaves. "I couldn't hear much. It couldn't have been too bad. You're still a free man."

"Ha. Funny. There wasn't much to hear. This was a fact-finding mission. They weren't sharing information, that's for sure."

"They probably don't have a lot of information to share."

"Yeah, well. Whoever the victim was, he seems to have been shot. I'm not sure if they deliberately let that slip or not."

"Good," J.X. said with bloodthirsty cheer. "That means they're going to have trouble connecting the murder weapon to you, assuming they continue to regard you as a suspect."

"I don't think they missed the significance of the fact that Dicky lived to cash his final paycheck, but they also didn't seem to regard it as a Get Out of Jail Free card."

"It's way too early to rule anybody out." I think he intended it to be comforting, but I'd have preferred to be automatically ruled out by virtue of obviously being innocent.

J.X. studied me for a moment. "This is routine procedure, Kit. You know that."

"I know."

"Don't let it rattle you."

"Do I look rattled?"

He bit his lip, clearly torn between diplomacy and his natural—distressing—inclination to always tell the truth. "Just don't let it spoil our day, okay?"

"No, no," I assured him. "I believe the Halloween Hootenanny will accomplish that."

J.X. chuckled and looped his arm around my shoulders, hauling me in to nuzzle the side of my face. "Come on. Let's have breakfast. The hootenanny is going to be more fun than you imagine."

The hootenanny is going to be more fun than you imagine. Now there was a phrase I never expected to hear in connection with myself.

I sighed. "Well, it could hardly be less." I kissed him back.

* * * * *

Sponsored by the Haight Ashbury Street Fair, the 13th Annual Halloween Hootenanny was held at the skate park in the Stanyan and Waller Street cul-de-sac. By eleven in the morning, the event was already packed. By eleven-thirty, I was ready to leave.

Needless to say, I was outvoted, and we continued to mill around with the throngs of costumed kids and parents—some of the grown-ups also in costume (although this *was* San Francisco, so who could say for sure)—wandering from booth to booth to enjoy the games and contests and performers.

This year's theme was Clowns and Carnivals, and there were a disconcerting number of pint-sized Pennywises as well as the occasional benign Bozo.

Ten minutes in, Gage, dressed like a miniature Zorro, had his face painted in the Day of the Dead style, which was probably culturally inappropriate, but what do I know? My family background is Swiss and English. Anyway, the kid looked very cute in a gruesome-child-corpse kind of way—which, IMHO, would be his fate if he continued to eat everything in our path. On top of the pancakes he'd had for breakfast not more than an hour earlier, Gage consumed popcorn, peanuts, cotton candy, and a premonition-green slushie before his uncle finally called a halt.

"We're going for pizza later, remember?"

Gage did remember but clearly still felt thwarted, which he vented by jabbing me a couple of times with his rubber sword.

"Ow," I said, parrying his jabs with my hand.

"*Hey.* Not cool," J.X. intervened. He frowned. As looks of displeasure went, that was a formidable one. "*Not* okay."

The ghastly stitched outline of Gage's mouth turned downward in embarrassed hurt at being scolded in public, and I felt an unfamiliar affinity—as well as the equally unfamiliar desire to earn uncle points by saying *nah, never mind, no problem*. I recognized in time that undercutting J.X.'s authority was not okay, and equally not okay was becoming Gage's favorite outlet for frustration, and instead settled for looking grave while glancing around uncomfortably for some useful distraction.

My gaze happened to light on a group of clowns standing near the photo booth. Two of them were, of course, variations on Pennywise—complete with Queen Elizabeth I hair and pointy fangs—a third one was an impressively vintage Pipo de Clown, and the others had no identifying marks or characteristics other than being...clowns. With them was a man not in costume. He was attractive enough: average height, slender, curly brown hair. Something about his smiling profile caught my attention. My heart skipped a beat. I looked more closely.

Was that—? He looked an awful lot like…

It couldn't be.

No. It was impossible. He was in jail, awaiting trial.

As though feeling my gaze, the curly haired man turned his head and stared directly at me.

The sounds and sights of the street fair seemed to fade away into a stark, echoing silence. There was no one on the street—in the world—but me and the guy across the way.

He did not smile. Did not look away. Did not so much as blink.

It *was* him. There was no mistake. It was Jerry Knight.

My biggest fan in the world.

The man who had tried to kill me.

CHAPTER FOUR

Granted, I had tried to kill Jerry back.

Had he seen me? Was this a coincidence, or was he following us? What the hell was he doing out of prison?

"You feel okay?" J.X. asked behind me, and I jumped.

I threw him a quick, harassed look. "What?"

His smile faded, his eyes narrowed in warm concern. "You look sick, Kit. What's wrong?"

I stared at him, but it wasn't J.X. I was seeing. "I-I think I just spotted Jerry Knight."

"What?"

"Jerry Knight. He's here."

"That's not possible. It must be someone who looks like him."

"I know, but I think it was him."

J.X.'s face took on a hard, tight look as he scanned the crowd around us. "Are you sure?"

"Yes. He was over there. *Wait.* Don't be obvious." I stole a peek at the group near the photo booth, but now there was no sign of Jerry. "He was standing there with those clowns."

J.X. glanced automatically at a group of teenaged boys jostling each other near a hot-dog stand, and I said, "Not *those* clowns. The other clowns. The real clowns."

"The *real* clowns," J.X. repeated in a funny voice.

I jerked my head in the direction of the clowns. "I don't see him now, but I'm positive…" I glanced at J.X. and then did a double take. "He's not out, right? He couldn't afford bail."

"Right," J.X. said. He definitely looked strange.

"But?"

"Nothing. Kit, Izzie would make sure we got a heads-up if Knight was out on bail."

Izzie was J.X.'s former partner at SFPD, and they were still good friends. Izzie would certainly give us a heads-up if he learned Jerry had been bailed out—but what if he didn't know?

"In theory, yes. But I've been watching *Obsession* on Investigation Discovery, and you would be horrified to learn how many times the system fails to protect victims of stalkers." I surveyed the crowd, trying to spot Jerry. Where had he gone? I had only looked away for a second.

"Kit—"

"I've seen at least three episodes in the first season alone."

"You've *got* to stop watching that stuff. Anyway, Knight is more than a stalker. He's being held on Homicide and Attempted Homicide charges."

I nodded, only half listening. Jerry had completely disappeared, seemingly having melted into the milling crowd. That was the advantage of looking so abnormally…normal.

"I think we should talk to those clowns," I said.

"Why?"

I threw J.X. a look of surprise. "Because it seemed like he knew them."

"You don't think maybe they were just being friendly? As part of their job?"

"No. Well, I don't know, but it didn't look like that to me. They greeted him like they knew him."

J.X. said nothing. I couldn't quite read his expression.

"What's wrong?" I asked.

"Nothing!" J.X. sucked in a sharp breath. "All right. I'll do it," he said. "You keep an eye on Gage."

I kept half an eye on Gage, who was taking his frustrations out on some kind of knock-the-hell-out-of-the-Jack-o'-lanterns game, but most of my attention was on J.X. Even at a distance I could see he wasn't getting anywhere. There was a lot of shoulder shrugging and shaking of red, blue, and green heads going on.

"Look, Uncle Christopher!" shrieked Gage as several orange-painted rolls of toilet paper went sailing. "*Look!*"

"Great," I said. ·

J.X. strode back to where I waited. He shook his head. "Dead end. Three of them denied talking to anyone. The fourth one claimed someone came up and asked for directions to the restrooms, but he didn't know the guy and didn't keep track of where he went."

"A likely story."

J.X. said patiently, "It *is* a likely story."

"Take my picture!" cried Gage. "Uncle Julie, take my picture!"

"He can't remember someone he spoke to four minutes ago?" I protested.

J.X. pulled out his phone and snapped a string of photos of Gage beaming among the scattered square heads. "Kit…"

"The thin polka-dot line," I said.

"Honey—"

"Don't use that diplomatic tone. I know what I saw. Who I saw." Honesty compelled me to add, "I think."

"Knight's a common physical type. Average height, average build, brown hair. Isn't it possible you maybe mistook someone who looks like him for him?"

"No."

But yes, of course I thought it was possible. And with each minute that passed without catching sight of my number-one fan and former stalker, I thought it was even likely. Except I couldn't quite discount that moment of instinctive, horrified recognition. It was pure *Animal Kingdom*. Intraspecies recognition.

J.X. glanced back at the remaining trio of clowns, who were staring our way. He shuddered.

I studied him more closely. "You okay? You seem…"

Shaken, frankly.

He said tersely, "I don't like clowns."

"Does anyone *really* like clowns? I wonder."

"No, I mean…it's…" He cleared his throat.

"It's what?"

"It's kind of a thing with me." He met my eyes, looked away. His expression was almost…stricken.

Enlightenment dawned. See? I *knew* he couldn't be perfect. It was actually a relief to hear this.

"You mean like a-a phobia?"

He nodded glumly. "It *is* a phobia. It's called coulrophobia."

Whoa. J.X. had actually gone to the trouble of researching his *bête noire*. Or in his case, his Beppi noire.

I tried to be comforting. "If it's got its own phobia name, it means a lot of people have the same reaction."

J.X. winced. "Please. I know how ridiculous this is. I know it's a cliché, but…"

"Cliché or not, fear is fear." Yeesh, I sounded like the flip side of one of those schmaltzy *love is love* memes. Only instead of a rainbow, my meme would have lightning bolts and a graphic indicating fried wires.

J.X. said irritably, "And there isn't any reason for it. It's not like I had a bad childhood experience at the circus or an evil clown showed up at my birthday party. I've just always found clowns…disturbing."

"You don't have to explain. A lot of people don't find clowns funny. Me included."

"There's a difference between not finding them funny and…what I experience when I see a group of clowns."

I regret to say I laughed. I did manage to turn it into a cough at the last moment, so it came out sounding like I'd swallowed my gum. Not that I chew gum, and not that I'm completely insensitive—I hope—but compared to seeing the guy who tried to kill you loose on the street, J.X.'s fear of clowns seemed kind of…frivolous.

I mean, it's one thing to see a lone clown standing by the road in the middle of nowhere. *That's* creepy. But this was a street fair with the theme Carnivals and Clowns. J.X. *had* to have known what to expect when he dragged us here.

I tried, though. I tried to find something sympathetic to say. "Sure. Of course. And all these weird clown sightings we hear about on the news can't have helped."

He muttered something and stared bleakly into the distance.

I said, "I...guess it must have made your career in law enforcement challenging."

J.X. swung his head back in my direction and looked at me like I was crazy. "Uh...how many crimes do you imagine are circus-centric?"

I opened my mouth, but Gage interrupted with exhortations to photograph him stabbing toilet-paper heads. J.X. seemed only too relieved at this change of subject, and I was able to return to watching the crowd for the moment Jerry might leap out at me.

Which, for the record, did not happen.

If Jerry was at the street fair, he was watching us from afar. Afar enough that I couldn't spot him, and I spent a lot of time looking and worrying about it. In fact, I'd have preferred that we left the fair immediately, but since I'd been pushing for that from the moment we arrived, my wishes were not taken seriously.

We strolled around some more. Gage tried his prowess at knocking down a variety of inanimate objects, and J.X. coaxed me into having our "portrait" live-sketched by one of the street artists. It turned out all right. I looked a little wild-eyed, but J.X., as ever, looked handsome and stoic. He vowed to frame the thing and hang it in his office.

Finally, *finally* the delights of the Halloween Hootenanny were exhausted for the year, and we departed to catch a matinee showing of *Smallfoot*.

I don't remember much of the film. I believe it was cute and probably amusing. Gage laughed a lot. J.X. occasionally chuckled. He was holding my hand throughout the film—something David and I had never done: hold hands at the movies—and though he was not saying anything, I could feel his silent reassurance. *It's okay. It's okay...*

And if it were up to J.X., it would be okay. But it was not up to him.

If Jerry really was out on bail, I couldn't help feeling that it would *not* be okay.

After the movie we continued on to Rosario's Pizzeria, which was Gage's second favorite place to dine.

His first favorite place was the home of Ronald McDonald, the Hamburger-Happy Clown, and I now felt I had insight into J.X.'s antipathy toward that relatively harmless establishment. But maybe tonight it had nothing to do with clowns. Maybe it had everything to do with me being along for the ride.

One thing I like about J.X.—well, there are many, many things I like about him—but one thing I especially like is the fact that he understands some of us need adult beverages with our kiddie meals. And by adult beverage I don't mean wine or beer. I mean G&T and keep 'em coming.

Okay, two G&Ts. And maybe an after-dinner coffee drink.

We were having our after-dinner coffee, and Gage was putting his final touches on his placemat-in-Crayola masterpiece (which would doubtless find its way to our refrigerator door), when Izzie finally returned J.X.'s earlier phone call.

I could tell by J.X.'s expression the news was not good.

"When was he released?" J.X. asked. This was followed by what felt on my end like a lengthy explanation. "Jesus Christ," J.X. muttered.

His eyes, dark with anger and apology—not that he had anything to apologize for—met mine.

I grimaced and considered ordering another drink.

J.X. restrained himself to a few terse comments, thanked Izzie and apologized for interrupting his weekend, before he finally ended the call.

"So he *is* out," I said.

J.X. nodded. "He's been out since the fifteenth."

I was trying to match his straightforward tone, but that got me. "That's almost two weeks!"

"I know."

"For God's sake."

His eyes grew still darker and more apologetic. "There's no excuse. We should have been notified. It's just sometimes things fall through the cracks."

"Crack? This is kind of a fissure. This is more like that two-mile-long, thirty feet deep *crack* in Pinal County, Arizona."

"I know, Kit. It's troubling."

"*Troubling?* Yes. It is troubling. It is fu—" My gaze fell on Gage, tip of his tongue poking from between his teeth as he concentrated on getting every layer of his rainbow solid black. "—reaking terrifying."

"His being there today could have been a coincidence."

"Seriously?"

"I know it seems unlikely, but he'd have to be—"

"Crazy?" I suggested. "Check. Obsessed? Check. Homicidal? Check."

"Yes. Kit—"

"How did he get out, anyway? He couldn't make bail. How is it he's walking around the streets of San Francisco?"

"He's apparently formed a relationship with some woman who began writing him while he was incarcerated. She came up with the money."

"She came up with a million dollars in bail money?"

"She came up with the required ten grand."

"He shouldn't even be eligible for bail, given that the facts are evident and the presumption great."

This was an old rant—er, topic—and J.X. sighed. "I know Knight's conviction seems inevitable to you, and I think he will *be* convicted, but he's still permitted due process."

"*Whatever!* Who is this woman who bailed him out?"

"Her name's Violet Sanderson."

"Violet Sanderson," I repeated. "Why is that name familiar to me?"

"I don't know. It isn't familiar to me."

"Violet Sanderson sounds like a turn of the last century lady sleuth."

J.X. shook his head. "All I know is she's been writing him letters almost daily and eventually came up with the bail money."

"Hybristophilia," I said glumly. It seemed to be our day for bandying phobias about.

"*Gesundheit.*"

"You know. Bonnie and Clyde Syndrome. Seemingly normal people who are sexually or romantically attracted to criminals. There are all kinds of reasons behind the attraction, but the bottom line is, some women really do like bad boys. Very bad boys."

"It seems Ms. Sanderson is one of them. Listen, we'll file a restraining order against Knight first thing Monday morning."

Gage piped up in a clear, carrying voice. "What's a restraining order?"

That earned a few interested looks from our fellow diners.

I said, "It's what happens to kids who talk with their mouths full."

Gage opened wide to demonstrate exactly how full his mouth was.

J.X. frowned. "That's disgusting."

And, of course, both Gage and I laughed, because as much as I hated to encourage the little hooligan, there was something entertaining about J.X.'s occasional attempts at severity.

Gage and I exchanged looks of smug fellowship, and I did my best to put aside all thoughts of my impending doom for the duration of our evening out.

It was not quite seven when we returned home to Cherry Lane.

J.X. unlocked the front door, Gage darted inside, and we followed, turning lights on as we went.

"...to spoil your weekend with this..."

I tensed at the sound of a woman speaking in the kitchen, but then realized the voice was leaving a message on our answering machine.

"...Legally, I don't think they have a leg to stand on, but a lawsuit is a lawsuit. Maybe if you could talk to them..."

I recognized the voice as belonging to Rina, the realtor who had handled the sale of my Chatsworth home, and I squeezed through the kitchen doorway ahead of Gage and J.X. and picked up the phone.

"Hey, Rina. It's Christopher."

"Oh, thank goodness!" The relief in her tone carried up the length of the state. "*Thank goodness* you're there. I can't tell you what a shock this whole thing has been. A dead body!"

"I know. I'm a little shocked too."

"But then you write mysteries."

"I don't usually…" I was going to say *live them*, but the fact of the matter was, over the past year, life had sometimes been alarmingly meta.

"I've been selling real estate for twenty years, but this is a new one on me. And on the Kaynors, of course, which is why they're trying to claim the sale of the Hiawatha property is invalid."

"*What?* Why?"

She said cautiously, "Because of the, er, body in the backyard."

"But I mean…it's not like I knew there was a body in the backyard when I put the house on the market."

"I realize that. They're upset, of course. And being kicked out of the house while the police investigate isn't helping."

"Right. Of course. But…" I recalled the second part of her message. "If you think my talking to them would help, I'm more than willing—"

"Yes!" She leaped on this immediately. "I do think it might help. They were so impressed when they met you. Mrs. Kaynor's mother being such a fan sealed the deal, I think."

"I remember." That had been one of the nicest parts of the transaction, frankly. The nine hundred grand the house had gone for had been another nice part. That money allowed me financial freedom and independence during this lull in my career. I did not want to waste so much as a dime of it in a dumbass lawsuit.

"Honestly, I don't believe they would win any such suit—unless you did have something to do with the body being there."

"I course I didn't have anything to do with it!"

"No, of course not!" She seemed to relax ever so slightly at my offended tone. "But regardless of the eventual outcome, a legal battle is so expensive, and the publicity wouldn't do any of us any good."

Rachel would have disagreed, but I said nothing.

"And the fact that the house would be standing empty all that time would just make it harder to sell down the line. So, if you *could* see your way to speaking with them, it might be possible to resolve the situation without further action."

"I agree. I'll make arrangements tomorrow."

Rina said, "Just a thought. The element of surprise might be useful."

I glanced at J.X., who was listening in with a less than delighted expression.

"Really? Well, there's a lot of that going around right now," I said.

CHAPTER FIVE

I had been happy in that house.

It was just an ordinary 1970s single story in an ordinary neighborhood in the San Fernando Valley, but it had been home. In some ways it still looked like home. In some ways it didn't. The black plastic bats hanging from trees were new and added a grimly festive touch—as did the grinning skeleton hanging in the front window. Now there was irony for you.

Otherwise the house was mostly as I remembered it. The fountain in the front yard was adorned with what appeared to be a large, lone trout—but was presumably supposed to be a dolphin—the double entryway doors were dark oak with leaded glass, but the formerly lush-green lawn, like a couple of others on the street, had been allowed to go to seed whether out of cheapness or in a nod to the ongoing drought.

Really, the only *not* ordinary thing about the house was the fleet of crime-scene vehicles and squad cars parked out front and taking up every available bit of parking on the street.

As I strode up the sidewalk, I saw crime-scene technicians in coveralls milling in the doorway of the residence. A middle-aged couple were in the process of lugging suitcases across the white stone gravel garden and down the driveway.

"George," I called. "Gina. May I have a word?"

They stopped walking, turning warily to face me. I could see they didn't recognize me. I barely recognized me. I didn't often wear a suit, and this one was a little large through the midsection now. But as I drew nearer I saw realization dawn.

They glanced at each other. Gina raised her chin. George straightened his shoulders.

"Mr. Holmes," Gina said in frosty accents. She was a roly-poly blonde, usually amiable-looking, with bright blue eyes and short, spiky hair. She wore magenta Fabletics and pale-pink acrylic nails; she did not look amiable today. George was also fair, round, and not looking amiable.

He said, "I'm surprised you'd show your face around here, Holmes."

"Christopher, please," I said, exuding charm—or whatever scrapings of charm I had left after yesterday's long-ass drive from the Bay Area. It would have been easier to fly, except I hate flying even more than long-ass drives. "Of course I'm here. I'm as anxious as anyone to know what's going on."

"What's going on is you sold us a house with an attached graveyard," Gina said.

"So I've heard. I certainly didn't do it knowingly."

They both looked openly skeptical. I don't think I'm unduly touchy, but it's hard not to take offense at people acting like nothing you say can be trusted.

"They're spraying the house with Luminol," George said.

"Ah. I see. I don't think it stains, so that's the good news."

"That's your idea of good news?"

"I think it's probably standard procedure," I replied. "Spraying for—er, with Luminol."

Gina said, "Not for us!"

"No, I realize that. And I realize it's very inconvenient and that you're upset. But I wanted to give you my personal assurance that I had no knowledge of the body they've discovered, and certainly nothing to do with whatever befell him."

"We can't stay at the house until they've signed off on the crime scene—whatever that means."

"You wouldn't want to stay here, believe me."

"That's not the point! No, we wouldn't want to stay here. We'll never stay here again. But we also don't want to go stay in a hotel for who knows how long."

George thrust his chin out pugnaciously and said, "We're canceling the sale on the house."

"See, that's the thing," I said. "Escrow closed forty-five days ago. You've been living here for over a month. You've started making changes to the property." I nodded at the dead lawn. "As much as I want you to love the house the way I did, it's a bit late for second thoughts."

"The property was misrepresented to us," George said.

"It wasn't misrepresented. It turned out to have features I was unaware of, but that's not—"

"*Features!*" exclaimed Gina.

"Well, in a manner of speaking."

"You can keep your features, and you can keep this house you loved so much. We want our money back."

George nodded agreement.

"Unfortunately, that's not possible. And even if it were, once all this"—I gestured broadly to the crime-scene personnel and cop cars and crowd of gawkers—a number of whom I recognized as former neighbors—gathered behind the yellow and black crime-scene tape—"is over and done, everything is going to be back to normal."

Gina began, "Maybe that's your idea of normal. You write mysteries. The rest of us—"

I interrupted, "It's the same house it was last week, same neighborhood, same everything. This is inconvenient and uncomfortable, but I don't feel there are legitimate grounds for canceling the sale."

"It's not up to you," George returned.

"It's not up to you either. It'll be up to the courts."

George shrugged. "So be it."

"And that's going to be expensive and time-consuming. Are you sure you want to go that route?"

"It won't be expensive for us because you'll be paying our legal fees." He glanced at his wife. "Come on, Gina."

They marched away without another glance in my direction. I watched them go, lumbering down the sidewalk with their bulging bags.

Hell. That could have gone better. I let out a long, exasperated breath. Now what? Having had a couple of days to cool down, I really hadn't expected the Kaynors to be quite so unreasonable. Clearly, it would take more than a few minutes' schmoozing and gifting copies of my latest book—not that I had a latest book—to change their minds.

Some of the crowd gathered behind the yellow and black tape were now looking my way and whispering. One or two people pointed. I couldn't help a twinge of unease. If J.X. was correct, someone on this street—maybe someone in that very crowd—had dumped a body in my yard when my back was turned.

Someone on this street was very possibly guilty of murder.

It was like being on the set of *Fear Thy Neighbor.*

No wonder Gina and George were having second thoughts. I'd be having second thoughts too.

"Mr. Holmes?"

I glanced over my shoulder and spotted Detectives Dean and Quigley picking their way across what was left of my former lawn. They ducked under the crime-scene tape and came to meet me.

I said, "Before you say it, this isn't me returning to the scene of my crime. This is me trying to keep my buyers from returning the scene of the crime."

Quigley chuckled. "They do seem to believe you're somehow involved."

"They choose to believe that because they want to back out of the sale."

Detective Dean, wearing a body-hugging dark suit that made her look like a sexy undertaker, said, "Is there some reason you chose not to approach the Kaynors over the phone?"

"Yes. For one thing, I'm more charming in person."

And for a second thing, the knowledge that Jerry Knight was loose in San Francisco provided strong incentive for me to leave town.

Dean allowed herself a polite smile at the idea I could be charming in any form. "Have you located Dickison's contact information yet?"

"Not yet." In fact, I hadn't looked. I'd had more pressing matters on my mind, like averting a potential lawsuit and postponing my inevitable homicide for as long as possible.

"Has the body been IDed?" I asked. "Are you sure it's Dicky's?"

"The body has not yet been officially IDed," Dean returned. "We'd like to get in touch with Dickison's family."

DNA sampling. That's what she was after. My stomach rolled over like a cruise ship right before it sank to the bottom of the sea.

"Right," I said. "That's not information I ever had, though. Dicky was estranged from his family."

That caught her interest. "Is that so? Any idea why?"

"He was from some backwoods town in one of the Carolinas. I think his father was a minister." I frowned. "Or maybe he was a banjo player. Maybe it was the one before Dicky with the minister father. Anyway, whichever it was, Dicky's father threw him out of the house when he came out."

Dean looked confused. "When he came out of where?"

Quigley said, "You can't remember if the man's father was a minister or a banjo player?"

"*The closet*," I told Dean, who blushed—and rightly so. After all those hours of taxpayer-funded sensitivity training? To Quigley, I said curtly, "I've had a lot of personal assistants through the years."

For some reason, he didn't seem to want to take my word for it. "Is that so? How many is a lot?"

"Twelve. At least. Twelve who stayed at least a year. There were a few who didn't last more than a few months—and not because I didn't pay them well, for the record."

"Going by Dickison's final paycheck, you paid 'em okay." Quigley said it as though there was something suspicious about how well paid my personal assistants were. What nefarious things did he imagine I demanded of them?

Dean wrenched back control of the runaway interview. "How long did Mr. Dickison work for you?"

"Two and a half years. He was definitely the best of the batch."

"And his employment ended when he and Mr. Gordon decided to..." She hesitated.

"Don't bother being tactful at this late date," I said. "His employment ended when David informed me he was leaving me to be with Dicky."

She tried to be tactful anyway. "What kind of an employee was Dickison?"

"Treacherous, it turns out. Though if you'd asked me at the time, I'd have said exemplary. He was smart, efficient, good in a crisis and, well, fun." Yeah, that was what hurt. We had laughed a lot in between the regular publishing crises. I had liked Dicky. I had hoped he'd want to work for me forever. I thought he had liked me too. He had certainly seemed to enjoy his job.

Anyway, I had been mistaken. In many things. Life goes on.

Quigley said, "How do you think your ex would have reacted if Dickison told him he'd changed his mind?"

"Loudly."

"Do you think he might have become physical?"

"You already asked me this on Saturday. The answer was no then, and it's still no. I don't believe David killed Dicky. David has a temper, but he's not violent."

Dean said, "And yet, interestingly, he thinks *you* might have killed Dickison."

Yes, David did apparently think there was a good possibility I'd committed murder. It was truly disconcerting.

I shrugged. "Turns out neither of us actually ever knew the other."

Quigley said, "It's kind of suspicious—"

He was interrupted by one of the white-garbed crime-scene technicians, who joined us to announce, "We've found another set of remains!"

"*What?*" I think I might have actually rocked back on my heels. I felt like I'd been punched.

And it didn't help to see the look of glee on Dean's face. In fact, it was terrifying. *Career-making case*, that was what Dean was thinking. I think blood-spattered stars twinkled in her eyes for a second or two. Quigley just looked bewildered. Like a walrus that finds himself on an ice float surrounded by killer whales.

"Animal," the technician added apologetically before they could get too worked up. "It was buried in the roses outside the pool yard."

Dean's face fell.

My horror gave way to ire. "Are you kidding me?" I yelled. "That's my *cat*! Those remains belong to Marple!"

"It is a cat," the technician admitted. "Was."

"You goddamned *barbarians*!"

Dean said coldly, "I'm going to have to ask you to calm down, Mr. Holmes."

"Ask away!"

Quigley bristled on her behalf. "Were you aware that LA municipal code states: 'No person shall bury an animal or fowl in the city except in an established cemetery'?"

"No." And it wouldn't have made any difference to me. I didn't say that, though. I was even less tactful. "Are you aware you're an idiot? I'm thinking probably not."

"OKAY. TIME OUT." Dean put a hand on her partner's beefy arm. "We're sorry about disturbing the remains of your pet, but unfortunately this is a murder investigation. It's our job to—"

"Dig?" I snapped. "Yes. Got it. I'll leave you to it."

That was an exit line if there ever was one, and I took advantage of it before Quigley could come up with another LA municipal-code violation worth throwing my butt in jail over.

I crunched my way over the dried straw of my former lawn, narrowly missed tripping over the spike of a small Jack-o'-lantern solar light, and started down the sidewalk.

"Hey there, Mr. Holmes!" shouted Reggie Chow, who once upon a time had delivered the *LA Times* to my front door. That was nearly a decade ago, and Reggie had since moved on to less wholesome occupations like breaking into mailboxes and stealing UPS parcels off unguarded front porches. Still, it was nice to see him out of jail again.

I raised my hand in greeting but kept walking. I was not feeling sociable, and the uneasy knowledge that one of these neighborhood lookie-loos might be a homicidal litterbug did not warm my heart.

"Christopher!" another voice called.

My heart jumped.

The voice was male. Familiar. I turned, on guard, to see a tall, silver-haired man in jeans and a yellow Lacoste polo shirt crossing the street toward me.

Though I knew the voice, it still took me a second to recognize him—his hair had grayed considerably in the past year. Worry over his missing boyfriend? Guilt for having done away with his boyfriend? Regret for having unceremoniously dumped me? Or just an unlucky draw from the gene pool?

"David," I said.

I turned my back on him and started walking again.

CHAPTER SIX

"Christopher, we need to talk."

"No, we don't," I said without turning around.

I heard his footsteps speed up. I stopped walking, turned, and waited for him.

"What are you doing here?" he demanded.

"The same thing as you. Returning to the scene of the crime. By which I don't mean Dicky's demise. But thanks for thinking I'm capable of murder."

David seemed to redden, but maybe that was just the warmth of the autumn day. He had never been prone to regrets, let alone blushing over them.

"It was just the initial shock," he said. "I don't really think that."

"Believe it or not, I don't care. But you should know the cops consider you every bit as much a suspect as me."

"Me?"

His genuine astoundment (yes, it's a word) was almost cute.

"Of course *you*," I replied. "The romantic partner is always the number-one suspect. You know that. You read mysteries. You used to."

He'd used to read my mysteries, as a matter of fact. Hard to believe there had been a time I'd valued his opinion.

Here's a strange thing. When I'd spoken to David on the phone, all my defenses had been in place. Seeing him unexpectedly like this, live and in color, shook me. My heart rate had ratcheted up unpleasantly, and the palms of my hands were suddenly cold and damp. The phone conversation had been about the past. This meeting was very much in the present—and, unsettlingly, it felt like I was seeing David for the first time.

He was a handsome guy.

Not as handsome as J.X., but then he was a completely different physical type. J.X. was good-looking in a careless, naturally gorgeous kind of way. He looked as hot in jeans and a motorcycle jacket as he did in one of his black Carlo Pignatelli suits—or as he did stark staring naked. The staring being done by yours truly.

David's brand of good looks was more...calculating corporate executive. In fairness, I hadn't always thought so. There was a time when I'd thought he was distinguished and dashing and, yep, handsome as all get out. And get out he had. Eventually.

Anyway, he was a couple of years older than me, but he worked a lot harder at holding back the tide, and it had paid off. He got the kind of haircuts that required an actual budget, and he had gone in for skin treatments in the days when only *GQ* discussed such frivolities.

Unlike J.X., when David didn't shave he looked like a bum on a bender. He was shaved today and, despite the casual wear, as groomed as if he was headed for the office.

When he didn't reply, I put my hands on my hips and jutted my chin pugnaciously. "Anyway, what are *you* doing here?"

To my surprise, his face worked. He got control at once, though. "I had to come. I have to know if it's..."

Dicky.

I felt an unexpected pang. Had David *really* cared for Dicky? I'd figured by now they'd be at each other's throats. Easier on my pride to think that, of course. But also, I'd had long experience with David's peccadillos. They were a lot like lightning strikes. Sudden, intense, and over quickly. Nothing left to do but sweep up the charred and blackened bits of broken hearts.

With unwilling sympathy, I said, "Okay, but hanging around the crime scene isn't going to solve anything. It's not like the cops are going to hold a press conference here. And they're sure as hell not going to report to you."

"They told me they'd keep me posted. I figured I'd make it easy on them."

That drew a not very kind laugh from me. *"We'll be in touch* does not mean *we'll keep you posted."*

He said stubbornly, "I have a right to know."

"Maybe. And when the cops are good and ready, I'm sure they'll bring you up-to-date. In the meantime, don't you have a company to run?"

He retorted, "Don't you have a book to write? Why *are* you here?"

"I'm trying to keep the couple who bought the house from suing me."

David looked startled. "They think... They can't think..."

Really? Because *he* had thought it.

"They claim to think. I think they're probably overstating their abilities. Anyway." I stopped in the face of his sudden silence. I felt unexpectedly uncomfortable beneath the intensity of his gaze.

"You...look good," he said slowly, as if only noticing, as if it was a surprise. *"Really* good."

I did not want to hear this. Not any variation of it. I said briskly, "It's the Botox."

He laughed, but in fact, I had been getting Botox for my migraines. The injections helped, and since I was already there... Now the frown line between my eyes was a thing of the past, as were the previously perennial knots in my eyebrows, and the beauty of modern Botox treatments was, I could still scowl all I liked, which I was currently doing.

I said, "For what it's worth, I don't believe that body is—was—Dicky."

David was momentarily distracted. "Then where is he?"

I shook my head. "I don't know. But I didn't kill him. I don't think you killed him. So, chances are high it's not him."

"But then who is it?"

"J.X. thinks a former neighbor probably tossed a pesky corpse into the construction site when no one was looking."

We both glanced uneasily around the tidy suburban street.

"That seems a stretch. They'd need a key to the back gate. Plus, you were always at the house. Even if they dumped the body in the middle of the night, that would be taking a hell of a chance."

"True." I hadn't debated the theory with J.X. because I wanted him to be right.

In afterthought, David added, "J.X.? Who's J.X.?"

"J.X. Moriarity. My...well, my fiancé." That was a slight exaggeration. We weren't formally engaged.

David's jaw dropped. I had never seen him look quite so...flabbergasted. I assumed it was at the idea I had managed to snag another poor fish, but I should have remembered his tiresome love of thrillers.

"J.X. Moriarity? *The* J.X. Moriarity? The author of the Dirk Van de Meer books?"

"The same."

"Where would you meet— Oh." His face changed. "When you solved that murder at the author retreat in Northern California. I remember reading he was there too."

On the one hand, I was sort of flattered that David had followed my exploits enough to know even that much about my life post-him. I knew zero about anything that had befallen him—and I hoped there had been plenty of befallens—since we'd parted ways. On the other hand, it was typical of him to assume the only way I'd have the opportunity to get to know someone like J.X. was if we were trapped in an isolated mountain resort, being stalked by a killer, and with no way of escape.

I saw a chance for payback that I had thought long gone—and I grabbed it.

"No, I've known him for years," I replied, and I even drummed up a spiteful little smile. "I met him the weekend before you and I tied the knot. In fact, we had quite the fling, he and I."

That gaping, gulping, landed-fish look of extreme astonishment was not exactly complimentary, but the hurt expression that followed was balm for my still tender ego. Yeah, the wounds David had inflicted had scarred over, but the scar tissue was pretty thin, and I was small enough and petty enough in spirit to enjoy my moment of triumph.

"You... I s-see," David said with the little stammer he only got when he was really flustered. "I had no idea."

"Well, no, how would you?" I was still smiling with a hard, bright cheerfulness I didn't actually feel.

"You never said a word. You used to make fun of his books." He repeated, "I had no idea."

That's the problem with revenge. It cuts both ways. However much he had it coming, I didn't like feeling I'd slammed David over the head with a blunt instrument. My revelation affected him more than I'd expected. I'd been thinking tit for tat. In execution, it felt more like I'd brought a bazooka to a knife fight.

I said briskly, "It was just a fling."

"It never occurred to me you weren't..." He sounded almost dazed.

Faithful? Loyal? Honorable? Too dumb to know what he was up to?

Ugh. And it was bullshit anyway. I *had* been faithful to him. The, er, transgression with J.X. had occurred during the very brief window when we had officially broken up.

"I was hurt after finding you in bed with Marc— *Anyway*, ancient history. I don't want to drag all this up now. My point was J.X. thinks someone took advantage of my home-improvement efforts to get rid of a problem. If he's right, DNA tests will prove that the body is not Dicky's and that this unfortunate incident has nothing to do with either of us."

"Yes. Of course." David nodded—and kept nodding—like someone trying to hide the fact he had no idea what page we were on. "But then where *is* Dicky?"

Oh. *That old thing again.*

"I repeat. I don't know."

"He didn't change his mind. I know he didn't."

I sighed. "Okay. Well, stuff happens to people, and maybe something happened to him."

"Like what?"

"Maybe he had an accident."

"But we would know that. We would have been informed."

Would we? Perhaps. As Dicky's employer, perhaps I would have been informed. But perhaps not. Wouldn't it have depended on what identification he was carrying at the time? I didn't know if David would have been informed, because their relationship had been both fairly new and clandestine. Again, it would likely come back to what ID Dicky was carrying when whatever had happened to him happened. Assuming *anything* had happened to him.

Unlike David, I wasn't so sure Dicky wouldn't have changed his mind. I had changed *my* mind.

"Yeah, well. Time will tell. I'm sure the cops are going to keep us apprised, whether we like it or not, so..." I gave him a brisk *see-you-around-campus* nod and took a couple of steps toward my car.

David stepped after me, which sort of defeated the purpose. I tried for a smile, hoping to convey the appropriate synthesis of *keep your chin up* and *see ya!*

"Christopher..." he began in a hesitating kind of voice.

Oh, for God's sake!

"Was there anything else?" I asked crisply. I even glanced at my watch.

But David managed a whole sales team. It took more than restless shuffling and glancing at archaic timepieces to convince him to abandon his prey. "Would you want to..."

I stopped inching and stared at him warily. "What?"

"Go have a drink somewhere?"

"No."

"I just...feel like we should talk."

"No. About what?"

"About this." He waved at the house and the crime-scene technicians bustling to and fro like ants following a trail of breadcrumbs. Which is kind of what they were.

"What is there to talk about? I didn't kill Dicky. You didn't kill Dicky. What is there left to say?"

"Seriously? We haven't spoken since—"

"You walked out? Sure we have. We spoke Friday night."

He looked pained. "There are things I've needed to say to you, felt you deserved to hear."

"Oh, believe me, I *know*. I felt the same way for a long time. But letting go of all that has been very good for my, er, karma."

He actually smiled. "Look, I would like to buy you dinner. I would like to apologize, yes, and I would like to talk about this situation with the house and with Dicky. I think there's plenty to say and we'd be smart to get our stories straight before we're interviewed by the police again."

"*That's* the first genuinely suspicious thing you've said," I told him. "'Get our stories straight'?"

"You know what I mean. Anyway, aren't you at all concerned or even curious about what happened to Dicky? You've solved four murders in the past year. Why wouldn't you want to solve this one?"

"Because this one is too close to home. Literally."

"All the more reason to try and figure out what happened. I don't know about you, but I *need* to know what happened."

Goody for you.

But I didn't say it. I *was* curious. Morbidly curious. Granted, less about Dicky's fate than about what David wanted to say.

"It's just dinner," David coaxed. "We never have to see each other again after tonight if you don't want to. But surely we've reached a place where we can at least be polite."

"I've been polite for nearly twenty minutes," I said. "This is already a test of my endurance."

He laughed. He laughed in the old way, a warm appreciative chuckle that brought back way too many memories of happier times. "*Come on, Christopher,*" he said, as he had said a million times before.

"Fine," I said ungraciously. "I'm staying at the Radisson. They have a restaurant on site. You can buy me dinner and we can talk."

His smile broadened. "About six?"

"Make it five-thirty. I'll meet you in the lobby."

"I'll see you then," he said, and irritatingly, was the first to turn away.

I like hotels.

Staying in hotels was one of the few things I never minded about book tours. Yes, the art is bad and the pillows are never quite right. And yes, I've heard the horror stories about black lights illuminating semen on bedspreads and maids washing glasses with toilet brushes, but I'm good at convincing myself that doesn't happen at hotels *I* stay at.

I had just finished unpacking and was settling down to give J.X. a call when Rachel rang.

"*Christopher!*" she greeted me. "How is the investigation coming?"

"Slowly. They still haven't identified the body. It could be weeks before they know if it's Dicky or not."

"But what about suspects? Suspects are the interesting part. How many suspects are there?"

"It's hard to narrow the list of suspects when you're not one hundred percent sure who the victim is. The good news is if the victim *is* Dicky, the cops suspect David every bit as much as they suspect me."

She said impatiently, "The cops! Who cares about the bloody coppers? I'm asking about *your* investigation!"

"My—? Rachel, I'm not investigating this."

"Of course you are! We've already discussed it. I can *sell* this book. I could sell it *tomorrow if we had a proposal ready.*"

"When did we discuss it? Wait. Never mind. It doesn't matter. I can't get involved. Even if I wasn't a suspect, I can't get involved."

"Nonsense! You've solved four murders this year alone. It is *imperative* that you get involved. The fact that you're also a suspect merely raises the stakes."

"Getting involved the last time nearly got me killed!"

"I'm not saying get *that* involved."

"I don't want to get involved at all!"

She said sternly, "You *are* involved. You're already involved. Why would you be in LA if you aren't investigating?"

I tried to answer, but the question was clearly rhetorical. Rachel was hitting her stride. "It only makes sense to capitalize on your work on this case."

"But I haven't done any work."

"*Exactly!*" she shrieked. "That is exactly my point. You're going to have to write *something*, Christopher. We can only tread water for so long."

My heart, apparently weary of treading water, sank. "I know."

"A hiatus is one thing. A sabbatical is one thing. This is starting to look like *dropped out of sight*. That's not good. That is the kiss of death in this business. We *cannot* drop out of sight. You need a new book."

"I know."

"If you're not going to write a book about how you solved this murder, very well. But I need something from you. I need a proposal."

"Okay. Yes." I couldn't help adding, "You know, I haven't solved this murder yet."

Rachel returned with ruthless cheer, "You will, Christopher. You will!"

CHAPTER SEVEN

J.X. answered on the second ring.

"Hey. Are you still mad at me?" I asked.

"Of course I'm not mad at you," he replied. "I'm just…"

"Please don't say disappointed."

"I'm not disappointed, Kit. But I do think you should have waited to leave town until *after* filing a restraining order against Knight."

Surprisingly, J.X. and I did not argue a lot, but we'd had words Saturday night after Rina had phoned. J.X. did not see the urgency in my decision to travel back to SoCal. In fact, he seemed to take it sort of personally. Like I was looking for any excuse to flee back to my home turf.

I said in what I hoped were mollifying tones, "I know, honey."

"The sooner that's done, the safer you'll be. You need to get it on record that you don't want him anywhere near you. He's still claiming you invited him to the house the night Beck was killed."

"I know."

"Otherwise…"

I sucked in a breath, but let it out quietly, measuredly. "I hear you and I agree."

"But yet you chose to leave town on Sunday."

"Because this is also important," I said. "The Kaynors are threatening to sue me."

I was careful not to let my impatience creep in. I had not been careful Saturday night. In fact, I had used one of the words you never want to use in a romantic relationship. Well, really, in any relationship. *Nag.*

J.X. had been hurt, and when he was hurt, he closed down.

He had barely been speaking to me when I left on Sunday.

"Let them," he said. "They'll lose in court."

"I'd rather it didn't get that far."

"Sure, but I don't see how you're going to stop it. If they're determined to sue you—"

"I can't afford a lawsuit!"

"Honey, it's just money."

"It's *my* money, and I'm not working right now!" I was trying, *trying* not to use exclamation points, but they were creeping in against my best effort.

J.X. said with maddening reasonableness, "But I am. We're fine. If worse comes to worse, I'll do an extra book this year."

!!!!!!!!!!!!!!!!!!!!!!!!!!

I put my hand to my throat and physically held in place the words—and punctuation—I would regret. He wasn't speaking out of anything but the desire to reassure and comfort. The last thing he intended was to rub my nose in the fact that my career was at a standstill—*dropped out of sight!*—while his was booming. Literally booming, if we took into account the sort of thing he wrote.

Anyway.

When I could speak without screeching à la Gage's favorite YouTube vid—the one where cartoon characters do nothing but scream for four very long minutes and thirteen seconds—I said mildly, "And don't think I don't appreciate it. But I would still prefer to head off a lawsuit, if possible."

He said grudgingly, "Okay. Were you able to talk to them today?"

"Yes. And no, I did not manage to change their minds. So far."

"Are you coming home tomorrow?"

"Probably. That's the plan."

"Probably?"

Why had I said *probably*? Because the plan *was* that I would return home on Tuesday. I guess I was more freaked out about Jerry being loose again than I wanted to admit. But also, Rachel had made her point. Getting involved, even peripherally, in several homicides within the space of a year was kind of a lot. Maybe there *was* a book in that.

I said, "The police are still excavating the backyard at the house."

"Yeah? So? What does that have to do with you not coming home?"

"I didn't say I'm not coming home." I heard the testiness of my tone. God almighty. Were we about to get into *another* argument? "I'd like to take one more crack at the Kaynors. That's all."

But that wasn't all. And I realized I was about to step into a very big, very deep hole.

"By the way—and by the way, this segue has nothing to do with me staying longer in LA, which I don't *plan* to do—David is here."

I winced at the tiny but resounding silence that followed my words.

J.X. said, *"David?* Wait. He's there with you *now?"*

"What? No. Of course not. I mean, he was at the house today."

Just like that, and despite my best intentions, I was teetering on the brink of a lie. Because I could see—hear—that the truth was going to upset him. Because, bewilderingly, it seemed J.X. had some completely unexpected and unfounded doubt where David was concerned.

No way was I going to risk what we had, however awkward the truth—and it *was* awkward as hell—so I just said what needed to be said.

"We're having dinner tonight."

It came out more bluntly than I'd anticipated.

There was another of those fractional pauses that made me want to go back to chewing my nails as I had when I was seventeen. J.X. repeated in the dazed tone of someone picking himself up after being hit by a runaway trolley, "You're having dinner with David?"

"It wasn't my idea, but yes. He wants to talk about Dicky. He thinks if we put our heads together, we might be able to come up with something useful."

"You do realize if Dicky's dead, David killed him."

"You're the one who said Dicky wasn't dead."

"How the hell do I know if Dicky's dead?" he cried. "*Someone* is dead. For all either of us know, it *is* Dicky. And your goddamned ex killed him."

For someone normally even-tempered, he was getting pretty worked up. "Wait. What? What's going on here? You told me you didn't think Dicky was dead."

"Kit, I was trying to reassure you by showing you there were other possibilities. I don't know what happened to Dicky, but if something *did* happen to him, David did it. That much I'll guarantee."

"That's quite a guarantee, given you never met either of them."

"I don't believe this," J.X. said. "After everything that asshole did to you, you're having *dinner* with him?"

"What the hell, J.X."

I mean, on the one hand, I did *sort of* get it. On the other hand, I put up daily—weekly, at the very least—with J.X.'s convoluted familial relationships, which included tolerating the regular demands for his time and attention by his ex-wife-quasi-sister-in-law-yeah-don't-ask Nina.

He said, "*What the hell* is right!"

"Why are you being like this? It's just dinner. You have dinner with old friends all the time. Do I come unhinged?"

"Since when is David your friend?"

I'll be damned. We really *were* fighting again. Just like that.

"This is ridiculous," I said coldly. "I'll talk to you tomorrow."

"If you can find the time," J.X. retorted.

The bastard hung up before I could.

"To absent friends," David said, and clinked his glass against mine.

"Hear, hear," I said. "Although obviously they aren't."

David chuckled.

It was 5:35, and we were in the mostly empty dining room of the Radisson's Caprese Restaurant. Having placed our orders with the waitress, we were making awkward small talk, and I was deeply regretting arguing with J.X.

I mean, I'd regretted it three minutes after we hung up, but I especially regretted it sitting here with David and being forcibly reminded of how lucky I was to have found J.X. again.

David was almost painfully unchanged—other than his now silver hair, which made him look unfairly sagacious and sophisticated—and it brought back a lot of not-so-good memories of other times and other meals when I'd spot that same predatory gleam in his eyes and know he was once more on the prowl.

Even his aftershave was the same. Grey Flannel. I did not like that fragrance, never had, but it was weird the way scent evoked memory.

Granted, the only reason my aftershave was different was because of last year's makeover, which I'd had to endure when Rachel decided I needed to reinvent myself. Take it from me, you need more than new aftershave and a couple of additional and unnecessary piercings to kick up your book sales.

"Were you able to contact the new owners again?" David asked.

"No. They've moved to a hotel. Rina is trying to hunt them down for me."

"I'm sure once the house is released as a crime scene they'll feel differently. It's no wonder they're upset with all these strangers trooping through the house and yard."

I nodded and sipped my drink.

"So J.X. Moriarity, huh?" He winked. "Holmes and Moriarity."

"Yep."

"You've heard that one before."

"Yep."

"I have to admit, I'm surprised." He met my look. "Not that you ended up with J.X. Moriarity. That you ended up with anyone. All that time I was thinking it was you. Maybe it was me."

"Maybe it was both of us," I said.

"Maybe." He raised his glass, and we clinked again. I foresaw a long night ahead and mentally apologized to J.X. Again.

The silence that followed was unexpectedly somber. We drank for a few moments, and David said, "I noticed there haven't been any more Miss Butterwiths. Are you working on something new?"

"I'm taking a little break."

"After sixteen years, you deserve a break. Too bad…"

He didn't finish it. At my look of inquiry, he said, "How's it work with two writers in one house?"

"So far, so good. How are things going for you?"

He flashed me a big, white, toothsome smile. "I finally got that regional sales manager position."

"That's great." That was a prize David had been after for practically as long as I'd known him.

"Yep. The corner office, the company BMW, and that 300K bonus are all mine. Now if I just had someone to share my success with."

I managed not to choke on my drink.

As though reading my mind, he said, "Sure, I have plenty of company when I want it. It's not the same as having someone to share the bad times as well as the good times."

"True words."

We had both downed our drinks—there was an area of compatibility that remained unchanged—and I signaled to the waitress for another round.

"When was the last time you saw Dicky?" David asked abruptly.

"The Monday after you and he took off. He came for his final paycheck."

"He did?" David's surprise seemed genuine. "What happened?"

I scowled. "What do you think happened? I paid him and he left."

"I didn't mean— I'm just surprised he went back to the house. He was afraid of you."

"Afraid of me?"

I had to stop there because the waitress returned with another round. I fumed as she set our drinks down, collected our empties, and then finally departed.

Before I could continue, David said, "I don't mean afraid for his life. I mean he was…intimidated." He grimaced. "He was embarrassed, truth be told. Maybe even kind of ashamed. He thought a lot of you. Really admired you."

"He had a funny way of showing it." Dicky had not been contrite that final meeting. He had been rude and defiant. "When was the last time *you* saw him?"

"That same Monday. I left for work that morning, and everything seemed fine. He didn't say anything about planning to see you. Maybe he knew I wouldn't like it." David's blue gaze met mine. "Hey, I might not be the most sensitive guy in the world, but even I can see that was too much like rubbing salt in the wound. That's what I would have told him."

"He cashed the check," I said. "So for the record, he survived our encounter."

David rolled his eyes. "Christopher, I'm sorry for what I said on the phone. I don't really think you had anything to do with Dicky's death, or I wouldn't be sitting here with you now. And I did *not* tell the police I thought you killed Dicky. They jumped to that conclusion on their own when I told them you wrote mysteries."

I grunted, only partly appeased.

He asked, "Were you able to give them the contact info they needed?"

"No. I'm not sure I still have his contact info. I'm not sure I ever had any background info on him."

"He was kind of secretive about his past," David said thoughtfully. "I remember that."

I couldn't remember if I'd thought Dicky was secretive or just wounded about the way his family had reacted to his coming out. In fact—uncomfortable to admit this even to myself—I couldn't remember much about Dicky that did not relate to me and our own interactions. I had been at my most unhappy during the years Dicky had worked for me, which meant I had been at my most self-absorbed.

"You must have met his friends," I said.

"Are you serious? Even if I wasn't supposed to be mar— Dicky was twenty years younger than me. What would I have had in common with his friends?"

That time I did choke on my drink.

"Okay, okay," David was saying when I stopped coughing. "But Dicky was very mature for his age. *We* did have a lot in common."

"Like what? Me?"

He opened his mouth and then closed it.

"Honest to God, I don't even care anymore." I pushed my chair back. "Thanks for the drinks. I'm not in the mood for—"

At that strategic moment, the waitress arrived with our meals. She deposited the plates, raised the cover on mine, and I got a whiff of shrimp primavera. Shallots, white wine, Romano cheese, and a hint of basil. I hadn't eaten since the night before. My salivary glands started watering. My stomach growled loudly, my knees seemed to melt, and I sat down again.

"You need another drink," David said.

I nodded and picked up my fork.

Oddly enough—or maybe not so oddly, because I did have that third drink and then a fourth—it was easier from that moment on. David and I were able to talk about Dicky and even our own past almost like old friends. It probably helped that he was so complimentary. No, not that he was complimentary, because I didn't trust his compliments, but that he was genuinely bowled over by the change in me. It was funny really. What a difference a good haircut and a few pounds made. Not just to David. To me. Because I was confident in a way I hadn't been for years.

But then that wasn't really about new clothes and fancy-schmancy moisturizer. It was about J.X. About the way he made me feel. Valued. Cherished. Loved.

I resolved to call him as soon as I got back to my room. To hell with who was right and who was wrong. I missed him like crazy. And I wanted him to know that.

"They dug up Marple," I told David.

"What the hell?" he was instantly and satisfyingly appalled, and I realized this was something I shared with him and only him. He had loved those two cats nearly as much as me. "Did they get Dashiell too?"

"Not so far." I said gloomily, "Apparently it's illegal in LA County to bury your pets in your backyard."

"Fascists," David pronounced, and once more we were perfectly in accord.

We ate in silence for a minute or two.

"I know you don't want to hear this," David said suddenly, "but you're the perfect person to find out what happened to Dicky. You've already solved four murders that I know of. And this happened in your own backyard."

"First of all, I didn't solve four murders." It was more like six if you counted secondary and appended victims. "And definitely not on my own. Anyway, are you so sure he's dead?"

"Yes." David's eyes were dark and sad. "I think I knew something was wrong almost from that first day when he never came home. I tried to talk myself out of it. Tried to convince myself he changed his mind, but I *knew*."

"Okay, maybe you're right. It's alarming that he's never turned up in all these months. But neither of us has any useful information as to where to even start looking for what could have happened to him."

"You must have his old résumé and his job application somewhere."

"Maybe in a box. I might have dumped it all, though."

"Not you," David said. "You always kept everything in case of a tax audit. Remember all those arguments we had about you hoarding business papers that were more than ten years old?"

Oh yes. We'd always found plenty to argue about. From the real to the manufactured.

"I guess I could have a look," I said reluctantly. "The police are asking for whatever contact info I had on Dicky, so I have to go through those boxes anyway."

"Exactly." David leaned back in his chair, smiling. "And if something brilliant should occur to you while sorting through those papers, well, it can't hurt to make a couple of phone calls. Right?"

"Hm. I suppose not."

He grinned. "Elementary, my dear Holmes!"

I felt a twinge as he said it because that was J.X.'s little joke with me. Then, with an uncomfortable flash, I remembered it had been David's joke first.

Funny I'd forgotten that.

I glanced at my watch and was surprised to see it was nearly ten. We'd been drinking and talking in the dining room for over four hours. The dinner crowd had come and gone, and it was back to just the two of us.

I said, "Wow. Look at the time. I should say good night. I've got a long drive home tomorrow."

David looked surprised and disappointed. "Are you sure?"

"Yep. But thanks for dinner." I rose, and he rose too.

He said, "My pleasure—and I do mean that."

"Yeah, it was…good." Good to confront old ghosts, good to let go of the old anger, the old bitterness anyway. Not an event I was in a hurry to repeat, however. More like a rite of passage.

I started to turn away, and David said quickly, urgently, "Christopher."

I looked my inquiry.

"I owe you an apology. Not just for Dicky, though for Dicky, yes. That was the worst one, I know. But for…all of it. All the times I hurt you. Whatever I felt, whatever you did, you didn't deserve that."

I hadn't expected an apology—or rather, I'd figured this dinner *was* his apology—so I didn't know what to say. Especially since I didn't miss the whatever-you-did comment.

I finally came up with what I thought was a gracious, "It takes two people to ruin a relationship." Which actually isn't true. One determined and resourceful person can do it all by himself.

David offered another of his stock smiles. "True. Well, then…" He came around the table to hug me. I think I stood there about as responsive as one of those blank-faced department-store mannequins they prefer these days.

He whispered into my ear, "What about one last time? For old times' sake."

I drew back. "What about—huh?"

His smile grew rueful. "You *know*. We never got to say goodbye."

"Yeah, we did. I gave you Dicky as a going-away present."

He leaned in, still smiling, charming and purposeful. His breath was warm against my face. "No, I mean *really* say goodbye."

"I think get-the-hell-out-of-my-life *is* really saying goodbye."

I'm not sure he even heard me. "You have to admit, the sex was always good between us. *Really* good."

Yeeeeaah. About that. The sex with David had been fine. I hadn't had any complaints. But back then I hadn't known how incredible sex could really be. J.X. had taught me that. He had taught me a lot of things. A few things I still struggled with. And it was hard for me to ask for what I wanted—really wanted—in bed, but I was learning. J.X. was helping me accept who I really was, face up to what I really *needed*. People talk about mind-blowing sex, but under J.X.'s—okay, I'll say it, *tutelage*—I really *had* had my mind, or at least all my preconceived notions and biases, blown away.

So yeah. No. Thanks, but no thanks.

And even if sex with J.X. had been the worst ever, I still loved him too much to ever think of hurting him the way I'd been hurt. Not in a million years.

I laughed, but not unkindly, not mockingly. "Man, you really are incorrigible," I said.

David heard me that time. His shoulders slumped, and he sighed. "Yeah. I am. But I mean, we *were* married."

"It was a commitment ceremony."

"Same thing. To me, anyway."

Did he really not see the irony? I said, "Uh...yeah. Okay. Your point is?"

"We're allowed to have goodbye-forever sex."

"I'm sure we had it, we just didn't notice it at the time."

He scrutinized my face. "I can't tell when you're laughing. Was that your *final* no or—?"

I was still laughing. "That was final."

"Maybe one more drink would help?"

"One more drink and I'll pass out. Besides, these people want to go home." I nodded at the waitress and bartender, who were watching us with weary wariness.

David gave another of those heavy sighs. "All right. Have it your way."

We bade farewell to the relieved-looking staff and walked out to the lobby.

At the elevators, I turned to him and said, "Good night, David. Thanks again for dinner."

"You're sure you don't want to—?"

"I'm sure."

"Absolutely, positively—?"

I said firmly, "'Night, David."

I stepped into the elevator, punched the button for the third floor. I nodded cordially as the doors closed on David's glum expression.

I chuckled quietly to myself as I strolled down the brightly lit hall and let myself into my room. I flipped on the lights and moved to pull the drapes across the windows.

I was buzzed but not drunk, and I felt pleasantly…pleasant. I'd have a leisurely hot shower, get in bed, and phone J.X. If all went well, we could maybe even manage a wee bit of phone sex. Phone sex with J.X. was still better than live and in-person sex with anybody else.

These agreeable plans evaporated at the tentative knock on my door.

I stopped smiling.

I admit being propositioned by David—urgently propositioned at that—had been good for my ego, but this was not flattering or amusing. Jesus Christ. He couldn't be *that* desperate to get laid.

I yanked open the door, prepared to tell him that very thing.

But it was not David standing in the garishly bright hallway.

Or maybe it wasn't the hall that was garishly bright. Maybe it was the green-haired guy wearing whiteface and a blue polka-dot clown suit.

CHAPTER EIGHT

The clown said nothing.

He gazed at me with his sad clown face, complete with painted downturned mouth and eye drips. His costume was one of those ruffled, old-fashioned things—I forget what they call them—and he was holding a single red heart-shaped balloon.

I stared silently back at him. I was thinking—and at this time the defense wishes to call upon the four G&Ts, two of which had occurred on an empty stomach—that maybe J.X. had sent some kind of weird floral-delivery apology. Except I did not see any flowers and J.X. did not like clowns.

I transferred my gaze from the clown's black eyes to his red balloon. I said, "Where are the other ninety-eight?"

The clown's blue-gloved hand released the string of the balloon, which went sailing to the ceiling, bouncing against it with an eerie whispering sound.

Belatedly, I registered his gloves were latex—the kind of thing cops wore at crime scenes—and that he was wearing boots. Durable hiking boots, not funny, oversize, floppy shoes. He thrust one of those well-made hiking boots between the door and the frame as I tried to shove the door shut.

"What do you want?" I gasped, trying to force shut the heavy door. "What the hell?"

He threw his weight against the door, which flew back, taking me with it. I recovered fast, slammed my shoulder against the solid surface, and shoved the door forward a couple of inches. I couldn't close it completely, though, because his body was now wedged halfway inside the room. It was stalemate as we both struggled for leverage.

He didn't speak, and after that initial shocked protest, neither did I. I don't know why I didn't yell for help. It was the obvious thing to do, but somehow the idea that it was late and people were trying to sleep remained uppermost.

Plus, the bizzarity of the situation overruled customs and norms. My whole day had been weird, and the fact that a clown was trying to force his way into my room seemed to be par for the course.

The clown grunted, swiping at my head with his gloved hand. His fingers latched in my hair and pulled. I yelped and tried to punch him, but he was at a weird angle, so I was only able to knock on the rubber baldpate middle section of his head with the heel of my fist.

Knock, knock!

Who's there?

Clown.

Clown who?

Clown for the count!

He winced, trying to duck the blows, but kept squeezing through the doorway.

"*Get out*," I panted. "This isn't your room."

I'm pretty sure he already knew it wasn't his room. It's amazing the dumb things that pop out of your mouth at moments like these. Not that most people have moments like these.

The clown's rubber scalp slipped forward, and I grabbed at the green tuft of his hair—not his real hair, obviously. He grew desperate and body-slammed the door. It bounced back, and I gave way with it.

The clown leaned against the closed door, breathing hard. He righted his hairpiece—and I jumped into the bathroom and locked the door.

I was bathed in cold sweat. My arms and legs were shaking. I felt like we'd been fighting for hours, and yet I knew it couldn't have been much more than a minute since he'd knocked on my door. I tried to catch my breath.

He would have to give up now, right? Give up and go away?

No. He began to kick at the thin wooden barrier between us.

For some reason that frightened me the way nothing else had. I think it was the realization that he didn't care if anyone heard or not. He had one goal, and that was to get to me, whatever the consequences.

I looked desperately around my gleaming white cell. A wall phone hung next to the shower. I'd always thought of phones in the bathroom as an abomination, but I fell on this one gratefully and punched the numbers for the front desk with shaking fingers.

The phone seemed to ring for an eternity.

Bam.

One ringie dingie.

Bam.

Two ringie dingies.

Bam.

Three ringie dingies.

Slow, steady blows landed on the door, punctuating the pauses between each leisurely ring.

"Front desk," replied a vague-sounding voice at last. She sounded about a million miles away, like she had been peacefully napping on another planet.

"Send someone up here right now," I cried. "There's a clown in my room!"

"What?"

"There's a—" Sanity reasserted itself. I could not afford for her to decide this was a prank and hang up. I tried to steady my voice. "Someone is breaking into my room! Send security!"

"Sir, we don't have security," she replied patiently. "They probably just have the wrong room—"

"No. *No.* He's already *in* my room. He's after *me*. Send someone up here!" I took the handset and held it in front of the door so she could hear the heavy, rhythmic blows of boots on flimsy plywood.

"Sir? Sir? There's no one to send!" She sounded wide-awake now and nearly as alarmed as me.

"Call the police!" I yelled.

"I could send Hector!"

"*Huh?* What? Who the hell's Hec—?" I dropped the phone to the tiles as the door splintered and a booted foot crashed through.

Wildly, I looked around for some kind of weapon and spotted the guest-use iron, which I'd left sitting on the sink counter after pressing the wrinkles out of my shirt that morning.

I snatched up the iron, prepared to make my last stand—and realized my intruder's foot had caught in the door.

I lunged forward, unlocked the door, and shouldered it open, using the iron to swipe at the struggling clown. He hopped back a couple of steps, somehow managing to keep his balance. He blocked my blow with his raised arm.

I heard him gasp in pain as the iron connected. He grabbed for the cord and tried to yank the iron out of my hand. I hung on and tried to hit him again while scrabbling with my free hand for the entrance-door handle.

I pulled the handle—but he'd slipped the security bar into place, and the door caught and sank back into the frame. Still clumsily swinging the iron, I let go of the handle and flipped the security bar.

Finally, I managed to throw the door open—except you don't really throw hotel doors open. They're too slow and too heavy. I did get the damned thing open, but by then the clown had managed to free himself from the bathroom door.

He tackled me, knocking me to the floor. I fell halfway into the hall and kicked at his head. I swung the iron like a club, but hit the door. It took out a chunk of wood.

Bada book, bada boom, as they say in the hotel biz.

"What the hell?" David's astonished voice spoke from overhead.

Unbelievably, the cavalry had arrived in the form of my lecherous ex.

"Help," I gulped. "Help!"

My assailant planted his knee in my midsection and shot out of my hotel room, crashing into David, who had bent to help me up. They grappled awkwardly.

David made an *ooof!* sound.

"Hey, stop!" he staggered back, and the clown burst through the crowd of people gathering in the hallway.

"What happened? What's going on? Who is that? Has anyone called the front desk?"

Everyone seemed to be talking at once.

"Don't let that clown get away!" I called feebly. I tried to roll onto my side, but at the ominous twinge in my back, fell back. "Goddamn it. Somebody grab that clown!"

A simple enough directive, and yet it seemed to only raise more questions in the minds of the onlookers.

"What's he talking about? What did he say? Was that a clown? Why is he laying there on the floor?"

"*Lying*," I protested. "There's no direct object."

I could hear the clown's footsteps pounding down the hallway as he escaped. The distant *ding* of an elevator followed.

"Christopher, are you okay?" David bent over me. "Did you hit your head?"

"Probably. I think I hit everything else."

"What in God's name *was* that?"

I blinked up at his worried upside-down face. Over his shoulder I could see a red heart-shaped balloon bobbing against the low ceiling.

"A clown," I said. "An evil clown. Look, he left his calling card."

David and the crowd of onlookers obligingly looked upward, gazing at the balloon as it began to bob its way farther down the hall.

"An evil clown... Did he say evil clown? He must be on something. Did you call the front desk?"

"But how?" David protested. "*Why?*"

I didn't bother to answer. Mostly because I didn't *have* an answer. I reached my hand out and let him pull me up, getting painfully to my feet just as a newcomer joined the throng of astonished and alarmed guests. A tall, lean, weary, but well-dressed newcomer.

J.X.'s wide, dark eyes stared into mine.

"It was a clown," I said to him. "An evil clown." I reeled across the few feet separating us. The crowd parted instinctively, and J.X., equally on instinct, I'm guessing, opened his arms to me. I collapsed against him, and his arms locked around me, strong and supportive— also surprised.

"Kit, what happened?"

"It can't be a coincidence," I told him earnestly.

"Honey—"

"Jerry has to be behind this."

"I think he hit his head," David said helpfully from somewhere behind me.

"And you are—?" J.X. inquired.

"David Gordon," David said promptly. "Christopher's ex. No need to ask who you are. I'm a big fan of your work."

"I'm afraid I can't say the same," J.X. said coldly.

"Did you not see the clown?" I interrupted. "You must have. He must have got in the elevator as you were getting out."

"No one got in the elevator."

"He took the stairs," a woman in an oversize blue-striped men's pajama shirt volunteered. "He ran past the elevator and took the stairs."

"*Who* took the stairs?" J.X. asked bewilderedly, looking from one to the other of us.

"*The clown*," I cried.

He didn't exactly flinch, but I think maybe he lost color. His lips parted, but he had no ready reply. And who would?

"Everybody, this is J.X. Moriarity," David informed the crowd. "You've probably read his books. Oh, and also Christopher Holmes.

He writes the Miss Butterwith mysteries. Christopher and I used to be married."

"J.X. Moriarity, I've heard of him! Oh, they were married! That's so sweet. They're making a movie of his latest book, you know."

"I've read those," the woman in the pajama shirt said to me. "She's a retired art teacher."

"That's Miss Seeton," I said irritably. "Miss Butterwith is a botanist. *Never mind about that right now.* We need the police—"

But it was too late. Pretty much everyone in the hall had read—and loved, OF COURSE—J.X.'s latest book, and they crowded round, asking for his autograph, and assuring him they couldn't wait to see his movie when it came out, and wanting to know who would play Ace Andrews, his protagonist, and was the next Dirk Van de Meer book already written because they had a great idea for it.

Eventually a small Hispanic man in khaki work clothes showed up, wanting to know who had called for maintenance. And still more eventually the cops showed up, and we all took turns giving our statements.

A couple of hours later I thanked the police, bade good night to David—who departed reluctantly and with unwanted promises to stay in touch—and closed the door of my battered hotel room.

J.X. stood by the window, gazing out at the twinkling city lights, but he turned at the sound of the lock.

"I don't know how you're here or why you're here," I said to him, "but thank you."

He opened his arms again, and I walked into them and wrapped my own around him. We held each other, not speaking for a moment or two.

"Kit, do you really not know why I'm here?" he asked softly, at last, his breath stirring my hair.

"It can't be jealousy because you have to know you're the only guy for me."

I felt his smile. "Yeah. Well."

I looked up and read the wryness in his eyes. "You *can't* be serious," I said.

He shrugged. "Nah."

Nah. Except he'd jumped on the first available flight after we'd argued that afternoon.

I said, "I'm sorry I was a jerk earlier. I'm not even sure why I got so mad. It was stupid. The last thing I ever want to do is fight with you."

"I'm sorry too. You have a right to have dinner with whoever you want. The last thing I ever want to be is…" He swallowed. "A *nag*."

That raw little gulp crushed my heart to powder. "You're *not*. Honey. I know you're just trying to look out for me. Honest to God, I'm not used to anyone caring so much."

"I do care," he said roughly. "I don't know what it is, but I've never felt like this for anyone. I can't help it. If I lost you, if something happened to you…" He stopped, too shaken by the very idea to continue.

It was fascinating. I mean, that he could say emotional things like that without sounding corny or overwrought. Whereas I…no. I did not have that gift. Not that I didn't feel it, because the idea of anything happening to J.X. stopped my heart.

I said, "What could happen? I mean, aside from the police wanting to pin a murder rap on me. And homicidal stalkers. Oh, and evil clowns—although the last two are probably the same person."

He smiled faintly, but then shuddered. "Was he really dressed like a clown?"

"You heard me describe him to the police."

"And you believe it—he—was sent by Jerry Knight?"

I hesitated and then just came out with it. "I believe he *was* Jerry Knight."

J.X.'s eyebrows hit the widow's peak of his hairline. "You think *Knight—*"

"Yes. I do. Absolutely. It's too big a coincidence otherwise."

One minute he was professing love without end and the next he was giving me that skeptical look that made me think he wanted to write me a ticket for jaywalking.

"Oh, come *on*," I said. "We see Jerry talking to a bunch of clowns, and two days later I'm attacked by a vicious clown?"

J.X. cleared his throat.

"It's not funny. He was probably going to kill me."

"I don't think it was *remotely* funny," J.X. said, and his stern tone went a long way to smoothing my ruffled feelings.

He just had to add, "But."

"But what?"

"It could be coincidence. It could be some weird random attack. I know the odds are against it—"

"Boy, I'll say!"

"But it's not impossible. You yourself told the officers you couldn't identify your assailant. He never spoke. He wore gloves. He wore a disguise. Average height, average build. You admitted you weren't even sure about the color of his eyes."

True. All true. Even after viewing the hotel security footage, I couldn't say for sure I recognized my attacker.

"It doesn't matter. He could have worn contacts."

"Yes, okay, I'll give you that. And maybe it *was* Jerry, but you have to keep an open mind."

"No, I don't."

J.X. sighed.

"Your mind is open enough for both of us," I said. "I know what happened here tonight was not a coincidence. Jerry is the only person with a motive to get rid of me. Or at least the only person who's currently out on bail."

"Okay, think about that for a minute." J.X.'s ebony gaze held mine. "Jerry wants you out of the way before he goes to trial. Correct? No you to testify, and the charges get dropped. That's your theory?"

"Correct."

J.X. said grimly, "Then why didn't he kill you tonight? He had plenty of opportunity. He could have stabbed you when you opened the door to your room. He could have shot you any number of times, including through the bathroom door."

I opened my mouth but had to swallow the words. Because J.X. was right.

Brutal, but absolutely right. It hadn't occurred to me until that very moment.

If Jerry really had come after me, why wasn't I dead?

CHAPTER NINE

"How did you and David meet?" J.X. asked as we were climbing into the Radisson's king-size bed sometime after midnight.

He had packed light for this flying—literally—trip, and I couldn't help admiring how nice he looked in his pale-blue boxers and crisp, white T-shirt. He smelled nice too. Always. Like summer on the Mediterranean. And that wasn't his cologne; that was *him*.

"Funny thing," I said. "Pretty much the same way you and I did. At a mystery convention." I flopped back into the nest of pillows and tried not to groan my relief.

Already the alarming events of the evening were starting to feel far away and long ago. The whole incident had been so incredible, had there not been witnesses—and plenty of them—I'd have been tempted to think I dreamed it.

J.X. frowned. "No way is that dude a writer. What is it he does?"

It occurred to me that he'd never bothered to ask before. Never asked a single question about David. Almost as if he preferred to pretend David had never existed.

"He's the regional sales manager of a dental supply company. At the time we met he was a sales agent. I was attending Left Coast Crime in Vegas, and he happened to be using the hotel lobby's free Wi-Fi."

J.X. made a sound of disapproval. Was that for stealing bandwidth or the Fates working their matchmaking skills on David and me? After a moment, he said sourly, "He does have nice teeth."

"He does."

"You both do."

"Thank you. Anyway, when he discovered there was a mystery convention going on, he wandered up to the convention bar, ran into me, and the rest is history. Right there with the Great Chinese Famine, forced extinction, and the sinking of the Titanic."

J.X. made another of those spluttery snort sounds as he stretched out beside me. "He really is a mystery fan?"

"He really is. He's *your biggest fan*."

He winced. "I think I prefer Jerry."

"Not me. I'll trade you David over Jerry any day."

"Yeah, well. I just can't see you two together. He's so...corporate."

"Hey, no need to get nasty." I was amused. "David is corporate, but that doesn't make him a bad guy. In fact, he can be a great guy. In his own way. We had some very good times together." I shrugged. "And some very bad times."

J.X.'s expression was troubled as he met my eyes.

"Why did I stay with him?" I guessed.

"You deserved so much better than that, Kit."

I sighed. "Maybe. The first time I caught him cheating on me, I was devastated. I really did love him. I wasn't ready to give up on our relationship. Even after meeting you, connecting with you, I couldn't face the fact that it was over with David. I wasn't ready."

Still J.X. said nothing.

I made a face. "The problem is, I don't think I was able to ever really forgive him. I never trusted him again. I never again felt about him the way I'd felt before."

"I'm sorry."

I smiled at him because he really *was* sorry. J.X. was a genuinely nice guy. He was also a truly kind and decent man.

I said, "When I suspected he was cheating again—this was about a year after we'd signed the commitment papers—"

J.X. acknowledged that with a faint sound of amusement.

"Instead of confronting him, I ignored it. I was struggling to hit a deadline, and I told myself that work was more important, that work was the *only* important thing. That became our pattern. My pattern. My career was my life."

J.X. shook his head. "When I think of the time we wasted."

"Please let's not think of that," I said. "Let's just focus on where we are now. Here. Together. In this very comfortable bed."

He bent to kiss me, and I looped my arm around his neck and drew him down. His eyelashes flicked against my face, his breath was warm, his skin soft where it was smooth and softer still where he was bearded. His lips brushed mine with a touch as light as, well, *light*.

The light in his eyes when he was laughing. The light in his eyes when he first woke in the morning. The light in his eyes when we made love.

He said softly, "Are you okay, Kit?"

He was not asking for sex. He really was simply making sure I was okay after all I'd been through.

I nodded, whispering, "I am now." It was funny how just that... tenderness could make my eyes sting. David and I had not been tender with each other. We had loved each other, we had been affectionate and passionate and often good to each other, but we had not been tender.

I'm not sure I even knew what tenderness was before J.X.

He kissed me again, and I opened my mouth to him. His tongue probed mine with almost courtly finesse, and I pushed back with a murmur of approval. There had been a time I had not liked this, but that was a lifetime ago. The life that had belonged to a sad, snarky, solitary man old before his time.

It had been a tiring and stressful day and a dramatic and terrifying night. Our lovemaking was quiet and gentle. We held each other tightly and moved with pleasurable efficiency.

"I love you," he whispered. I'm not sure we ever made love that he didn't say it, but it wasn't something I got tired of hearing.

Nipple to nipple, groin to groin. The intimacy of shared breath and mingled fluids. The fireworks were small and bright, the afterglow warming to heart and soul as well as body.

Afterward, we continued to hold each other while our breathing slowed and the wet on our bodies dried. His heart thumped with solid, steady certainty against mine, and now and again he dropped a tiny, afterthought of a kiss on my temple or ear or corner of my eye.

I was just starting to drift off when he said suddenly into the darkness, "How was dinner with David?"

"Hm?" I blinked that over. "Okay, I guess."

David? Again? Really?

"How did he happen to be up here when the clown attacked?"

I smiled sleepily. When Clowns Attack! It sounded like one of those cheesy FOX television specials. Then his words sank in. Sleep fled.

I lifted my head, the better to try to read his face. I said slowly, incredulously, "Are you asking what I think you're asking?"

After a fraction of a pause, he said stiffly, "Of course not."

"But?"

"It's a legitimate question."

"*Which* is the legitimate question? The question you're asking or the question you're not asking?"

"What? *Kit...*"

"Yeah, but what is it you really want to know? Why was David outside my room? Or did I ask David up to my room?"

I could feel my heart banging against my collarbone as I waited for his reply.

He said, "You didn't want me to come with you on this trip."

"It wasn't because I hoped to hook up with David. I had no idea he'd be lurking around like the Ghost of Infidelities Past. I didn't want you to come with me because you've got less than a week to finish the new book before you leave on your tour for the last book. I remember how crunch time works. I was trying to be considerate."

Another of those freaky pauses followed before he bumped his face against mine. He didn't kiss me. He whispered in a pained, husky voice, "I know you wouldn't ask him. I do know that. But did you..."

It seemed he couldn't finish it.

"*No*," I said. "J.X., you can't seriously believe there's *any* contest."

He seemed to think that over before saying without emotion, "You chose him over me once before."

"And it was a huge fucking mistake that I paid for a hundred times over. Okay? If I had it all to do over...well, I'd do things differently. That's all. We wouldn't have wasted ten years."

"Okay," he said at last. "What *was* he doing up here?"

I groaned. "I think he was going to ask if I wanted to have good-bye-forever sex."

J.X. swore. Proof of his distress, it may even have been in Spanish.

"To which I would have said no—even if I hadn't been in the middle of being attacked by a killer clown."

He gave a muffled laugh and hooked his arm around my neck, pulled me closer still. He kissed me. "I love you, Kit. I just *do*."

I muttered, "Well, you don't have to sound like it's against your will."

He gave another huff of amusement.

"Or against your better judgement. Or like it's a guilty secret. Or a fatal health condition."

His kiss was sweet and coaxing. I liked the taste of his apologies. "Sorry. I'm sorry, honey…"

"I can guarantee it's not contagious!"

J.X. laughed again.

We left early Tuesday morning and had a surprisingly enjoyable trip back to San Francisco. One of the useful things about long drives is the opportunity to just talk. And that's what we did. We talked, almost without interruption, for hours.

Some of it was mundane stuff: Should we bother with buying candy for Halloween? Would there be trick-or-treaters on Cherry Lane? How to best arrange so I—standing in for J.X., who would be leaving Saturday for his book tour—could attend the Halloween party Nina was throwing for Gage. Should I go ahead and get estimates on resurfacing the pool while J.X. was away? Were we still having dinner with my dad on Thursday? How was J.X.'s book coming along?

Some of it was less mundane: Were the Kaynors really going to sue me? Did they have a chance in hell of winning in court? Where could Dicky be if he wasn't dead? If Jerry hadn't come after me, who had—and why? Would the news media pick up the story of the clown attack?

We talked about the last time we had made this trip together, and exchanged wry smiles. J.X. reached out his right hand, we linked fingers, and the next miles rolled by in companionable silence broken only by Jack Johnson's "I Got You."

When we arrived back in town, the first thing we did was head to the Civic Center Courthouse to file a Civil Harassment restraining order against Jerry Knight.

I dutifully filled out all the forms in my packet, and then we left to make the required copies, after which we stapled the copies to the originals and then brought the request for the restraining order, the copies, the Confidential Information form, the Notice of the Court Hearing, and the *temporary* restraining order back to the courthouse for filing.

Because we were filing after ten a.m., we would have to wait until the following day to pick up our temporary restraining order and the Notice of Court Hearing so that Jerry could be served.

"I didn't realize the process was quite so complicated," I told J.X. as we left the courthouse. "Thank you for not saying I told you so."

"I told you so," said J.X.

By four o'clock I was knee-deep in boxes I hadn't bothered to look at since I'd shipped them from Los Angeles. I found a lot of cheery notes and smiley Post-it stickies from Dicky attached to old manuscripts and book notes, mini snapshots of my day-to-day work life back then.

Our day-to-day work life.

Trader Joe's chicken salad you like in fridge read one note. *Picking up David's dry cleaning. Will stop by bank and pharmacy* read another.

All those colored pieces of paper with smiley faces and *xoxos* reminded me of things I'd chosen to forget. How much I'd relied on him, for one. How much I'd trusted him. How much non-writing-related running around for me he'd done. Unwillingly, I recalled how much I'd liked him and what a good PA he'd been.

I thought you were my friend. I smoothed out a crumpled orange square.

But that was childish. Dicky had been my employee and eventually my romantic rival. Not even my rival really, because I'd put up no fight for David. And I probably *had* been a pain in the ass to work for. Exacting and opinionated and a complete workaholic who, unrealistically, expected of him the same dedication to my interests that I had.

I picked up a manila folder and found the notes and initial chapters of the Butterwith novel I'd been working on when my life had fallen apart—and by my life falling apart, I don't mean when David left me. I mean when Wheaton & Woodhouse dumped the series.

I thumbed through the initial pages of *Miss Butterwith's Seeds of Doubt* and read the final paragraphs.

Miss Butterwith gathered up her bag, pulled on her gloves, and nodded to Mr. Pinkerton, who was lazily watching butterflies from the window seat overlooking the rose garden.

"Unless Mr. Fothergill is a good deal more ruthless—and clever—than I believe, I shall be back in time for tea."

Mr. Pinkerton meowed, showing all his sharp, white teeth.

"I'm always careful," Miss Butterwith assured him.

The cheerful pipping of a car horn outside the gate informed her that Inspector Appleby had arrived at last.

She turned toward the door, then glanced back in afterthought. "Mind you leave those songbirds alone," she warned.

Mr. Pinkerton yawned a wide and delicate yawn.

Miss Butterwith bestowed a reluctant smile upon him, and locking the door behind her, bustled off, a diminutive Athena in sensible shoes and a brown tweed suit.

I realized I, like Miss Butterwith, was smiling, and I wondered why I hadn't finished the book.

No, I knew why I hadn't finished it. Being dropped by my publisher had certainly played a role, but there were other publishers out there. In fact, Rachel had lined up a new publisher within a month after we'd returned from the writing retreat.

It was more about feeling that nobody cared if I finished the book or not. Publishing had changed a lot since I'd written the first of Miss B.'s adventures: *Miss Butterwith Closes the Case.* Reader tastes had changed. Now the heroines of cozy mysteries were all young, sexually active professional women (though, seriously, some of those jobs! Sudoku champs, wedding planners, NASCAR drivers, genealogists!), all with large, tiresome extended families and troublesome comic-relief pals—or, occasionally, a completely stereotypical gay best friend. It was depressing how few readers still seemed to care about elderly, retired Englishwomen with zero sexual experience and yet an uncanny understanding of the human heart—oh, and also a helpful feline companion.

I removed my glasses, wiped them on the tail of my T-shirt, and slid them back on.

Sure, I had always written for myself, but nobody *publishes* for themselves. I had published for others. I had published for my imagined audience. Now that audience seemed truly imaginary. In fact, it seemed to have disappeared in a puff of smoke.

Or had it? Maybe I was the one who had disappeared, disheartened by the lack of enthusiasm I perceived in everyone from Rachel to J.X.

It was hard to know, because I had never been exactly…engaged in promotion and publicity. I had been writing professionally long before there was anything like social media, and the marketing department at Wheaton & Woodhouse had taken care of the reader interaction end of things. I had simply written the books and occasionally shown up for signings.

I had *loved* writing the books.

Was I ever going to love writing anything again?

It seemed less and less likely, and yet I longed to rediscover that old excitement, the old passion for storytelling.

I gazed down again at the printed page.

Miss Butterwith bestowed a reluctant smile upon him, and locking the door behind her, bustled off, a diminutive Athena in sensible shoes and a brown tweed suit.

Were those really going to be the final words of fiction I wrote?

I mean, Miss B. had never even had a chance to solve that final case—or change out of that uncomfortable suit.

I laid the manuscript aside and picked up the phone to call Rachel before I could change my mind.

Although it was after seven in New York, I knew Rachel would still be working, and sure enough, Jordan Lombard, her latest assistant, picked up the phone at once. When I asked to speak to Rachel, Jordan put me straight through—so some things had not changed. I still carried some clout.

Rachel came on the line, demanding, "Christopher! Have they caught the clown who attacked you?"

"Not so far. At least, not as far as I know."

"How is the investigation coming?"

"I don't think they have a lot to go on. It's not like the description I gave is going to be of much use once he takes his costume and makeup off."

"Not *that* investigation! *Your* investigation."

"Oh, right. I'm still sorting through boxes, seeing if I can find any contact info for Dicky. That's not why I'm calling, though."

"No? Why are you calling?"

"Rachel…"

For the first time in our relationship, I didn't know what to say to her. It was hard to ask. It felt like begging. Like begging her to go begging for me. And the last time we'd tried that, it hadn't gone so well. We'd both ended up as murder suspects.

"Christopher?" she said sharply. "Christopher, are you there?"

"Yes." I drew a long, shaky breath. "It's just…in three years Miss Butterwith turns twenty. *Twenty.* That's a milestone in any series, and the Butterwith books made a lot of money and won a lot of awards in their time."

"That's true." Her tone was neutral. "What's your point?"

"It just seems like…"

She was silent. She *had* to know what I was asking. Couldn't she say *something*?

"I still love the Butterwith books. That's all. I enjoyed writing them, and I wish the series could have ended properly instead of being dropped."

After a moment she said, "Have you been working on a new Butterwith book?"

"No."

"Do you have a proposal for a new Butterwith ready to go?"

"No," I had to admit again.

"Millbrook Prime Crime is ready to contract another Butterwith book when you're ready to write the proposal."

"Yes."

She prompted, "But?"

"Rachel, I know perfectly well Millbrook doesn't care if I send them a book or not. I know you twisted arms to get that deal, and I know you did it as a favor to me. And I know this phone call is a waste of your time. It's not that I don't want to write anything new. I do. I just would have liked...more for Miss B. That's all."

Okay, this was truly ridiculous. And embarrassing. I wasn't quite sure what I was trying to ask of her. But the idea of Miss Butterwith's inevitable fade from the halls of publishing was getting me even more choked up than the idea of my own.

"I see." After a moment Rachel said briskly, "Thank you for calling, Christopher. Touching base with the client is never a waste of time."

I said feebly, "Okay. Well. Great."

"Keep me informed of your progress into the investigation of that little rat Dicky's death."

Rachel had taken Dicky's defection nearly as badly as I had.

"Uh, yes. I'll do that."

"Toodle-oo. Talk to you soon." She disconnected with a clean, clear *click.*

I stared at the handset. That was *it?* No *lemme see what I can do?* No *lemme think about it?* No *put together a proposal and then we'll talk?*

Maybe J.X. was right. Maybe I did need to change agents. Rachel was getting even more eccentric than me. Except, what would be the point of a new agent when I wasn't currently writing?

I put the phone to rest in the cradle and picked up the manuscript to stick it back in its manila folder. A lime-green Post-it square fluttered down to my desktop like a torn butterfly wing. I picked it up, turned it over.

In Dicky's neat writing read the message: *Going to movies with Joe E. Call if any problems,* followed by a phone number I did not recognize.

CHAPTER TEN

"What can I do for you, Mr. Holmes?" Detective Dean was brisk as a winter's morning in Iceland when she returned my phone call later that evening.

J.X. had joined me for dinner but was now back in his office, racing to hit the deadline on his current book. I returned to my own office and continued sifting through boxes and boxes.

I said, "I haven't been able to find Dicky's original job application or his résumé, but I did come across a phone number for one of his friends. I don't know if the number is still good or how close a friend this person was, but—"

"Not necessary," Dean cut me off. "The victim in your former backyard is not Dicky Dickison."

"What?" Despite telling David there was a chance the body did not belong to Dicky, in my heart I had been pretty sure Dicky was buried beneath the pergola. The fact that he'd been MIA for over a year seemed like too much of a coincidence.

Dean said, "The ME's preliminary findings indicate the skeleton belongs to a well-nourished, middle-aged Caucasian male."

"Middle-aged?"

"Correct. It looks like our victim was six feet tall and somewhere between fifty and sixty years of age. Does that sound like Mr. Dickison to you?"

"No. Dicky was twenty-three, slim, and about my height."

"Furthermore, our vic predates Mr. Dickison going missing."

"Predates him? How could he? The pergola was built less than a year ago."

"Actually, I wanted to discuss that with you," Dean said. "According to the ME—again, these are only preliminary findings—our vic has been dead and buried for nearly two decades."

"I-I don't see how that's possible."

"Well, in fact, there are a couple of possibilities. One, the victim was already buried in your backyard when you bought the house. Two, the victim was originally buried elsewhere but was moved to your backyard when you began construction on the pergola."

Into my silence, Dean added, "Three, you killed someone who was not Mr. Dickison and buried him in your garden."

That woke me up. "Are you kidding?" I demanded.

"Yes," Dean said without any hint of humor. "It's highly improbable you murdered someone twenty years ago and brought the body with you to the Hiawatha property—although it has been known to happen. Previously you rented an apartment in Northridge, so it would have taken effort to safely store the body in the interim before moving to Chatsworth. We can't find any record that you ever rented a storage facility."

They had actually explored that scenario!

I spluttered, "Then where's Dicky? Who's buried in my old garden?"

"Mr. Dickison's whereabouts remain unknown. That's a case for Missing Persons. As to the identity of the body in your backyard, we've not yet been able to identify him. We're hoping you might be able to help us with that."

"Of course I can't help you! I tell you I had nothing to do with it!"

She sighed. "Mr. Holmes, by *help*, I mean we're looking for information on the history of the house. According to the property records, you purchased the home from a Mr. Zachary Samuels."

I felt a twinge of guilt. *Zag.* God. I hadn't thought of him in years. "That's correct."

"Samuels lived in the house for seven years, which places him on scene within the time frame we're looking at."

"There's no way," I said. "I knew Zag. We were friends. He was not a killer. And I know everyone says that, but I mean it. He was *not* a killer. He was one of the sweetest guys you could ever hope to meet. He wrote cupcake mysteries, for God's sake."

"I'm sorry?"

"Just...you have to take my word for it. Zag is not who you're looking for. Assuming he's even still alive, which, sadly, probably not. Is it possible the body could have been buried *more* than twenty years?"

"It's possible," Dean acknowledged. "It could have been buried *less* than twenty years too. As I said, these are preliminary findings, and it's sometimes difficult to pinpoint exact dates, particularly in residential situations where the environment is relatively controlled. The question, of course, is if the body was already buried in your backyard by Mr. Samuels—or, for the sake of argument, someone else—why was it not discovered when the pergola was built?"

I said, "I think I mentioned this before. Originally there was a garden shed in that spot. It was kind of a weird place for it. Inconvenient, for one thing. For another, why take up that nice view—"

There was a tinge of exasperation in her, "Mr. Holmes, what does the *view* have to do with anything?"

There was probably equal exasperation in my, "I'm *getting* to that."

"Go on."

"It was a weird place to put a garden shed. That might be a clue."

She said with dangerous restraint, "Really? I'll make a note."

"Anyway, the shed had a cement floor. I don't know for a fact that the floor was broken up and removed. It's possible the contractor knocked down the building but retained the original foundation and built the pergola over it. It was just a small pergola. I used to have my coffee out there on sunny mornings."

"Are you telling me now that you believe the foundation to the pergola was part of the earlier, older structure?"

"I have no idea."

"How is that possible?"

"I had a lot on my mind at the time. I wasn't out there supervising. I hired a company with good ratings, told them what I wanted, and left it to them. I had a book to write." And a broken marriage to grieve. Mostly I had a book to write.

Dean's voice rose ever so slightly. "You didn't think to mention this earlier?"

"No."

"It didn't occur to you that might be significant?"

"It didn't occur to me at all."

"*Why wouldn't it occur to you?*" she cried.

I was rather taken aback by her vehemence. "Because you already seemed certain of the time frame and the victim's probable identity. I wasn't thinking about the history of the property. I did mention there had been a previous structure. And for all I know, the contractor *did* break up the old foundation and replace it. You'd have to ask him."

Dean had regained control of her voice as she answered, "I don't suppose you have the company's contact information?"

"No, but I remember their name. The Metal Petal. They did hardscape and softscape."

"Thank you for your help," she said as though slicing each word off a frozen loaf. She disconnected before I could share with her Zag's horror stories about the house's previous owners. Tip and Etta Coopersmith. He'd even used them as the killers in one of his books, *A Deadly Dozen*.

In my humble opinion, if anybody had committed murder and buried their victim in the backyard, the Coopersmiths were the most likely villains. But hey, if Detective Dean didn't want to hear my theories, fine.

I picked up the green Post-it with Joe E.'s phone number.

The good news was Dicky was not dead. At least, probably not dead. That was an enormous relief. In fact, I hadn't realized how distressed I was about his supposed murder until now when it turned out to be a false alarm.

But then where the hell was he?

I picked up the phone, but hesitated.

It had been one thing when I believed Dicky had been murdered and dumped in my backyard. I had felt guilty about that, even though I'd had nothing to do with it and he'd no longer been my responsibility. But now that things were back to status quo—i.e., Dicky was the little rat who had betrayed my trust and run off with my husband—his situation, whatever it was, was no longer my concern. Whether he'd had a change of heart or mind or had simply been thrown down a well was David's problem, not mine.

So instead of phoning the number on the green Post-it, I phoned David.

"I have good news and less good news," I said.

"I could use some good news," David replied. He sounded uncharacteristically down.

"The person buried in my old backyard is not Dicky."

He gasped. "Are you sure? How do you know that?"

"I just spoke with Detective Dean. She said the ME's preliminary indicates the victim was middle-aged."

"Middle-aged?"

"Yes. And that whoever he is, he's been dead for about twenty years."

"*Thank God.*"

"Yes."

He was silent for a moment. "So, this is a creepy thought, but that body was in our backyard the whole time we lived there?"

"It sounds that way."

"Holy shit."

"Yes. Well, on its way, at least."

"Do they have any idea who the victim is?"

"No. Right now their main suspect seems to be Zag Samuels."

"Why do I know that name?" he mused. "Wait. Was he the cupcake guy?"

"Yes."

"I remember him. He wrote about the ex-cop who gave it all up to become a baker who specialized in cupcakes and solving crimes."

"The Sweetie MacFarland series," I agreed.

"Right. Right. He always brought cupcakes everywhere he went. You used to drive together to conferences and signings."

"Yes."

"Whatever happened to him?"

I felt another of those guilty twinges. "I don't know. We lost track of each other after I bought the house. I heard he had a stroke and was living with family."

"But if it's not Dicky buried in the backyard, where is he?"

"I have no idea. As far as Dean and Quigley are concerned, Dicky is a case for Missing Persons. So I guess you should file a missing-persons report. Or no, you must have already done that." I stopped. *"Did you file a missing-persons report?"*

It seemed to me that David hesitated. "Uh, no. I didn't," he admitted.

"Why?"

He sounded defensive when he replied, "I told you. I figured he must have changed his mind."

"No, you said from the very first you had a bad feeling. That you knew Dicky would not have willingly left your side. Or some such muck."

"Sure, but *then* I realized that was unlikely. I figured he probably *had* changed his mind."

"Didn't you consider any other possibilities?"

After a moment he said, "No. Not really."

I was getting more confused by the second. "But didn't you want to know for sure?"

"Of course!"

"And yet..."

"He took his stuff," David said.

"When? From where?"

"From the hotel. I had moved into a hotel, remember? The plan was he was going to stay with me while I looked for a new place, but he only brought a few items. I had the feeling— Anyway, his toothbrush and everything was gone when I got home that night."

"The night he disappeared? The Monday he came to see me?"

"Yes."

"He'd cleared his things from your hotel room?"

"Yes."

"And when Detectives Dean and Quigley came a-callin', you didn't bother to tell them that?"

"Well..."

"You let them think he disappeared after talking to me!"

David said hotly, "He *did* disappear after talking to you!"

"But it was obviously planned. He took his belongings with him. He left *voluntarily.*"

"*Maybe!*"

I said, "What are you talking about *maybe*?"

"He would have had his keys on him. So whoever killed him could have come back to the hotel and cleared his things out to make it look like he left."

"Whoever... You mean *me*?"

David didn't say anything.

"Are we back to this? Didn't you just say... What you're telling me is you *do* think I had something to do with Dicky's disappearance?"

"Not anymore, no. But at the time, I thought maybe we'd..."

"We'd—you'd—*what*?"

"Driven you to it."

I could only make random vowel sounds for a few seconds. Finally, I got control and said, "Let me get this straight. You thought Dicky might have changed his mind *or* I might have killed him, but you didn't bother to check up in either case?"

Once again David said nothing.

"You didn't care enough to find out?" I demanded.

He protested, "I did care, but…"

"But *what*?"

"I also thought maybe…we'd made a mistake. And that he saw it too."

It was my turn to say nothing.

David said, "If you had done something, then it was partly my fault. I didn't want to know."

"You didn't want to know if I'd *killed your boyfriend*?"

"No. I didn't."

"I don't believe what I'm hearing."

"It's not like I thought that was what happened," David protested. "It went through my brain, of course. I read mysteries. But mostly I figured he'd changed his mind. And frankly, that was a relief."

"*A relief?*"

"Yes."

"But what about all that guff about finally having met your soul mate? What about what you were saying on Monday about missing someone who could share the good times and the bad?"

"I'd already had that. And thanks to Dicky, it was all fucked up. So…"

"I can't believe this."

I could hear the shrug in his silence.

"If you'd changed your mind, why didn't you tell me?" I pressed.

David gave a weird laugh. "If I'd told you I'd made a mistake, would you have taken me back?"

"Hell no!"

"Exactly. So what was the point?"

"Wow. I just…wow."

David said, "Which brings us back to the question of what *did* happen to Dicky."

"Okay, well, that's your problem," I said. I had my breath back by then and planned to put it to good use. "He was your boyfriend, and you lost him. So if you want to find out at this late date what happened, I suggest you file a police report."

"I will. But in the meantime, maybe you could look for him. I could help."

"What? No, I really couldn't."

"You're good at this kind of thing, Christopher. You're a natural."

"No, I'm not. I've never looked for a missing person, and I'm not going to start with Dicky. I can give you the phone number of one of his friends. I don't know if it's any good, but you can start there. Or not. This is *not* my problem. I do *have* my own problems and plenty of them."

"Christopher, wait—"

"Here's the phone number." I read the number from the Post-it note.

"We could work together," David was saying. "We'd make a great team. I always wanted to—"

I hung up.

CHAPTER ELEVEN

"Thank God for that," J.X. said after I'd filled him in on the latest developments. And then, belatedly, "What did I tell you?"

I had been in bed, reading, when he finally finished the day's work and tiptoed upstairs. As much as I'd wanted to run straight to him with my news, I remembered only too well what it was like to be interrupted when you were deep, deep into the zone.

Now I tilted my head sideways, considering him. He looked tired and frazzled as only a writer in the homestretch can look. There were shadows under his eyes, his five-o'clock shadow now looked like two a.m. in the drunk tank, and his hair was standing up in tufts like he'd been tugging on it in despair.

I asked, "Did it ever cross your mind that I might have murdered Dicky?"

"No." He answered without hesitation. "Never. It crossed my mind David might have."

"Sure, before you'd actually met him. But now that you have met him, do you still think *David* would be a likely suspect?"

"I didn't think it was likely, but certainly, between the two of you, David is the logical suspect."

"Really? You don't think I could kill someone?" I recollected slamming Jerry over the head with that adorable—and murderously heavy—

reading-bear bookend. In that moment, I hadn't been unduly concerned whether I killed Jerry.

Maybe J.X. remembered that too because he said, "I didn't say that. You could kill if you had to. But you wouldn't be so dumb as to plant the body in your own backyard. The fact that the body appeared to have been dumped on your property seemed to indicate malicious intent. And that, to me, implicated David."

I thought of my earlier phone call with David and his suggestion that we take up amateur sleuthing together. I was not going to share most of that conversation with J.X. He was edgy enough on the topic of David without adding to his list of grievances.

"He wouldn't have had any reason to feel malice toward me," I said. "He was doing the dumping. I was the dumpee. Between the two of us, I had a much stronger motive. On paper at least."

"Maybe on paper."

"Anyway, he's not a murderer. I'm not sure he could kill even to save his own life. You should have seen him wrestling that clown. It was pathetic."

J.X. shuddered at the word *clown*. "In any case, it's moot."

"Yes," I said slowly.

J.X. watched me. "What are you thinking?"

"Something David said. If that body is a couple of decades old, it was there when I bought the house. All those peaceful mornings I sat drinking coffee up there under my pergola, and *that* was underneath my feet."

J.X. was silent. "Not necessarily," he said at last. "It's not yet been determined whether the original cement slab was left in place or not."

"True."

"This is a bit gruesome, but I recall a case where a husband held on to his wife's remains through several moves across the state. He stored her in an oil drum, and he faithfully took that drum with him every time he changed addresses."

"Sure," I said. "I've seen a number of episodes like that on Investigation Discovery. In the instance you're talking about, the guy was finally undone by a nosy son-in-law."

"Yes," J.X. said in surprise.

"I can think of eleven cases right off the top of my head where women's bodies were left in barrels. It's not so common with men because it's a lot harder for a woman to get a man's body into a barrel than it is a man to deposit a woman—and most of these times the killer is a disgruntled spouse or partner."

He paused in the middle of pulling off his T-shirt, offering me a very nice view of his muscular chest. Silky dark hair swirled across the brown, satiny planes, setting off the rosy hue of his small, flat nipples. I rested my book on my lap.

"You've got to find another channel," he said. "What about Acorn? What about BritBox? You used to love watching polite English people kill each other."

"I still do. But ID gives me great ideas." He raised his brows. I said, "For writing, that is."

J.X. made an unconvinced noise and finished yanking off his shirt. He lifted the lid on the hamper in his half of the closet, dropped the shirt in, and replaced the lid. Yep, that was the attention and care his *dirty* clothes received. No ordinary laundry basket for his garments!

"Anyway, I see where you're going with your theory. Someone decided to get rid of the incriminating contents of a barrel or a burial in their own backyard under cover of the construction on my property."

"It's still a possibility."

"It is, I agree. Although, it's very hard to picture the Olsens on the left or the Jászis on the right resorting to murder, let alone illegal dumping. Both families were so conscientious about recycling."

"You never know what goes on behind your neighbors' front doors."

"True. If rather a sinister outlook."

"Hey, you're the fan of *I Wanna Kill My Neighbor* or whatever that show is called." He climbed into bed and stretched out with a groan. "God, I'm tired. My brain is tired. My back is tired, my butt is tired…"

"I get the message." I picked my book up again. "You're too tired."

The book was plucked out of my hand and went sailing across the room.

"I didn't say *that*." J.X. reached past me to snap out the lamp.

Inspector Ishwar Jones of SFPD's Investigative Bureau—Homicide Detail—phoned the next morning as we were having our coffee, scrambled eggs, and toast. Izzie was not contacting us in his official capacity. He was calling in his capacity as J.X.'s former partner and perennial pal.

They had a brief and cryptic—at least from my end—conversation, and then J.X. promised to phone Izzie later that morning. He bade his brother-in-blue goodbye.

"What was that about?" I asked as J.X. returned to the table.

"Jerry Knight's girlfriend has alibied him for Monday night."

I chewed that over. "Maybe she's lying."

"Maybe she is, but Izzie says she's credible."

"What does that mean?"

"Credible? It's an adjective meaning worthy of belief or confidence; trustworthy. For example, a credible witness."

"Thanks, smartass. This girlfriend is the jailhouse pen pal with the Victorian slew-foot name?"

"Violet Sanderson. She and Knight are currently living together."

"Unbelievable."

"I know. I figured he was gay."

I shook my head. "No. He's not gay. Interestingly, you can be obsessed with someone and yet not sexually interested in them."

"True. There are all kinds of stalkers."

I said, "Jerry could have hired someone to come after me."

"It's possible. But to what purpose?"

"You know, there doesn't have to be a practical purpose. Terrorizing me could be purpose enough."

"Yes, but in that case, I think Knight would want to experience that firsthand, not contract it out."

I grunted. "Point." I put my fork down. "Okay. Well, speaking of psycho stalkers, I should get down to the Civic Center to pick up my paperwork. I want Jerry served as soon as possible."

J.X. lowered his coffee cup, said casually, "No worries. Leave it to me."

"No way. You've got a book to write. It's my problem. I'll deal with it."

"The thing is," J.X. said in that careful tone he got when he was about to tell me something he figured I didn't want to hear, "Izzie's going to serve Knight."

"Izzie? Why? I thought that was something the Sheriff's Department did."

"Because we want to make sure it's done ASAP. Sometimes these things have a way of falling through the cracks. Especially—" He cut himself off.

I eyed him uneasily. "Especially what?"

"The Sanderson woman is apparently well-connected."

"You mean like mob-connected?"

"More like Nob-connected. As in Nob Hill. She belongs to one of the oldest and most wealthy San Francisco families."

I could see by his expression that this was liable to be more of a potential problem than he wanted me to know. "Terrific."

"It doesn't matter. Knight is getting served today."

After a moment, I nodded.

I spent the morning working in my office, continuing to unpack the boxes I had put off dealing with since I'd made the move from Southern California.

My reluctance seemed odd in retrospect. Why had it been so painful to sort through these old files and folders? Why had it felt like I was putting my old life into mothballs instead of what it was: preparing to take active part in my new life?

As I moved around the room, I'd occasionally glance at the Post-it lying on the desktop. Would David bother to phone Joe E.'s number? It hadn't sounded like it. Even if he did phone, would he know what questions to ask? Would he say the wrong thing and scare off our only lead?

I mean, not that *we* had a lead. There was no lead because there was no investigation. Not on my part.

Although…

Why not admit it? I was a little curious.

Okay, a lot curious.

Curiosity was killing me.

I sat down at the desk, picked up the phone, and punched the numbers on the piece of paper.

The phone rang a couple of times, and then someone picked up. A male voice said, "Yep?"

"Hi, I'm looking for Joe E."

"Joey? He moved out about six months ago."

"This isn't a cell phone?"

"Nope. It's the house phone."

"Do you have a new phone number for him? Or even his last name would be helpful."

"Who are you again?"

"My name's Christopher Holmes. A friend of Joe's used to work for me, and I've been trying to get in touch with him. I thought maybe Joe might have his address or a phone number."

"I don't know."

"His name is Dicky Dickison."

"Nope. Doesn't sound familiar."

"Okay, well, do you have a new number for Joe?"

"What company did you say?"

"I don't work for a company. I'm a writer."

"Huh."

I waited. Nothing seemed forthcoming.

"So do you have a number or maybe a forwarding address?"

"Somewhere, maybe."

"I don't want to be a pest, but it's kind of important. Do you think you could look and maybe phone me back?"

He seemed to think it over. "If you want to hang on the line, I'll have a quick look now."

"Yes. Thank you. That would be great."

I waited. The minutes ticked by on the clock on my desk. I absently admired the woodwork on the heavy hand-carved ball-and-claw writing desk. It was a beautiful piece of furniture, originally belonging to my former mentor, Anna Hitchcock. I had come to regard it as spoils of war.

The front door bell rang. I ignored it. If it was the mail or UPS, they'd leave their package or redeliver. If it was Girl Scouts bearing cookies, damn, damn, damn. Anyone else could come back another time.

Another minute passed. The doorbell rang again.

"Go away," I muttered.

"Here it is," the voice on the other end returned. "I don't have his cell, but this is where he was staying. It's from six months ago, so he might not still be there." He recited a number with a 213 area code, which I took as a promising sign. Six months ago Joe E. was still in the Los Angeles area.

"Thanks very much for your help."

He said cheerfully, "No prob, Rob."

I hung up and went to the front door. I looked out the peephole, but no one loitered on our doorstep. I opened the door and glanced out. No package sat on the small porch. No notice had been stuck to the door.

I went back to working in my office.

About an hour later I heard the front door open. J.X. shouted, "Kit? *Christopher?*"

Christopher? Since when?

"Right here."

My voice must have been muffled because his footsteps pounded down the hall. "*Kit,* are you here?" J.X. called again, and his tone was odd. Sharp. He sounded almost, well, scared.

"Here. In my office." I rose from behind the desk as J.X. skidded to a stop in the doorway.

"Kit!" He actually closed his eyes and leaned against the door-frame. "Thank God."

"What's going on?" I came around the desk to meet him, and he locked his arms around me and buried his face in my hair.

"Hey, hey. I missed you too," I said, patting his back.

He raised his head, and his eyes looked black in his pale face. "I thought—" He stopped, swallowing.

My unease grew. "You thought what?"

"Did anyone come to the door?"

"The doorbell rang a couple of times. I was on the phone. Why?"

He gave another of those jerky swallows.

"Were you expecting a delivery?" I asked.

He shook his head. "There's a red heart-shaped balloon tied to the front gate."

CHAPTER TWELVE

You don't solve four or so murders in a year and not make a few enemies.

People who hate your guts kind of comes with the Amateur Sleuth gig. That's not me being nonchalant; that's me explaining why the police couldn't immediately arrest Jerry, despite my exhortations to do so at once.

"Who else would it be?" I demanded of J.X. after the cops had departed. We were watching the footage from our home security cameras for the fourth time. "I tell you, it's the same clown who assaulted me."

(Now that was a sentence I never thought to hear myself say.)

The jaunty black-and-white figure of a clown in ruffled polka dots climbed the steps to the portico, waved at the security camera, and rang the doorbell with an exaggerated index finger pressed to the button.

"*Asshole*," J.X. growled, as he had growled at the same spot in our three previous viewings.

Definitely, but as J.X.'s former colleagues had regretfully pointed out, there was nothing remotely threatening in the clown's behavior. Nor was it illegal to try to deliver a balloon or even leave the balloon tied to a garden gate. Even the *Catch you next time* message scrawled on the attached card was arguably innocuous.

Violating a restraining order was illegal, but to prove that, we had to prove the clown was, in fact, Jerry.

The clown waited, pretending to examine the fingernails of his gloved right hand, and rang the doorbell again, before finally waggling his fingers at the security cam. He sauntered down the steps and out of view of the camera.

"It's Jerry," I said. "I know it's Jerry."

"Tell me how you know it's Jerry."

I stared at J.X. in disbelief. He stared back, unmoved.

"I *know*. Jesus Christ. It's *obvious*."

"*How* is it obvious?" he asked with infuriating patience.

"What do you mean *how is it obvious*? Who else would it be?"

"Kit, listen to me. Is there anything we can use to identify this clown as Jerry? Something about the way he walks? His facial structure? His height, his build?"

I glared at the monitor. The height, build, and facial structure were all similar to my memory of Jerry, but it was crazy how effectively the exaggerated makeup disguised him.

"I believe you," J.X. told me. "I think it's Jerry. Izzie believes you too. But if we haul him in based on nothing more than your conviction that it's him—and his girlfriend alibis him again... Do you see what I'm saying?"

I said tightly, "Yes."

I felt his gaze but continued to scowl at the screen.

"Please don't kill the messenger."

"I'm not going to kill the messenger," I said.

"Please don't make the messenger sleep on the couch tonight."

I grunted, trying to acknowledge the effort at humor, but none of this was funny. The sight of that red balloon tied to our front gate and bobbing merrily in the autumn breeze had scared the shit out of me. I was still scared, and that made me angry. There's nothing worse than feeling helpless. Well, being actively tortured is probably worse, but this felt like a kind of torture.

"So what do we do? Wait until he tries to get into the house again? Obviously, the restraining order had no effect."

"Practically every house on this street has a security camera on its front porch. Maybe one of those cameras picked up something like our visitor getting into or out of a vehicle. If we can get a license-plate number, we might have him cold."

I nodded.

"The balloon and card are being examined for fingerprints."

I made a pained sound. "There aren't going to be any useful fingerprints on that balloon. Or the card. And they won't be able to match that block-style print to Jerry's handwriting."

"And you call yourself a fan of true-crime TV? You have to know how often a partial print is enough to ID a criminal."

As a regular viewer of *The Forensic Files* I was forced to acknowledge that.

J.X. kept talking, trying to reassure me. "Nobody is about to let this go. Okay? We're looking into Knight's past employment records. And we're looking into how he's currently spending his time when not at Sanderson's home."

"Try the circus," I muttered.

By *we,* J.X. meant Izzie and his old pals at SFPD. Within five minutes of J.X. phoning SFPD, we'd had so many cop cars on the street, it looked like a hostage situation going down at 321 Cherry Lane. Which was probably how most of his friends thought of our union anyway.

I must have heard, "We've got your back, man," four times at least in the first half hour of the investigation.

I was grateful for the extra care and attention we were being afforded, but it didn't change the fact that there was not a hell of a lot that could be done for us. Not yet. Not until Jerry was caught actually in the middle of breaking the law. Like maybe the next time he came to kill me.

Reading my thoughts, J.X. said, "A patrol car will be driving past the house every few hours."

"I know. I know everybody is doing what they can."

J.X. drew a breath. "And I'm going to postpone my book tour."

That got my attention. I transferred my glower from the monitor to him.

"Uh, no. You sure as hell are not."

"Yes. I've already decided. I can't leave with this going on."

"You can undecide, then, because one of us needs to keep his career in good shape, and it's clearly not going to be me."

"First of all, that's bullshit about your career."

I said hotly, "*Really? B*ecause I haven't written a word in over a year!"

He continued to regard me with full and serious attention. "You're not going to distract me with an argument about your career versus my career. You're on sabbatical, and my career is fine. If I need to cancel a book tour, I will. You come first."

Well, hell.

I hadn't even realized I was doing it, but he was right. I was instinctively starting an argument as a diversionary tactic—a pattern David and I had developed through the years. By the end, we had argued constantly, but never about what was really on both our minds.

J.X. said, "Of course you're scared, Kit. I'm scared. This is something we need to deal with as a team."

His gaze held mine. So serious. So sincere. So hard to sidetrack.

I exhaled slowly. "Okay, you're right. We do need to deal with it together, but that doesn't mean you can't go on tour. I mean, come on. What sense does it make, you sitting around here on the off chance Jerry shows up again?"

"It makes sense because it's the right thing to do."

"No, it isn't. It makes me feel like you think I can't look after myself."

He got that mulish look that reminded me of Gage at his least endearing: squinty eyes, outthrust jaw, thinned mouth.

"What sense does it make leaving you here alone to deal with this?"

"We've got a good security system, and the cops are on standby. I'm not sure what more we can really do—what *you* can really do—until we can somehow prove Jerry has violated the restraining order."

Or Jerry was caught in the act of coming after me again.

J.X. said nothing.

"Right?" I said. "Isn't that what you've basically been telling me for the last half hour?"

He said reluctantly, "Maybe."

"As much as I hate the timing on this, signings and book tours are part of the writing gig. Correct?"

He nodded reluctantly.

"It's only for two weeks. I can handle that."

"It's not a matter of *whether* you can handle it. It's a matter of you shouldn't *have* to handle it."

I so totally agreed with him. But they tell me adulthood is about putting other people first, so…

"Let's say you postpone for a week or two and the situation still isn't wrapped up. Are you going to postpone again? Cancel? Come on," I scoffed. "Let's be realistic."

There went the chin again. His gaze grew steely. "I've got no problem canceling, if that's what it takes."

"But it isn't what it takes. I can manage on my own for a couple of weeks. Seriously. I'm offended you think I can't survive two weeks of my own company."

His face twisted. "You know that's not what I'm saying."

I sat back, smiling, though smiling was not how I felt. "Then we're agreed?"

J.X. still looked troubled. "If this is how you want it, but I am *happy* to cancel that tour and stay here with you."

"You're happy to cancel the tour so you can ask for an extension on the book."

"No." He wouldn't be distracted by weak attempts at humor. "I want to be here for you. Kit. Whenever you need me—"

I leaned over to stop him with a quick kiss. "Don't be a goof. You *are* here for me." I kissed him again. "Even when you're not, you know, physically *here*."

Despite the fact that the evening was cool and a bit damp with fog rolling in from the Bay, I grilled a plank of salmon and we had dinner on the patio. You really can't beat fresh Alaskan salmon brushed with olive oil, garlic, and a dash of smoked paprika. I had pretty much given up on cooking by the time I'd reconnected with J.X., but he was not content eating out of the freezer section of the grocery store, and gradually I was rediscovering my love of good food prepared well. Which didn't mean I wasn't stocking our freezer with plenty of my favorites to tide me over while he was away. In fact, my taste buds were already snapping in anticipation of ice-cream sandwiches and frozen pizza.

"I guess summer's over." J.X.'s tone was reflective as I set his plate in front of him.

Our first summer together. It had been a good one, despite the occasional dead body.

"Maybe we should get a couple of heat lamps for out here," he added. "We could extend our outdoor eating for another month at least."

"Sure." I took my place across from him and watched the blossom-shaped solar lights along the brick walk come on. This garden—our garden—was a magical place at dusk. I sighed. "It's going to be too cool to swim before long."

He was amused. "It's already too cool for most humanoid life forms."

"Ha."

"I haven't been in that pool since Labor Day. It must be your Scandinavian heritage." He winked.

I was part Swiss, not Scandinavian, but that was one of our little jokes.

I helped myself to a summer salad made of fingerling potatoes, shelled English peas, asparagus, fennel, and arugula. "Or that very efficient pool heater."

"True." J.X. rose to get another glass of wine. "Did you want your G&T topped up?"

I shook my head. Tempting as it was to get blitzed, I would be keeping the drinking to the necessary minimum until the situation with the creepy clown, whoever he was, was resolved.

Across the hedge I could see lights shining cheerily in the upper-story windows of the home of our neighbor and friend Emmaline Bloodworth. If anyone had noticed anything amiss that day, it would be Emmaline. Had the police talked to her?

When J.X. returned from the kitchen, I said, "Was Emmaline interviewed?"

"They interviewed everyone on the street."

I nodded and then sighed. "How did it go with Jerry today? You didn't say."

J.X. had accompanied Izzie to the Sanderson mansion, but had not been present when Izzie served the restraining order.

He made a face.

"That bad?"

"Yeah. Izzie said Jerry struck quite the pose. *Why am I being persecuted by this crazy writer? Isn't it enough he had me falsely arrested? Normal citizens don't stand a chance against celebrities.* Blah, blah, blah."

"Celebrity? *Me?*"

J.X. said grimly, "That wasn't the worst of it. *Then* he broke down and cried. Pretended to cry, at least."

I gazed at him, aghast. "How would Izzie see all that? I thought process servers just handed the paperwork and walked away."

J.X. looked briefly uncomfortable. "They do. Usually. Izzie may have added a word or two of caution."

"*Oh.*" I thought that over, wondering uneasily if threats would be helpful with someone like Jerry or merely egg him on.

J.X. sipped his wine and then shook his head. "The Sanderson mansion is something. It looks like a historical monument. This place seems like a dollhouse by comparison."

I glanced back at our own brightly lit windows and the glimpses of the comfortable, cozy rooms beyond. Our pretty little gated three-story Victorian was set back from the street in a private, almost parklike Tommy Church garden. But everything is relative.

"I like our dollhouse. As dollhouses go, we've got a nice one."

He smiled faintly. "It really does feel like home now, doesn't it?"

"Yeah." I went back to J.X.'s earlier comment. "You never know. Maybe Jerry will wear out his welcome with Ms. Snob Hill."

"Maybe." J.X. did not sound convinced.

Most nights after dinner we would take a stroll around the neighborhood. The mix of small, historic houses—many of them, like ours, noted for their gardens—the nearly hidden park, and the phenomenal views of the Palace of Fine Arts and the Golden Gate Bridge made it a pleasant and tranquil way to end the day.

It was especially charming this time of year with all the Halloween decorations. Pumpkin lanterns and cats with glowing eyes peeked out from windows. Skeletons and ghosts drifted lazily from tree branches. The occasional witch readied for takeoff from a rooftop. Tidy lawns were decorated with resin gravestones and plastic coffins.

But J.X. was once again closed in his office, trying to complete his book before he left on Saturday, and after our afternoon visitor, I didn't feel comfortable walking the streets alone. That was one of the most aggravating things about being the victim of violence. Or even the victim of attempted violence. It damaged your confidence, undermined your sense of independence. I wasn't living in terror, but I was constantly uneasy, jumpy. Every squeak of a floorboard had me on my feet, braced for attack.

And it was going to be a hell of a lot worse with J.X. gone for two weeks, although I would never tell him that.

I worked some more in my office. I found a box of awards and trophies, closed it again, and replaced the container on the closet shelf. Those things had meant a lot to me at one point. I'd enjoyed the recognition, of course, but more, the awards had felt like confirmation. Validation. Now, with the unceremonious ending to my career and Miss Butterwith's legacy, the trophies felt counterfeit. Or maybe it was that they made *me* feel counterfeit. Like I hadn't really deserved them after all. Just the sight of them depressed me.

I moved on to another box of old manuscripts.

I'd managed to empty two boxes and either file or trash their contents, and was well on my way to finishing a third box when the phone rang.

"I've got it," I shouted, though it was likely J.X. couldn't hear me— or the phone—over the pound of the Black Keys.

"Hello?"

"May I speak to Christopher Holmes, please?" The voice was feminine, stiff and snappish. The voice of someone used to getting her way.

"Speaking."

"Mr. Holmes, you and I have not yet met, but I know all about you."

"Who am I speaking to?"

"Violet Sanderson. Jerry's fiancée."

Swell. And yet somehow, I was not surprised. It takes a lot to disquiet J.X., but something about Violet Sanderson had disquieted him.

"My condolences," I replied.

She replied, "Predictable. Jerry said you would be sure to make some cheap comment."

Predictable? Well, that hurt.

I restricted myself to a terse, "Why are you calling, Ms. Sanderson?"

"I'm calling to warn you, Mr. Holmes, and you can consider it a threat if you like. Jerry is not alone anymore. He is no longer your helpless victim—"

I sputtered, "M-m-my helpless victim!"

"I've known people like you. People who abuse their celebrity status and position in society to prey upon those with less power. You used Jerry. You tricked him and then made him your dupe."

"My *what?*"

"You took advantage of his admiration for your work and pretended a friendship simply to trick and betray him."

"I didn't pretend any friendship. From the first, I considered Jerry a stalker—and I still do. Why don't you ask him where he was about three o'clock this afternoon?"

"*You* are the stalker, Mr. Holmes."

"*Me?*" I couldn't help the note of indignance that crept in. Had she even read the official account of Jerry's attack on me?

"What is this so-called restraining order but a deliberate and obvious attempt to harass and bully someone who already fears you?"

"Fears *me?* Madam, you have got the wrong end of the stick. Your fiancé has a long history of stalking and harassment. I was just the latest—"

She had stayed pretty cool up to that point, but after I accused Jerry, her thin voice rose. "You're not going to get away with it. I know your boyfriend still has contacts within the police department. Well, I have contacts too, and they are far more influential and important than Inspector Ishwar Jones."

A chill rippled down my spine. Not so much for myself—well, not only for myself. I didn't want to bring potential legal trouble down on Izzie, let alone J.X.

"Jerry is going to have his day in court," Sanderson said. "We'll see who's crying then!"

CHAPTER THIRTEEN

"If you want to ditch dinner with my father tonight, it's not a problem," I said to J.X. as we stumbled around the kitchen the next morning.

He had not slept well the night before. That was mostly because I had not slept well the night before. True, I did not sleep well a lot of the time, but Violet Sanderson's phone call had rattled me, as it was no doubt intended to do. No doubt it was intended to rattle both me and J.X., but in the end I had made the decision to keep quiet about it until J.X. returned from his book tour.

As menacing as Sanderson's message was, she had not said anything we did not already know, and J.X. had enough on his mind. If I'd gone to him about her call, he'd have cancelled that damn book tour for sure, and as much as I privately wanted that very thing, there was no justification for it.

"No, I don't want to ditch dinner. I've been waiting to meet the man for a year!" J.X. held up the coffee pot in inquiry.

"Not a year," I objected, holding my mug out to be filled. "You can't count the months before we were officially together."

"Long enough." J.X. popped a couple of bagels in the toaster oven, then sat back down at the table. "I'm looking forward to tonight."

"It's just we both know you have this very tight deadline—"

He cocked an eyebrow. "You're a lot more worried about this deadline than I am."

"I noticed!"

"Life doesn't stop because I have a deadline."

I said ruefully, "It did for me when I was writing."

He shook his head. "That's not healthy."

"Maybe not, but it was efficient."

J.X. made a dismissive sound. "When you get back to writing again, things are going to be different. I'm not going to let you shut me out like you did David."

It was my turn to express disdain. "When I get back to writing? Ha!"

J.X. got all dark-eyed and earnest, as he always did when I talked about my writing career being over. "You will, Kit. You burned out, that's all. You needed a break, and that's what you're having."

I said testily, "I wasn't burned out. I was dropped by my publisher."

"There are all kinds of burnout," he answered, which was inarguable.

I stirred my coffee, glanced up, and he was watching me with that sometimes unnerving attentiveness. Attentive and sympathetic. A hard-to-resist combo.

"I think David was the reason I started shutting the rest of the world out," I admitted finally. "I didn't want to know what he was up to, and I used work to barricade myself from…"

"Being hurt."

"Maybe," I said uncomfortably. It still astonished me, the embarrassing confessions he dragged out of me. All because of his insidious gift of being able to really *listen.*

"It makes sense. But I'm going to give you plenty of reasons to keep that door—"

The phone rang, mercifully cutting short our conversation.

It was J.X.'s publicist, and he ended up excusing himself and taking the call from his office.

I buttered the toasted bagels, spread cream cheese on mine and almond butter and honey on his. I left his breakfast to keep warm on a plate under a pot lid, and headed for my own office.

When I tried the new number for Joe E. or Joey, whichever it was, I got an answering machine.

"This is Derek, Michael, Rafe, and Joey's phone," announced a cheerful chorus of male voices, bringing back long-ago memories of frat houses and first apartments.

I felt a surge of elation. Joey still lived there.

I debated leaving a message, but ultimately decided against it. Forewarned was forearmed, and I wanted my quarry defenseless and forthcoming.

Of course, the elusive Joey might not have any useful information regarding Dicky's current whereabouts. Nor was Joey my only avenue of investigation. There was always social media. I signed into J.X.'s Facebook account and did a search for Dicky Dickison. A couple of Richard Dickisons came up, but they all appeared to be too old to be Dicky. There was a Dick Dickison located in Florida, but the account was set to private.

To see what Dick shares with his friends, send him a friend request! advised Facebook.

It was tempting, but I didn't want to abuse J.X.'s generosity in letting me use his account—or involve him in a potentially sticky situation.

I tried a general internet search and found a slew of possible leads. Most of them led to deceased persons much older than Dicky. There was one YouTube channel belonging to a Dick Dickison, and the videos looked like the kind of thing Dicky had liked: Honest Trailers, book trailers, interviews with authors—including a very old interview with me. The music playlist was all stuff I remembered Dicky liking: Imagine Dragons, AWOLNATION, American Authors, and KONGOS. The account profile revealed nothing, but I felt pretty sure this was Dicky's channel and experienced another rush of excitement. Maybe I was closing in on him.

Unfortunately, the last time anything had been uploaded was over a year ago—before Dicky had announced he was leaving me for David.

My excitement wilted. The abandoned YouTube channel didn't mean Dicky was dead, though. Maybe he'd found other things to occupy his time.

My bird-dog instincts fully aroused, I went back to delving through boxes, trying to locate Dicky's résumé or job application.

I didn't find either, but I did come across the old deed to the Hiawatha property. I studied it unhappily.

I'd known Zag Samuels for a few years before we'd discussed the possibility of my buying his Chatsworth home. We had met through Sisters in Crime. We were around the same age and had instantly bonded over being the only two men in our local chapter writing cozy mysteries.

We weren't buddies, but we had lunch now and again, and we usually drove to chapter meetings together. On two occasions, we'd roomed together at conferences, but not only was Zag a very loud snorer, he liked his hotel room kept ice-cold. I wasn't crazy about sharing a room to begin with, so the bunkies thing hadn't lasted long.

An additional strain to our friendship had come from the fact that for the first few years we were always in competition for the same awards. At first the division of prizes wins had been pretty even. He'd won the Anthony for Best First Novel, and I'd won the Edgar for Best First Novel by an American Author. I'd won the Agatha for Best First Novel, and he'd won the Lefty for Best Debut Mystery Novel.

And so it had gone. But after Zag's agent convinced him to change publishing houses a couple of times, Sweetie MacFarland stopped bringing home prizes. I'd tried to convince him to drop his agent and go with Rachel, but the idea had not gone over well. Zag was loyal—and he also felt I had no business giving him advice when I hadn't been publishing any longer than he had.

Maybe he'd had a point because his agent's strategy of cranking out stories at a speed nearly unknown before the advent of Amazon paid off big-time. Though in my opinion the quality of the books had declined, Zag had done very well financially. So well, that he had decided to move uptown with his girlfriend Felicity, and had put his house on the market. The timing was great for me. I'd been looking to move out of my apartment, and I made an offer. A deal was struck.

But midway through escrow, tragedy occurred. Zag suffered a serious and debilitating stroke and had been hospitalized. After he'd left the hospital, he'd had to move in with his niece.

I had never seen him again.

Looking at his niece's signature with the underlying note "power of attorney" beneath *Pandora Pearce*, I felt a stab of regret.

Initially, Zag had been too ill for visitors, but why had I never made any effort to see him once he was out of the hospital?

I had meant to, but time had passed, and I'd been busy with moving out and then moving in and writing three books a year and then meeting David, and then writing three more books after that and then David's cheating, and then writing three more books and three more books after that and three more books after that… I had simply never gotten around to it—and then, eventually, I'd forgotten all about Zag.

No wonder David and I had gotten along so well. We were both heartless bastards.

Jeez. Well, hopefully, I had evolved over the years. I was trying. A lot of the time.

I went back to studying the Hiawatha deed.

You could never really know everything there was to know about a person. I didn't need J.X. to tell me that. The Investigation Discovery channel was full of stories about innocent persons being done in by what they didn't know about people they trusted. Just ask Lt. Joe Kenda. Come to think of it, Zag would have loved Lt. Joe. Though it was hard to picture Lt. Joe ever turning in his badge for cupcakes.

Even so.

Was Zag still around for the police to question?

I hoped so—hoped that he was still around—but from what I recalled, his prognosis had not been very hopeful.

My money was on the couple who had owned the house before him. The Coopersmiths. I still remembered some of Zag's stories about them, though obviously any information I had would be hearsay. In fairness, it had been a forced sale, and the Coopersmiths had, understandably, not been happy. Their unhappiness had manifested in worrying ways. Zag claimed Felicity had actually witnessed Etta trying to poison a neighbor's cat, and Zag had seen Tip dumping salt in the flowerbeds. Zag claimed they had carved out chunks of drywall throughout the house, placed dead fish inside, and sealed the walls up again.

So, yeah, I thought the Coopersmiths were candidates for the title of Homicidal Homeowners of the Year.

Detective Dean had not been interested, but was it maybe my civic duty to push harder? Or should I take J.X.'s advice and let the law run its course? If Dean and Quigley were able to interview Zag, he'd have plenty to tell them. Even if he had passed on to that prime real estate in the sky, his niece had probably heard some of his horror stories.

It was not my business. I was already poking into Dicky's disappearance when I had no good reason.

At the same time, it couldn't hurt to look. Right?

I typed *Tip and Etta Coopersmith* into the search bar—and sat blinking at the results.

Eviction notices, lawsuits, bankruptcies—

The phone rang, and I gasped.

I couldn't help feeling kind of like a Peeping Tom, even though my motives were pure.

I reached for the handset without tearing my gaze from the alarming search results.

"*Christopher!*" Rachel squawked in my ear.

"Nothing to report yet, but—"

"Never mind that now. Wheaton & Woodhouse is asking us to submit a proposal."

As the words filtered through my brain, I stopped staring at my monitor screen and sat back in my chair.

"What kind of proposal?"

"A book proposal. Surely it hasn't been *that* long."

"No, I just mean… Wheaton & Woodhouse? I thought we were with Millbrook House's Prime Crime now."

"Technically we are. But since you haven't actually delivered anything to them, including a proposal—and since W&W controls the entire Miss Butterwith backlist—Millbrook is willing to release you."

I'll bet. I'll bet they couldn't wait to unload me.

"Okay," I said cautiously. "But W&W dropped the series, so what kind of book proposal would they be looking for?" My heart leaped, and I stood up. "Do you mean for a Butterwith book?"

"Yes."

"But I thought— You said—"

"Now that Satan—er, Steven Krass—is gone, wiser heads have prevailed. As you've pointed out, we're coming up on Miss B.'s twentieth anniversary. Cozies are back in, especially series and especially—"

"Hold on. A year ago you told me the cozy was dead."

"I didn't say *dead*, Christopher. I said Cozy was suffering *malaise*."

"I'm pretty sure you pronounced it dead."

"Not at *all*. Cozy was in ICU. Cozy was receiving necessary medical attention. Happily, Cozy has survived and is on the mend. So that's brilliant news. It's especially brilliant news for you with your extensive backlist."

"Three books a year for sixteen years!"

"Your math skills remain unparalleled. Better yet, because of the plethora of sleuthing yoga instructors, pet sitters, flower arrangers, witches, butchers, bakers, and candlestick makers, W&W anticipates a demand for old-school snoop sisters."

"Snoop sisters?" I wondered uneasily if she was talking about a tie-in based on the 1970s mystery-comedy TV series on NBC. Was this what it had come to? Writing TV tie-in books?

"Old maids. Spinsters. Senior singletons."

"*Old maids?* You aren't allowed to say that anymore, Rachel."

"The point, my dear Christopher, is that W&W is looking to make a deal."

I said warily, "What kind of deal?"

"They want three more Miss Butterwiths. A holiday novella for this year—"

My knees gave at the words *three more*. I sat down again. *Thank you, God. Thank you…* Then I registered the rest of her sentence.

"*This* year? It's already October. It's the end of October. That's even worse!"

"Oh, come, come. You can do a novella in a week if you have to."

"In a-a *week?*"

"A holiday novella and two novels. One to be released in year nineteen and the final novel to be released in Miss B.'s anniversary year."

My throat closed, and I couldn't say anything for a moment.

Rachel wasn't waiting for me anyway. She said smoothly, "You'll be able to bring the series to a gracious and elegant end as befits Miss B. and Mr. Pinkerton."

"I see that," I managed.

"You're pleased of course."

I made a strangled sound.

"You'll be still more pleased to hear W&W is planning to put the entire series into boxsets."

"Are they? Is that— That's a good thing, right?"

"Of course. *And* they have finally agreed to purchase the audio rights, the bastards."

"For which books?"

"The entire series."

"The entire…" I had to sit down. Wait. I was already sitting down. I lowered myself to the carpet, lay back, and stared at the ceiling with its bronze Corinthian medallion.

"Ask me how much," Rachel demanded.

I asked faintly, "How much what?"

"How much they're paying for audio rights."

"How much are they paying for audio rights?"

She named a figure, and after a moment, I said, "Did I—did I hear that right?"

"You heard me."

I closed my eyes, lest I actually, unmanfully burst into tears. I finally managed, "Rachel, how did you *do* that?"

"Negotiating audio rights is one of my superpowers," she purred. "Until now, W&W has refused to even consider putting the series into audio. For that insult, *They. Shall. Pay.*"

I'm not sure she actually said *for that insult*, but she did snap out the words: *They. Shall Pay*, exactly like Colonel Saito in *The Bridge Over the River Kwai* barked out, *You. Would. Die!* I could almost picture her in a pristine kepi and glossy riding boots, facing down the quivering acquisition team at Wheaton & Woodhouse.

I whispered, "You are the best agent ever."

"I know. So this is the deal. A four-book contract—"

"Wait. Four books? What's the fourth book?"

"I'm getting to that. The fourth book is my anniversary present to you."

"Anniversary? We haven't even set the wedding date. I haven't even asked him yet."

"*Christopher!* I am speaking of *our* anniversary. It is not simply Miss Butterwith who is turning twenty. You and I will have been together twenty years as well."

"My God. You're right."

"My gift to you is the fourth book. Wheaton & Woodhouse is contracting a standalone novel. It doesn't matter what the book is, so long as it's a work of mystery or suspense."

"Rachel." I had to stop.

Her tone softened ever so slightly. "You can complete the Butterwith series properly, and you can launch the next phase of your writing career. Assuming your true-crime book isn't a bestseller."

I laughed and knew she could hear how shaky it was.

"I'm not even sure how to thank you," I began.

She said curtly, "Stop. You thanked me a year ago."

"I did?"

"At the lodge. When you chose to continue our association despite certain revelations about my past."

"Oh, but that was… Come on. Of course I wouldn't…wasn't going to terminate our relationship."

"It would have been extremely foolish, and now you know why."

"Yes."

"I take it the deal meets with your approval?"

"God, yes."

"And you'll get to work on putting those proposals together?"

"I will. Yes." I added huskily, "Thank you, Rachel. Truly."

She gave a loud and watery sniff—and hung up.

CHAPTER FOURTEEN

"There's something you should know about my father," I said to J.X. as we walked from the parking structure across the street to Fog Harbor Fish House, where we were meeting my dad for dinner.

"He doesn't know you're gay?" J.X. guessed, putting his hand on my arm as a green Porsche tore out of the garage. "Watch this guy."

I stepped back as the car roared past. "Huh? What? Yes, my dad knows I'm gay!"

J.X. raised his brows. "Okay. I did wonder, given the way you've stalled my meeting him. Meeting both your parents."

"I haven't stalled," I said uncomfortably as we resumed walking. "It just hasn't been…convenient."

"He's a racist," J.X. surmised. "He wouldn't be happy about you marrying a Hispanic."

I ignored the *marrying* comment because one battle at a time.

"First of all, you're half Irish, so it would make as much sense to say he was anti-Irish—which, given my English grandfather's views, might actually be true—*except*, secondly, hell no, my dad is not a racist!"

"What's the matter with him, then?"

"I didn't say anything was *wrong* with him."

"He's a Republican. He's a right-wing looney—"

"Would you stop? No. And they're not synonymous, you know."

"I know they're not synonymous." His own family was extremely conservative.

"Anyway, he is *not* a right-wing looney. He's just a little…corporate."

J.X. laughed. "Is he?"

"Yes."

"Did he and David get along?"

"Yes. They got along great. They both liked to golf and smoke cigars with their after-dinner brandies and bitch about how the morons at "Corporate," meaning the head office, had no clue of how it was out in the field where the real action was."

J.X. laughed again. "Okay. I'll keep that in mind."

Our feet thumped on the wooden walkway leading to the restaurant entrance. The briny scent of the ocean—and cooking fish—filled the damp evening air.

"Also, don't mention my mother."

"Why would I say something about your mother? I haven't even met her yet."

"No," I said. "I don't mean don't criticize her. I mean, don't refer to her. Don't mention her at all. Tonight let's pretend I was raised solo. By my father."

He gave me a sideways look. "Yeesh."

"Yeah, it's always worse when he's in the middle of a divorce and she's not."

He blinked. "How many times has your dad been married?"

"Three times. Not including the times he married my mother."

He stopped walking. "Your parents divorced more than once?"

"Three times."

"How is that even possible?"

"Apparently it's like murder. Once you've done it, it gets easier."

He said cautiously, "What about your mom? How often has she—?"

"Twice. Not including the marriages to my dad."

In answer to the look he was giving me, I said, "I told you the first time you brought this up that my family was not like your family."

"Not like *my* family? They're not like anyone's family. With maybe the exception of Henry the VIII's."

"So far no spouses were harmed in the making of their relationship."

He stared at me. "And you had the audacity to say *my* family was difficult."

I hooked my hand around his elbow and drew him on. "Come on, we don't want to be late. He likes punctuality."

My dad was sitting in the faux Tudor-style bar of the Fog Harbor Fish House, drinking his usual martini and gazing out at the sunset. He glanced over as we approached, raised his hand in greeting, and rose to meet us.

As befitted a guy who was in town for the Santa Rosa City Amateur & Senior Championship, he wore khaki shorts and blue and white striped golf shirt—despite the fact that it was October and the evening was chilly. That's kind of a SoCal thing. Clinging to shorts and T-shirts in the face of inclement weather. But then Southern California is home to both Hollywood and Disneyland, the twin capitals of make-believe.

I hadn't seen Dad for a few months, but he looked unchanged: a deeply tanned and reasonably fit guy in his late sixties. He was taller and broader and a grayer than me. I could see J.X. sizing him up and trying to decide if I took more after my mother.

And...not really. I'm shorter than my father but blonder than my mother. I have my dad's brown eyes and my mother's button-shaped mouth. My dad is...blunt. Blunt in features and blunt in manner. My mom is...pretty much the same.

"Long time no see, Christopher," Dad said as J.X. and I reached him. He thumped me on the back in greeting. "You look good. Lost some weight, I see."

I patted him back briskly. We are not a hugging type of family. "You too. Keeping healthy?"

"Always, always." He nodded cordially to J.X. "So this is the guy!"

"Dad, this is J.X. Moriarity. J.X. this is my father, Andrew Holmes."

I made the introductions, and as they shook hands, my father said to J.X., "I can't call a grown man by a set of initials. What's your actual name, son?"

"Dad, he goes by—"

"Julian," J.X. said calmly, giving me a look that said, *Chill the hell out.*

"Julian, there we go," my father approved. "And you're a writer too?"

"Yes, sir."

"Call me Andy. Everybody does. Are you as successful as my son?"

I said, trying to usher them toward the waiting hostess, "Our table's ready. If you want to postpone the third degree until we sit down..."

"I do reasonably well," J.X. said.

"He's being modest," I said. "He's enormously successful. They're making a movie of his first book, and a couple of the others have been optioned."

My father looked duly impressed.

We reached the hostess and were escorted to our table near the windows with their panoramic view of docked sailboats bobbing gently on the evening tide.

The candles were lit, drink orders taken, and we were off.

There was a bit of chitchat about the weather and Dad's trip up north.

"Christopher's…" Dad coughed and cleared his throat. "Reads his books. I'm not a reader. I don't understand sitting around reading books when you can be outside doing things. He got me a book for Christmas." He shook his head. "What was that damned thing called?"

"The Mysterious Montague: A True Tale of Hollywood, Golf, and Armed Robbery," I answered. "You'd like J.X.'s books for sure. Although you'll like the movie better."

My dad laughed. "He's always trying to get me to read books!"

"Christopher's books are very entertaining," J.X. said, ever loyal, ever misguided.

"Sure, if you like old ladies and talking cats," my dad agreed. "Do you golf, Julian?"

I opened my mouth to point out that Mr. Pinkerton did not actually talk, but let it go.

I love my dad. I love both my parents. But I don't have a lot in common with them, and frankly never did. Aside from their ongoing marital drama, I had a peaceful childhood and a relatively painless adolescence. I moved out as soon as I could and never looked back.

Well, when I say *never looked back*, that's not to say I cut off ties. I saw my parents a couple of times a year, we exchanged birthday presents and holiday greetings and still celebrated the occasional holiday together, but I didn't have anything near the close relationship J.X.

shared with his family. Which was fine with me. You don't miss what you've never had.

At least that's what I'd always thought until I met J.X. Until J.X., I had figured most marital relationships were some variation on what David and I shared—ideally, minus the serial cheating.

The first time I'd met J.X., I'd had a taste of what love and romance could be, and frankly it had scared the hell out of me. It still scared me sometimes.

But I was trying. I wanted this relationship to work. Wanted to believe it was forever. I can't deny that seeing David again had brought back memories. Not feelings for David. There was no comparison between what I felt for J.X. and what I'd once felt for David. But I had been reminded love is often not enough—and how much finding that out hurts.

Watching J.X. trying to charm my father made me smile.

It was actually a nice dinner. We had a good table with an excellent view of the evening harbor. J.X. was his naturally charming self, and I could see my father liked him, despite J.X.'s admission that he wasn't much of a golfer.

The food was great. We started with drinks and the shellfish tower, a stack of lobster, crab, oysters, and jumbo shrimp drizzled in cocktail sauce and light and tangy mignonette. We moved on to salad, which was followed by more drinks and then our entrees: linguine and clams for me, mixed grill for J.X., and New York steak for my old man.

"Seriously?" I said. "This is one of the best seafood places on the West Coast and you're having the steak?"

"I like steak," my father said.

J.X. grinned at me and said, "He knows his own mind. Who does that remind me of?"

"Gage?" I suggested tartly. My cell rang. I eyed the number suspiciously and then realized it was David's. My suspicions grew. I must have muttered something because J.X. gave me a questioning look.

"I'll take this outside."

"What's up? Do you need your plate kept warm?" J.X. asked.

"This won't take long. It's David," I said, and his face instantly shuttered.

I sighed inwardly and clicked Accept.

"Tell him hello!" my father called jovially.

I nodded distractedly. "What did you need, David?" I inquired.

As I threaded my way through the crowded tables, I could hear my father regaling J.X. with the tale of how he'd helped David correct his duck-hook shot.

"Hello to you too!" David's voice said in my ear.

"We're in the middle of dinner with my dad."

His tone changed instantly. "Oh hey. Tell Andy hi!"

I stepped outside and leaned against the railing overlooking the purple-blue water. "What did you need, David?"

"I remembered something. About Dicky. I was thinking about him last night. He had an older sister living in Florida."

It didn't ring a bell. I couldn't remember if Dicky had siblings or not.

"What part of Florida?" I asked.

"I don't know."

"Was she married?"

"I think so."

"Damn. If you don't know what part of Florida and we don't know for sure what last name she might be using, I'm not sure what good it does."

"We could start with her maiden name, right? I know what she did. I mean for a job. She was a RIPR coordinator."

"RIPR? What's that?"

"Reef Injury Prevention and Response. It had something to do with managing the coral reef."

I felt a flash of interest. That was a pretty uncommon job description. "So that would be where? Southeast Florida?"

"I think so."

I thought it over. "Okay. I don't know if it's useful or not, but thanks."

He said quickly, "Were you able to contact that friend of his?"

"Not so far."

"But you did try?"

"Yes."

"Have you made *any* progress?"

"Not noticeably." I added defensively, "It's not like I'm a PI. I'm not actively looking for him. It's just—"

"Yes, you are. If you're trying to reach his friend, you're actively looking."

Hard to argue with that.

"It would be much easier if we put our heads together," David urged.

"I appreciate the offer, but no."

"Why not? I just gave you your best lead so far."

Hopefully not. Because as much as I wanted to find Dicky alive and well and betraying other employers, it was going to be so very annoying if David turned out to be right about that.

"Thanks for calling." I disconnected.

When I got back to the table, J.X. said, "Everything okay?"

I nodded, picking up my glass. "Just David being David."

"I always liked David," Mr. Tact said.

"I know." I shook the ice in my glass and debated having another drink.

J.X. said, "I ordered champagne."

"Why?"

"Because we're celebrating." He said to my father, "Christopher's agent phoned him today with big news." J.X. beamed at me.

My face warmed. "It's not *that* big of news," I protested. Although it had felt life-changing that morning. It *still* felt life-changing, if I was honest. I'd tried to downplay it when I told J.X, but it seemed he'd seen right through that.

The champagne came—Dom Pérignon, for God's sake—we toasted, glasses clinking against each other with a sound as fragile as success.

"To Kit," J.X. said. "And the next fifty books." He was smiling, and the smile lit his eyes. All that warmth. For me.

"Hear, hear," my father said. He was getting plastered as he—we—usually did during such occasions.

I felt silly, but at the same time, I was touched that J.X. wanted to make a thing of this new contract. I felt warm and happy, even if he was fussing too much.

After the champagne, we had dessert. Well, I did. I ordered the warm chocolate-fudge cake, and J.X. shared a few bites, and then we had coffee. Finally it was time to say goodbye.

"It was a pleasure to meet you, sir," J.X. said as Dad's Uber ride pulled up.

I couldn't help smiling. He looked so earnest. Like a kid on his way to the prom. *Don't worry, I'll have her home by eleven!*

My father shook hands. "Good to meet you, Julian. I'm looking forward to that first round." He jumped into the car, and we waved him off as they sped away.

"First round where?" I asked as we walked back to our car.

"Of golf. At your dad's country club. The next time we're down in SoCal."

I tilted my head, directed a skeptical look at him. "Go on as you mean to continue," I said.

"I will." His smile was quizzical. "I don't hate golf. And I like your dad."

"Sure. But don't say I didn't warn you."

He seemed amused. "I won't." Then with less amusement, "What did David want?"

"Oh." I groaned. "He had a possible lead on Dicky's sister."

"What does that mean?" J.X. stopped walking. "Kit, you're not involving yourself in that investigation?"

"No. Well, not *that* investigation. Dicky's disappearance isn't part of that."

"Finding Dicky is a job for the police. It's a job for Missing Persons."

"I agree."

"Then what the hell—" We had reached the parking structure and were walking toward J.X.'s car. The building smelled of exhaust and oil and, more distantly, fish. Despite the grim lighting, there were a lot of shadows and dark corners at night, so it took a moment to see what had stopped J.X. mid-sentence and mid-step.

A tall figure stood by the Honda S2000. Impossible to know if it was male or female, but its face was painted white and a red ball protruded in place of an ordinary nose. The ball matched the bright red winged wig. The figure wore bright and baggy hobo-style clothes and purple, oversize, floppy shoes.

A clown.

The clown seemed to be searching through a yellow change purse and didn't hear our approach until J.X. made an inarticulate sound.

The clown looked up. He seemed startled to see us. He opened his wide red mouth and pointed with his white gloved hand.

I didn't hear what he said because at that moment J.X. made a guttural noise that was part rage and part fear, and launched himself at the clown.

The clown's eyes and mouth turned into a terrified triangle of wide O's, shaping the single word that escaped him: *NOOOooooooooo.*

Yes, a big cinematic NO! only this was the slow-mo gif version. As J.X. tackled him about the waist, the clown's hollow voice rolled down the rows of parked cars, echoing out across the ocean. And as the pair of them crashed to the cement floor of the parking structure, I echoed that howl of protest.

"J.X., *NOOOO.* It's the wrong clown!"

CHAPTER FIFTEEN

"Really, I can't tell you how sorry I am," J.X. said again.

"No, no!" Happy Harold said quickly. "An honest mistake. I understand!"

"Are you sure you don't need medical attention?"

"No! No, I'm fine. Mustn't be late for work!" Harold's shaking hands fumbled over his head, tugging at his red wings of fake hair. His mournful eyes moved from J.X. to me. "Is my wig on straight?"

"Yes," I said.

J.X. opened his mouth, met my gaze, closed it.

He looked genuinely mortified—like an illustration straight out of a graphic-novel version of *The Mortification of Sin*—and seeing all that dark anguish, Harold couldn't help volunteering, "You're not the first person who's reacted badly to the unexpected sight of a clown. It happens all the time in my profession. I've been spat on, cursed, and punched. I've been kicked by seven-year olds and even thrown up on by babies. And it's gotten worse since those creepy clown sightings began a couple of years ago."

"Exactly," I said quickly. "Those clown sightings really don't help matters."

J.X. flicked me a *nice-try* look and went back to his stricken observation of Happy Harold.

After realizing his mistake, J.X. had helped Harold to his wobbly feet and made him sit in the front seat of J.X.'s Honda, taking deep breaths with his head between his legs. Now fully recovered from being knocked flat on the cement floor, Harold climbed out of the car and brushed his costume down. He took his time about it. When he at last straightened, he looked directly at J.X. and said, "After what you people have been through, I can kind of understand your reaction. And I'll ask around in the community. See if anyone knows anything about this rogue clown. Guys like that give all of us a bad name."

Yep, in the first few shocked moments of realizing he had attacked an innocent bystander clown, J.X.—of all people—had poured out the whole sordid story of my being stalked and attacked by one of Harold's tribe. Proof that he really was rattled by the whole situation—more so than he'd let on to me.

"That would be really kind," I said.

"I believe it's my duty," Harold said with simple dignity.

J.X. handed him his card. "If you find that you're more seriously injured than you realize now, here's my number. And again, I'm so sorry for the…misunderstanding."

Harold brushed this aside as sheer nonsense, gave his nose a couple of squeezes, which caused it to honk loudly, and waddled away down the cement ramp leading to the street.

We watched until his baggy figure vanished into the night.

When we got home, I poured J.X. a couple of fingers of his favorite Jack Daniels and patched up his scraped hand in the master bathroom.

"I know you feel terrible about assaulting—" J.X. flinched, whether from the antiseptic or the word *assault.* "Happy Harold, but honestly, that was one of the bravest things I ever saw."

J.X. glowered. "Go ahead and laugh."

"I'm not laughing. I mean it. I know how you feel about clowns, and you didn't even hesitate. You just went for him."

J.X. groaned. "God. Don't remind me. It'll be a miracle if he doesn't sue me."

"I don't think he'll sue you. He seems like a-a kindhearted clown. The kind of person who goes into clowning to help people."

J.X. rolled his eyes. I can't say I didn't find the situation a *little* comical, but J.X. really *had* shown courage. Also, an unexpected impulsive streak. But then again, looking back, he'd tackled me once too. And with even less provocation.

When I had taped his hand to my satisfaction—and his bemusement—we retired to our chamber and undressed for bed.

I was just punching the pillows behind my back into a comfortable nest and reaching for the remote control, when he asked, "What did David have to say that was so urgent?"

"Something useful for a change. He remembered a couple of things about Dicky's sister that might make it possible to track her down."

"I thought you weren't going to get involved in looking for Dicky."

"I thought I wasn't either. But."

"But what? This is not a good use of your time, Kit."

"What is a good use of my time? Sitting around waiting for Jerry to kill me?"

He didn't say the obvious thing: *shouldn't you be starting those book proposals?* Instead, after a reflective moment, he asked, "Do you feel responsible somehow?"

"For Dicky? Hell no. I just…" This was kind of awkward. "I'm curious, I guess. It's probably all those years of writing mysteries."

J.X. said grimly, "Don't forget. Curiosity killed the cat."

"Then it's a good thing I'm not Mr. Pinkerton."

"You're not Inspector Appleby either."

"No. True." I turned that over for a moment or two, said thoughtfully, "I wonder if I should try spinning off Inspector Appleby?"

"You mean give him a series of his own?"

I nodded. "There really isn't a mainstream cozy series with a gay protagonist."

J.X. laughed. "I thought Inspector Appleby wasn't gay?"

"Ah." I smiled at him. "Things change."

He slipped his arm around my shoulder, tugged me over, and kissed me. I kissed him back and rested my head against him. It was nice like this. Being tender, romantic together even without having sex. I wondered if a time would come I would take having this for granted. I hoped not. That I would ever take it for granted, that is.

After a time, J.X. reached over and picked up one of the travel brochures on the nightstand. "You never said about Italy."

"I never said what about Italy?"

"About making the trip a honeymoon."

"I…"

I'd known this was coming. I just hadn't expected it to come so quickly. Wasn't it awfully soon to be planning another wedding? We'd only been living together a couple of months. It had only been a year since my relationship with David had ended.

I tried to think of something to say to play for time, but for once nothing came to me.

As J.X. studied my face, his own changed. His eyes darkened. His smile twisted. "No?"

I couldn't take it. I couldn't take the idea of hurting him. I mean, what the hell. I loved him more than I'd ever loved anyone in my entire life. Couldn't imagine my life without him now. Or rather, I could imagine and only too well what life without him would be like, and the pain of it was horrific. I'd known David for three years before we tied the knot, and it had still been a disaster. Could J.X. and I do any worse?

I sat up, dislodging his arm. "Yes," I said. "Of course yes."

It was a relief to see the light come back into his face. His smile was incandescent. He reached for me again, and I said quickly, "But Italy, no. I mean, yes. Italy itself, yes. Getting married, yes. Big fancy wedding trip to Italy with the families, no."

He looked confused. "No? Why?"

"I don't know. Maybe this isn't fair, but David and I did the big commitment ceremony thing, and I just don't want that again. I never did want it. He did."

Comprehension came into J.X.'s face. "I see."

"I wanted something small and private and meaningful. Instead, I got something big and showy and superficial, which pretty much defined our relationship. This time—if it's okay with you—I'd like to keep things real."

"Either way it would be real, Kit. The way I feel about you is as real as it gets."

"My feelings for you are real too. In fact...well."

J.X. said ruefully, "Come on. Throw me a bone. My ego could use some stroking about now."

I made a face. "I'm not good at saying these things, but I didn't even know I had it in me to care this much."

He beamed.

"Which probably sounds—"

"It sounds pretty nice to me," J.X. said.

"It's the truth. I never thought of myself as a romantic guy—I'm *not* a romantic guy."

"Well…"

"But the way I feel about you…" I cleared my throat. "If I was another kind of man, a romantic man, I'd be…doing romantic things for you."

His smile widened. "Would you? Like what?"

"Oh. I don't know. I'd send you flowers, or one of those oversize embossed cards, or maybe write you a poem or something."

J.X. grinned. "Roses are red, blood is too, I like to solve mysteries—sometimes with you."

I laughed. "Something like that, yes. Which is why I leave these things to you. You're the romantic in this family."

His smile faded. He said, "I am a romantic. And I want us to really be a family. I want to marry you, Christopher. I want to love, honor, cherish, and protect you—and take you to Italy on our honeymoon. Will you marry me?"

Somehow we had gone from laughter to solemnity.

I swallowed. A tiny little gulp of a sound I hoped he didn't hear.

"Yes," I said. "I will marry you."

Sex is rarely just sex.

When we'd first moved in together, it felt like every time I rolled over, J.X. wanted sex. Not just sex—penetrative sex, preferably with me being the one penetrated. According to J.X., that was how I preferred it, even needed it.

Which, as I pointed out to him in one of our occasional spats, was certainly opportune for him.

That hurt him. Quite a bit. So much so, that for a couple of weeks we had barely gone beyond a bit of frottage and petting. We had moved past the initial harm, but he'd still made no move to penetrate me during sex. He had offered himself to me, but to my horror—and for one of the few times in my life—I'd been unable to perform.

That had been a black night of the soul. Not to mention the penis.

Nor did my condition spontaneously clear up, no matter how much loving attention J.X. lavished on that area of my anatomy.

Finally, I got desperate enough to go to the doctor, who reassured me there was nothing physically wrong with the plumbing. It seemed it was all in my head.

In my other head.

A week of soul-searching had followed, and then J.X. and I had finally talked.

It had been painful but also freeing to admit he had been right about things I was still uncomfortable with, uneasy with. And harder still to confess I had trouble asking for those things even though I had been craving them since the initial argument.

He'd been solemn and serious. "You have to be able to say it, Kit. I don't ever want to feel like I've forced you into something you didn't want. I don't want to be that man."

"I know. And I don't want to be a man too afraid to ask for what he needs because I'm afraid of what people will think."

His bewilderment was genuine. "How the hell would anyone know? But more importantly, since when do you care what anyone thinks?"

"I don't know. I suppose it's some weird, lingering adolescent insecurity." I groaned. "Which doesn't mean it isn't actual."

"I'll say. You've actually second-guessed yourself right into impotency," he said bluntly. "And me into being afraid to touch you."

I winced. "The question is, where do we go from here?"

He was quiet, thinking it over. "Let's take it slowly. Let's just try being together without having sex. And let's promise to both share what we're feeling."

"That's *it?*" I was dismayed. "Your solution is no sex?"

He smiled reluctantly. "Just until we're both comfortable again."

"Okay. But…"

"What about this? Why don't I give you a full-body massage? With oil?"

I had immediately brightened. "That might work."

Yeah, that had worked all right. Long before the end of the massage, I was humping the mattress and begging J.X. to fuck me. Which he did with a gentle but inexorable dominance that left no room for doubt.

It had taken me forty years to figure it out. But there was no going back from the knowledge.

Nor did I want to go back from it.

I also didn't want it to define our relationship. As much as I loved sex—and finally having the kind of sex I craved—our life was about a lot more than sex. Nor did I want rules and rituals. Fetish was never going to be my thing—or his—and pain was a nonstarter for both of us.

Now our sex life was relaxed and happy, sometimes serious, sometimes silly, but always satisfying. So when J.X. pounced after I accepted his proposal, I had no compunction planting my hand in his chest and saying, "Not so much of the caveman stuff, if you please!"

He grinned, his smile white, eyes shining. "You kind of like the caveman stuff, though, don't you, Mr. Holmes?"

I sniffed in disapproval and then burst out laughing as he pretended to savage me, growling ferociously and covering my neck and shoulders with kisses and little bites. "Who are you supposed to be? The Werewolf of Lombard?"

J.X. knelt between my thighs, grinning. "Mm, mm, good. Christopher Holmes. The other white meat."

I laughed unsteadily, sucked in a couple of deep breaths of anticipation, and reached for a pillow to prop my head so I could watch everything he did. To me. Yeah, that too was a turn-on, once I'd learned to focus on what I was looking *at* versus what I looked *like*. His gaze rose to meet mine, and his eyes were so warm, they looked almost golden.

"You're beautiful, Kit."

I snorted. "Go on which ya!"

"I'm serious. You're beautiful."

"Maybe to you."

"Definitely to me. I love *every single solitary inch* of you..." He proceeded to demonstrate, wrapping his lips around the head of my cock and drawing me into the exquisite wet heat of his mouth, farther, farther.

I moaned, tried not to thrust, but it was like trying not to breathe. Your lungs start to burn, and you *have* to inhale or die. I grabbed a couple of fistfuls of the raw-silk comforter and rocked my hips up as pleasure kindled, caught light, and blazed into life. "Oh God. Oh God. *That*. Do that."

J.X. answered my shuddering moan, his hands closing around my ass, pulling me in deeper still.

I could see the silky, black shine of his hair falling over his eyes, the convulsive jerks of his throat muscles, little tremors shooting through my own thighs, and the root of my cock, nested in curling blond hair, thick and pounding with preorgasmic blood-surge, pulsing to the beat of this incredible deep-throat suck. The thunder in my ears drowned out all other sound, made this moment so intensely, fiercely isolated from the rest of the world. I forgot there *was* a rest of the world.

Pressure in my chest, a crowding tightness—the first couple of times this had happened I wondered if I was having a heart attack, my body succumbing to overwhelming sensation; now I knew to throw my head back and let orgasm roll through me.

But no. Not yet. J.X. drew back, withdrawing that delicious, wet wrapping of tongue, throat, lips.

He asked huskily, "You want me inside you, Kit?"

"Yes," I panted. "God, yes."

"How bad do you want it?"

Instinctively I raised my legs, giving J.X. entrance. "Bad. I want it so bad." I mean, to hell with grammar when you're on fire with desire and longing.

"Me too. *God*. And you think you're not beautiful..."

I gave another of those guttural, shattered moans as J.X. impaled me, shoving in, slick-hot inch by slick-hot inch, until I could feel the press of his balls against my backside. We shifted again, instinctively, practiced at this now, making room for each other, accommodating each other.

J.X. thrust cautiously a couple of times, making sure all was well, and I let him know with little cries and moans and writhing that all was *very* well indeed. He began to move more urgently. The bedsprings squeaked, the floorboards creaked, and I was distantly reminded of the first time we had done this, after a decade apart. I laughed, and he covered my mouth, wanting my full attention.

No worry there.

I wrapped my legs around his waist as J.X. increased the pace, shortening his strokes to quick, frantic slices that finally freed orgasm, that rich, rolling flood of pleasure like no other. I yelled, sinking my fingers in his shoulders, gasping as semen shot from me in hot spurts, spattering his chest and chin. Unsurprised when only a few strokes later, J.X. came too with a shout he turned into a prolonged wolf howl.

We finished with kisses and laughter.

I wasn't kidding. I am not a romantic.

But on Friday morning I woke with the unfamiliar and uncomfortable desire to do something romantic for my soft and sentimental soon-to-be husband.

Besides me, J.X. has one other weakness. Cake. He's a fiend for cake. And because he's also a fiend for fitness, we never have any on the premises. He finds the combination of flour and frosting too tempting for anything but the most special of special occasions.

So after he left to go running, I hied myself to our favorite local bakery to pick up a cake for a nice celebratory engagement dinner.

As usual the place was packed, but the line moved quickly and before I knew it, I was at the counter trying to choose from a selection of Halloween-themed pastries. That was something I hadn't figured on. I had the option of an orange Jack-o'-lantern cake, a purple cake with a giant black spider on top, an eyeball cake, and an elegant white cake with a haunted house on top.

I explained my dilemma to the girl behind the counter. "Can you scrape Happy Halloween off that and change it to Happy Ever After?" I pointed to the haunted-house cake.

She raised her brows, studying the drafty-looking chocolate mansion. "We *could*," she said doubtfully. "It'll take about half an hour to make the change. Are you sure you wouldn't like to special order a regular cake?"

"How long would that take?"

"Forty-eight hours."

I shook my head. "I need it for this evening."

"Okaaay, well… If you want to sit down and wait?"

I paid for the cake, ordered a coffee and something called a "mummy brownie," which was an ordinary, delicious brownie wrapped in ribbons of white icing with a couple of candy eyes, and sat down to wait.

I had just bitten the head off my brownie when the chair across from me was pulled out from the table with a jarring scrape and Jerry sat down.

Jerry. In the flesh. Looking unnervingly unchanged by four months of incarceration.

"Christopher, we need to talk." His blue gaze was wounded. "How could you *think* such terrible things about me?"

I closed my mouth in time to keep the brownie from falling out, chewed rapidly, swallowed, and said, "What are you doing here?"

"I'm picking up cupcakes for Violet's Halloween party."

"You're not supposed to come within a hundred yards of me."

"Christopher," he chided. "It's a bakery. I have a right to buy cupcakes."

"No, you don't. Not while I'm in the shop. And you sure as hell don't have a right to sit down at my table."

He chuckled at my naïveté. "That stupid restraining order is being challenged right now. It's *already* been dismissed, if I know Violet." He sighed appreciatively. "She's a go-getter. I wish you could meet her."

I opened my mouth, but in the Twilight Zone no one can hear you scream.

"I love her," he added. "I didn't know how lonely I was until Violet." He seemed dead serious, like he really wanted me to know.

"I… Great," I managed. "I'm glad. But that doesn't change—"

"I knew you would be happy for me because deep down inside you're a good person. I know you're doing all these terrible things to me to earn points with your cop boyfriend. But I believe you're better than that. I know we can work this out like grown-ups."

"What is it you think we can work out? You tried to kill me."

"I *didn't*," he said indignantly. A few people in line glanced over at us and then away. "I keep *telling* you, I was trying to *protect* you."

Jerry and I had not spoken since the night he'd tried to smash my head in with a meat hammer, so right there I took this insistence as proof he was either a pathological liar or nuts or both. He believed his own lies. I had no doubt of that. I also had no doubt he'd tried to kill me the night in question.

I said, "I remember it differently."

He continued to regard me with that eerily earnest expression. "Even hearing you say it to my face, I still can't believe you would think I could hurt you. You know how much I think of you and your work. How much I respect you. Our friendship was one of the greatest joys of my life."

"We weren't friends, Jerry. You harassed and stalked me, and then you attacked me."

"I gave you presents. I gave you compliments. I saved your life!"

Okay, there he had me, because yes, that was all true. He had given me presents and compliments, unwanted but accepted out of politeness. And he had very possibly saved my life that night too.

I said, "And now you're dressing up like a clown and—"

Jerry burst out laughing. "*Christopher*," he gurgled. "Did you really say that?"

We had the attention of everyone in the bakeshop. Jerry saw it too and played up to it. He guffawed and chortled and howled, "*A clown!*" He even hit the table with his hand, so that it jumped forward a couple of inches. I put my hands out to stop it from knocking into me. Two or three people at the end of the counter line abruptly left the shop.

Finally, he wiped at his eyes and sighed, shaking his head. I couldn't seem to tear my gaze away from the dark bruise on his forearm. That would be where I'd hit him with the hotel iron.

He said, "There's that wonderful sense of humor."

It was quite the performance, and that's all it was because as Jerry's eyes met mine, they were bone dry, cold, and unsmiling despite his wide, idiotic grin. "I'm sorry you're being stalked for *real* now. That must be awful. And by a clown." He continued to grin at me. "I know some people are afraid of clowns. Are you?"

"No."

"Holmes!" called the girl behind the counter.

I rose without another word, went to the counter, and said quietly, "Are your security cameras working?"

Her eyes widened. "Yes. Why?"

"You need to preserve the footage of the last ten minutes. In fact, since I walked in. The guy who's sitting at my table is violating a restraining order. The police are going to want to see those frames."

Her eyes went wider still. "Okay." She looked past me and said, "He's watching you."

"Yeah, well, that's what he does." I took the square pink box and departed.

Before the glass door closed, I glanced back at Jerry, but for once he wasn't watching me. He was studying the girl behind the counter.

I didn't like his expression.

I was still shaking when I got home.

Partly that was due to the brisk hike home—I hadn't been getting my workout in the past few days—partly it was altitude. Who the hell came up with the idea to build a city on a series of hills? Why wouldn't the people of the north simply razor off the hills and build cities in the dust like we do in the Southland?

Mostly, though, it was abject terror.

The whole walk home I had expected Jerry to come racing after me or, however unlikely this was, for a clown to jump out of the shrubberies and grab me.

I could hear the shower running overhead, and I shoved the cake in the fridge and went upstairs. I sat on the foot of the bed, waiting.

After a few minutes of tuneless humming, gargling, and flushing, the door opened and J.X. wafted out on a cloud of bath gel scented steam. Distressed as I was, I couldn't but admire the bronzed width of his shoulders and the muscular length of his legs. I'd never known a guy who could wear a damp bath towel like J.X.

"Hey," he greeted me. "Where did you go?"

"The bakery. It was supposed to be a surprise, but I ran into Jerry."

All trace of cheerfulness vanished. His face grew stony, eyes fierce. "You mean he followed you? Is he outside?" He dropped the towel and reached for his jeans with the air of an Old-West gunfighter buckling on his holster.

"No. I don't think so. I don't know if he followed me there either. Maybe not. Maybe it was a ghastly coincidence. He claims he was picking up cupcakes for his girlfriend's Halloween party. Anyway, he believes the restraining order won't stand. In fact, he seemed to think it had already been dismissed."

J.X. swore, finished buttoning his Levi's, and went to the phone.

There followed a few nail-biting minutes of tense and terse conversation before he threw over his shoulder, "They're contesting, but the hearing hasn't been held yet."

I had a million questions, naturally, but he was already punching new numbers into the phone.

"Izzie? That asshole Knight confronted Christopher at a bakery this morning."

Another terse conversation followed before J.X. put Izzie on speakerphone.

Izzie's deep voice boomed, "Yo, Christopher. How you holding up?"

"You know me. Like the Parthenon after the Venetians got done with it."

Izzie laughed heartily. "Tell me exactly what went down at the bakery."

The *what went down* sounded so dangerous and streetwise, whereas the actual encounter had been sort of pedestrian and suburban. *I was approached whilst purchasing pastries!* I felt silly by the end of my recounting—although I had not found it remotely silly at the time.

J.X. didn't seem to find it silly either. "Jesus Christ. This dude is a brazen-assed candidate for the psych ward."

"He doesn't seem impressed by my winning personality, that's for sure," Izzie agreed.

"What do you think?" J.X. asked.

That sounded innocuous but was clearly code, because Izzie made a soothing *nn-nn* sound.

J.X. was not soothed. "What about this broad he's shacked up with?" he demanded. "Is there a way in through her?"

This was an eye-opener. Not that I didn't know J.X. had to have a harder, more cynical side than the one I usually saw, but I realized there was a whole side to him that was a stranger to me.

"Violet Sanderson? No way. There's nothing on her besides the fact that she's a weirdo. She was adopted by the Sandersons when she was eleven. Private schools, debutante ball, the whole deal, but after her adoptive parents died, she went into seclusion. She turns up at the occasional charity do, dressed like Aunt Esther, and drops a shitload of cash when she's in the mood. That's all I could find on her."

They discussed the vagaries of rich white ladies for a minute or two while I debated whether to tell them Sanderson had called the house two nights earlier. I didn't want to, didn't want J.X. any more worked up than he was, but I also thought they'd better be prepared.

I broke into their conversation. "Violet Sanderson called here the other night."

"She what?" J.X. stared at me. Izzie was silent on the other end of the phone.

"She phoned to say I was not going to get away with harassing and bullying Jerry. And that her friends in high places beat my friends in high places."

"How fucking dare she," J.X. said, and the deadly quietness of his tone was kind of unsettling.

"Oh, did she?" Izzie boomed his deep, melodious laugh, though he didn't sound particularly amused to me. "Well, we'll see about that."

J.X. said, "You should have told me, Kit."

"It's not like we don't already know she's on Jerry's side."

"She threatened you."

I sighed. "Yeah. I get that a lot."

Izzie said, "Okay. Now we know. First thing I'm going to do is see if the bakery has security cameras."

"They do, they work, and I asked the girl at the counter to make sure nothing happened to that footage."

J.X. threw me a look of surprised approval. "Outstanding," Izzie rumbled.

"Any chance we can arrest this guy now on violating the TRO?" J.X. asked.

"Iffy," Izzie said. "We can try, if that's the way you want to go, but Sanderson hired John Kestenbaum to contest the TRO, so I'm guessing Bozo will be out again about fifteen minutes after we slam the door."

I had never heard of John Kestenbaum, but J.X. swore quietly, so apparently Kestenbaum for the defense was liable to prove a worry.

Izzie said, "I know, man. It might be better to play it cool. Hide our hand until we're ready to make our play."

J.X. glanced at me, and I said, "I agree with Izzie. Keep 'em guessing."

J.X. was unsatisfied with this, but he accepted being outvoted. "You'll keep me informed?"

"You'll be first to know, bro."

Izzie hung up, and J.X. turned to me. "Kit, you can't keep that kind of thing from me."

"I don't. I wouldn't. Seriously, she wasn't saying anything we didn't already know—and you've already been distracted enough by this."

"I'm *supposed* to be distracted by my boyfriend being—"

The phone rang, cutting him off.

This time it was Detective Dean.

"Mr. Holmes, were you able to locate that contact info for Zachary Samuels?" she demanded.

"Was I supposed to?" I asked blankly.

I mean, even taking into account my solving four-plus homicides in a year, God help the county of Los Angeles if the cops were relying on *me* to do their work for them.

"Yes," she said.

"Because I really don't remember you—"

She cut me off. "We've been able to locate Mr. Samuels' brother, but he tells us there was a riff between himself and other family members."

"Rift," I said. "Unless you're talking about the Partridge Family."

"I'm sorry?"

"Nothing. Go on."

"Were the Partridges particular friends of Samuels?"

"No. Please continue, Detective."

"Samuels was aware their sister passed away several years ago, but was unable to provide any information regarding either his niece or his brother. In fact, he wasn't aware he had a niece."

"I'm not surprised. I recall there was some kind of falling out between the siblings," I said. "But here's the thing, the people you need to be looking at for this crime are Tip and Etta Coopersmith."

"Who?"

"The couple who owned the house before Zag bought it." I began to regale her with the alarming tales I'd heard from Zag and Felicity.

"Mr. Holmes, is there some reason you neglected to share this information with me until now?" Dean broke in just as I was getting to the part about the dead fish in the wall.

"I didn't neglect to tell you; you weren't interested," I objected. "You cut me off when I brought it up. You were too busy trying to frame Zag."

"*Kit*," J.X. exclaimed.

I jumped guiltily, having forgotten he was in the room. I scowled at him.

"You can't say that to her."

I nodded, although I had just done so. Dean, meanwhile, was voicing her objections loudly on my choice of phrase—my term, not hers.

"Look, call it what you want," I said, "but in my opinion you made your mind up from the start that whoever was living in the house at the time the body was buried is your perp. First it was me. Now it's Zag."

"Why are you getting into this with her?" J.X. was saying in the background. "How does antagonizing her help?" This from the guy who five minutes earlier had been asking whether we could get to Jerry through one of the richest women in San Francisco.

"I realize you write mysteries, Mr. Holmes, but real-life police work is different from the fictional kind. In real life, crime is usually not complicated. The most obvious solution is usually the correct solution."

"How *convenient*," I said. That was payback for her same comment during our first meeting, but really it made no sense because in this case she was right. However, I had to take my frustrations out on someone, and Detective Dean had built up quite a pile of IOUs with me.

She was venting her own frustrations when a thought suddenly occurred to me—a thought which should have occurred before then.

"Have you tried to reach Felicity?" I interrupted.

"Felicity *who*?" Dean cried.

"Felicity Dann. Zag's girlfriend. Maybe she knows whether Zag's—what happened with Zag. Or at least she might know his niece's whereabouts."

"Until this moment I was unaware Mr. Samuels had a girlfriend," Dean said in that tight voice women get when they are trying very hard to show they are not about to scream at you, though you are certainly asking for it. "As I was unaware of the Coopersmiths and the Partridges."

"Yes, Zag and Felicity were together. Well, off and on. But they'd been off and on for years. I met her a couple of times. They were planning to move in together, but according to the niece, Felicity bailed after Zag's stroke. I'm not sure if that's a fair assessment. Nobody knows how they'll react in circumstances like that. We all hope we'll do the right thing."

My gaze wandered to J.X., who was listening to all this with an exasperated expression. As I studied his face, realization struck me. *I'd stand by you. Whatever happens, I'll be there for you.*

It was kind of shocking. Because it was true. Naturally, I would have wanted to be there for David too—back when I loved David—but I had never felt this kind of strength, this kind of certainty before.

In sickness and in health. Till death do us part.

They weren't just words. It wasn't just a formality.

Not that I'd ever viewed them as a mere formality, but that sudden strength and certainty? That was largely due to J.X. The way he treated me. The way he trusted me. The way he loved me.

I smiled at him, and J.X. blinked as though a constant star had suddenly flared up.

On the other end of the line, Dean was still talking, but I didn't care anymore. Maybe she would solve her case. Maybe she wouldn't. Maybe the Coopersmiths would be stuffing dead fish in walls from here to eternity. It didn't matter. I was out of it now. I had a new life and a new love, and the past was just practice.

CHAPTER SEVENTEEN

According to Amazon, Zag was alive.

On impulse, I'd gone online to see how my backlist was faring these days, and while studying those dismal results, it occurred to me to compare—er, *check*—Zag's backlist.

The results were staggering.

At the time Zag had suffered his stroke, he'd written eighty books under the pen name Sophie Snow for Millbrook's Prime Crime list. A lull of five years followed *Double Dutch Demise* and then boom! A new Sophie Snow mystery: *Murder with Sprinkles on Top.*

Zag was back—and he'd started writing again.

And how! In nine years he'd written an additional one hundred and twenty mysteries. Over thirteen books a year. Not only was he exceeding his old whirlwind production schedule, he appeared to have dumped Millbrook and turned to self-publishing. All his self-published titles were in Kindle Unlimited—and doing very well.

I was happy for him. I was relieved that he had not only survived his illness, he was thriving.

I scrolled to the abbreviated author bio. Because Zag was using a feminine pen name, he had chosen an avatar for his author photo—a variation on the classic pink and black Nancy Drew logo—so that was naturally unchanged. The bio itself had been updated.

> Sophie Snow loves tending her garden, baking cup-cakes, and, of course, reading mysteries.
>
> She is married and lives in the quaint town of Sunol, California, with three cats, two dogs, and a parakeet named Tweety.
>
> Sign up for Sophie's newsletter at: http://eepurl.com/b19qzz
>
> You can contact Sophie with questions and/or comments at: sscozygirl@gmail.com

Not exactly a mine of information, but it mirrored the bios of most of the other cozy authors I glanced at. Nor was it exactly accurate either. I remembered the bird—how long did those things live anyway?—but Zag had been allergic to animal dander. Then again, allergy medications had improved a lot in the last fourteen years, so maybe he was able to have furry pets now.

I debated for a minute or two—and then another minute or two—and then shot off an email.

> *Hey there!*
>
> *Remember me? So glad to see you're up and around and back to writing. I feel bad about not getting in touch for so long. I'm living in the Bay Area now, but if you're ever in town, let me know. I'd love to catch up.*
>
> *Christopher (Holmes)*

I'd love to catch up?

But yeah, I did want to catch up with Zag.

For one thing, I felt terrible about not ever having gone to visit him all the time he was sick. No, not even that so much as how easily I'd forgotten all about him. That was not okay. J.X. would never be so callous.

But also, I was kind of curious to see what Zag had to say about the body being discovered in his old backyard. As a fellow mystery writer, I knew he'd be as intrigued as I was, and I wanted to get his take before Detective Dean got hold of him and swore him to silence.

Minutes passed.

When I caught myself checking my email for the third time, I was amused. Was I really expecting an immediate reply? No. It took me days if not weeks to get around to answering fan mail. Especially after Jerry.

Instead, I tried phoning Joey again.

Once again, I got the house answering machine.

This time I gave in and left a message stating I was an old friend of Dicky's and was hoping Joey could help me get in touch.

Now what?

I gazed about my immaculately organized office and considered what to do next.

The obvious thing was to begin the first Miss Butterwith proposal. The holiday Butterwith story. I'd never done a specifically holiday story, so this was going to be fun.

No, really. It was.

I was eager to start. And yet...I was also a little nervous. Gazing at Amazon page after Amazon page of unfamiliar authors and book titles had thrown me. Who *were* all these people? With the exception of Sophie Snow, I hadn't recognized a single name.

Did Miss Butterwith and I even belong in this brave new world of .99 books and boxsets? And why the hell were so many of these amateur sleuths witches? Was that a Halloween thing? What had *happened* to my beloved genre while I was away solving real murders?

"Do you have a minute?" J.X. asked, startling me out of my apprehensive thoughts.

"Yeah. Of course. What's up?" I'd been so wrapped up, I hadn't heard him walking down the hall.

"I just talked to Izzie. He says they were able to retrieve the security footage from the bakeshop, but get this. Violet Sanderson tried to buy the footage first.

"Are you kidding?"

"No. Apparently she was irate when the shop manager refused to cooperate. Threatened to buy the place itself and fire every employee."

"That's crazy."

J.X. nodded grimly. "It is."

"Isn't that tampering with evidence?"

"Yes, but it's kind of a gray area."

By *gray area*, I assumed he was referring to John Kestenbaum. I'd looked him up online, and he was known in the Bay Area as the "Gray Fox." Kestenbaum was the attorney you hired when you were: a) rich, and b) probably guilty.

"So is that it? Jerry gets tossed back in jail for violating the restraining order?"

He grimaced. "Maybe. Sanderson's lawyer is filing a bunch of different motions to try to prevent that. Plus, Jerry's story—communicated through his lawyer—is he was trying to resolve this situation in a mature, civilized manner by speaking to you directly. He didn't realize the restraining order was already in effect—"

"That's utter bullshit."

"I know. He also claims he didn't understand the restraining order meant no contact at all. He thought it meant no private contact and no physical contact."

I rose. "That's not true. It's ridiculous. Jerry knows exactly what a restraining order is, and he knew exactly what he was doing. He specifically told me the restraining order was going to be challenged and had in fact probably even been dismissed."

"Which kind of supports Jerry's version of events, if you think about it." J.X. sounded apologetic.

"Goddamn it."

"Kit." J.X. left the doorway and came around the desk to wrap his arms around me. For a moment I stood as rigid as a pole; then I gave in and dropped my head on his shoulder. "It's going to be okay," he said against my ear.

"For who? Jerry?"

He didn't bother to argue, just held me.

That's the problem with an addiction to true-crime TV. Thanks to *Obsessed, Stalkers Who Kill*, and *Stalked: Someone's Watching*, I knew only too well how often restraining orders were not enforced, how often stalkers got off with repeated and ineffectual warnings, how often the system failed victims.

"It's not for sure," he said. "Ignorance of the law is no excuse, and depending on the judge, this might be enough to get him tossed back in the can. I just want you prepared if it doesn't go our way this time."

I nodded wearily.

"*This time.* All they can do is try to delay the inevitable. He is going *down*. If I have to take him down myself."

That was the tough, young ex-cop speaking. And while I appreciated the sentiment, I didn't want to hear it. I didn't want him even joking about putting himself and our life together at risk. Plus, he *wasn't* joking.

"Don't say that."

"I won't let anyone hurt you, Kit."

I nodded again. Raised my head. "I know. And I'm okay," I said gruffly. "It's just the bullshit is *wearing*." No lie. I felt like my nerves were being rubbed raw every time I remembered Jerry was out there somewhere, plotting God knows what.

"I know. Listen, I was thinking. Why don't you come with me on this book tour?"

"Huh?"

"I think it would do you good to get out of town for a while. You love bookstores. You love hotels. You love me." He grinned. "I think it would be fun."

I eyed him warily. "You think Jerry's going to try something, don't you?"

"No. Well, I mean, yes, we both do. But I don't have reason to believe he's planning to escalate. I just think it would be a good idea for you to have a break from worrying about all this. And I would love you to come. I'm going to miss you like hell."

I sighed. "Thank you, but no. It's not necessary."

"But why?"

"For one thing, I've got to start work on this holiday novella. It's already the end of October, and the thing is due next month. I haven't written in a year. I need warm-up time."

"Come on," J.X. said. "It'll come back to you. It's like riding a bike. It'll be like riding Miss Butterwith's bike. You'll be done in a week or two."

I freed myself, saying irritably, "What is it with you and Rachel? It's going to take me more than a week to write a novella. I know you don't think my work demands the time and attention yours does—"

"That's not what I'm saying."

Just like that my heart was pounding and I was flushed with anger. I glared at J.X., who looked baffled—and a little hurt.

I opened my mouth to say—I'm not sure what—but in the nick of time it occurred to me I was doing it again. I was picking a fight to avoid having to confront what was really eating at me.

"No, I know that's not what you're saying," I said, and I saw the relief in his eyes. J.X.'s shoulders relaxed, and I realized with chagrin he had braced for the onslaught. "But I'm out of practice, and it's going to take me longer than it usually would. I *can't* blow this. It's Miss B.'s last shot. I *have* to get that proposal in, and then I have to start work on the book ASAP. Going on tour with you *would* be fun, but I can't afford to take that time right now."

"You can't write while we're traveling?"

"No. I can't. I never could."

He sighed. "I was afraid you'd say that."

"Also, I refuse to be driven out of my own home by that asshole Jerry."

His smile was wry, "And I knew you'd say that too."

I was having my lunch of chicken salad on avocado at my desk when two emails *whooshed* in. One was from Rina, my former realtor, informing me the Kaynors were currently staying with Mrs. Kaynor's mother in San Diego. She regretted to tell me they still expressed every intent of suing me—and were now threatening to sue her as well.

"Fan-fucking-tastic," I muttered.

The second email was from Sophie Snow.

Dear Mr. Holmes,

I'm writing on behalf of my uncle. I remember you very well from the sale of the house on Hiawatha Street, and I know Uncle Zag will be delighted to hear from you. He used to talk about you often and how you both started your publishing careers together. Sadly, he recently suffered another stroke and is once more unable to communicate by typing or speaking, but he's still very much aware and alert of all that goes on around him. I plan to read your note to him when he wakes up from his nap. It will be the high point of his day.

Sincerely,

Pandora Boxleitner

My heart dropped. Jesus. Another stroke? That was sad. And a disappointment. I'd been so happy to think Zag had made a miraculous recovery. And judging by his expanded backlist, he had, but had eventually succumbed once again?

I reread the note from his niece.

Pandora sounded as pleasant as I remembered. Boxleitner would be her married name. Her maiden name had been Pearce. Pandora Pearce. I remembered thinking it sounded like a pen name.

Zag was lucky to have devoted family willing to look after him. Especially after Felicity had bailed.

Even so. Poor guy. What kind of a life was that? If a note from me was the high point of his day, not much.

Dear Pandora,

I'm so sorry to hear the news about Zag. Is he well enough for visitors? If he's able, I'd like to make the effort to see him.

Christopher

While I was waiting for her reply, David phoned.

"Now what?" I asked by way of greeting.

He was not offended. "Did you hear? The police arrested Reggie Chow! I always told you that kid was no good."

"Arrested Reggie Chow for what?"

"For murdering his uncle Van and dumping his body in our backyard."

"*What?* Wait a minute. The police think *Reggie Chow* is the culprit? Not the Coopersmiths?"

"Who are the Coopersmiths?"

"The people who owned the house before Zag."

"No. The cops nailed Reggie for it."

"But did they even interview the Coopersmiths?"

"How would I know? What does it matter? Reggie confessed."

"But-but *why*?"

"Because he did it. I guess he feels guilty about it."

"*No,*" I said impatiently, "why did Reggie choose our backyard? Why would he do that?"

"He said he had to put the body somewhere fast, and there was a big hole in our yard, so he waited till it was dark and did the deed."

"That's..." Weird. To say the least. Granted, Reggie had been evolving into quite the petty criminal over the years, but murder? I said, "But I thought forensics had determined the body had been buried for twenty years."

"That was a ballpark figure. They said it could be less."

True. Dean *had* said something to that effect. Still, the difference between one and twenty years was a lot to be off by.

"Case closed, I guess," I said slowly.

"Yes. I bet you're relieved."

"Yes. Of course. Although it's still hard to picture Reggie as a murderer. He seemed like a good-humored goof."

"Not to me. I always said that kid was a menace."

"Yes, you did. Why did he kill his uncle?"

"That, I don't know. He's claiming it was an accident."

"They all claim that," I said with the jaded certainty of the Investigation Discovery addict. "If they don't claim outright innocence."

"I guess so. Anyway—"

A sense of wrong occurred to me. "Why are Dean and Quigley calling you with this information? Why aren't they calling me? The house was mine."

"They didn't call me. I called them. I saw it on the news."

"Oh."

"Although on that note, what the hell did you do to Detective Dean? She talks about you like she thinks you're the devil. Did you really tell her the Partridge Family were potential suspects?"

I cleared my throat. "That was a misunderstanding."

"She thinks you're deliberately trying to make fools out of them."

I said shortly, "It wouldn't be hard. But no."

I was still trying to wrap my head around the concept of Reggie Chow as a murderer. Maybe it *had* been an accident. Maybe he'd done something stupid, panicked, and done something more stupid.

"Speaking of closed cases," David abruptly changed the subject. "How is your investigation into Dicky's disappearance going? Have you found his sister yet?"

"No, I haven't found his sister. I haven't looked for her."

"You're *ignoring* that lead?"

"I'm not ignoring it. I haven't got to it yet. How many times do I have to remind you I'm not a full-time detective? I've got a book proposal due."

"Oh, for God's sake," David said in disgust. "At the rate you're going, I might as well solve this case myself."

"*Ha,*" I snapped. "If you think you can, do so."

"You bet I will!"

Our phones slammed down in unison

CHAPTER EIGHTEEN

When J.X. saw the haunted-house cake, he started to laugh.

We were preparing dinner. Steak, creamy scalloped potatoes (recipe courtesy of our friend and neighbor Emmaline Bloodworth), bacon, avocado Caesar salad, and garlic butter and rosemary steak. J.X. had finished his book forty-five minutes earlier, so we had even more to celebrate.

"Kit, this is genius. Happy Ever After." He beamed at me.

I said offhandedly, "It's really a Halloween cake. There wasn't enough time to order—"

He cut me off by reaching across the cake and hauling me in for a kiss.

"Hey, hey," I protested when I could breathe again. "You'll squash the roof."

J.X. grinned. "Anyway, what were you saying about visiting this old friend?"

"It turns out he's actually living in Sunol, which isn't that far from here."

"Alameda County," J.X. agreed. "Sunol is about an hour's drive. Depending on traffic."

"Right. I thought I'd head out there and spend a couple of hours, er, brightening his day."

"That's a really kind thing to do. Who is this guy again?"

"Zag Samuels. We started out together. He wrote the Sweetie MacFarland series."

"No clue," J.X. returned. "Are those cozy mysteries?"

"Yes. It's a series about a homicide detective who turns in his badge to run a specialty cupcake bakery."

J.X. snorted.

"It was *very* popular."

"Sure. Who doesn't like cupcakes?"

"We know you're a fan."

"I am." He went back to seasoning the steak, unperturbed.

I put my hands on my hips, said, "You know, cozy mysteries are not actually any more unreal than noir or thrillers or—"

He was grinning at me again. "I know. I've heard you debate this before. Remember?"

Oh, right. The Murder at Midtown conference where J.X. and I had first met.

I made a face. "Right."

"I don't think cozies are—" J.X. broke off, and his expression changed. "*Waaait a minute.* Isn't Zag Samuels the guy you bought your old house from? The guy suspected of murder?"

I sighed. "I just told you five minutes ago that they've arrested a neighbor kid—well, he's not a kid anymore—but they've made their arrest in the case."

"You also told me you had trouble believing Reggie Chow was guilty."

One of J.X.'s more annoying traits is his ability to remember...too much.

"What does that have to do with anything? Reggie confessed. The police are satisfied. What do I know?"

J.X. cocked a skeptical eyebrow.

"What's that look for?"

"Suddenly, out of the blue, you think you should go visit your old friend who just happens to be a murder suspect in a case you privately believe has been effed up by the police."

I gaped at him. Not because he was wrong. Because he was dead *right*. How did he *do* that?

My expression was obviously a giveaway because J.X.'s own expression grew wry. "I thought so."

"Now here's where you're wrong," I said heatedly, because I felt he *was* wronging me in one aspect. "No way in hell did Zag kill anyone. I knew him, and yes, I know no one can ever *really* know another person blah, blah, blah, but there was *no* capacity for violence in that man."

"He wrote murder mysteries. He had *some* capacity for violence. He had the ability to visualize committing violence."

"His detective turned to baking cupcakes because he couldn't take all the bloodshed of his job."

"We can debate this all you want, but—"

"But I shouldn't visit an old friend because he was a suspect in an investigation that is now officially closed? *I* was a suspect too."

"Kit—"

"Would I like to talk to Zag about everything that's happened in the last week? Yes. But since he can't speak, it's moot. That's not what this is about. The truth is I feel terrible that I didn't go visit him when he had his first stroke. I should have made the effort, given that we were friends and I was buying his house. All these years, I figured he was dead, which is kind of an awful admission because he wasn't. He was alive the whole time. So, since I have another chance, I'm going to go see him."

"Okay," J.X. said.

"He's only an hour away. What's the excuse this time?"

J.X. said soothingly, "Okay, okay. I get it."

"I mean, how much of a threat can he be at this point?"

"You're right. I'm sorry I suspected you of amateur sleuthing when you're trying to do something very kind."

His mild tone diffused a lot of my agitation. I grimaced.

"Well, it's not like I wouldn't *like* to do a bit of sleuthing. But the opportunity is unlikely to arise. Plus, I'm serious. Zag is the least likely murder suspect on the planet."

That said, the more I'd thought about it, the more sure I had become that the landscape company I'd hired had *not* laid that concrete foundation. I vaguely recollected getting some kind of price break because the slab was already in place.

Except I couldn't think of any reason Reggie Chow would lie about such a thing.

But also, it seemed to me that the garden shed on the hillside had only been built *after* I'd made an offer on the house. I couldn't trust my memory on that because I'd only been in Zag's backyard once or twice. It was something I'd wanted to verify with him before I brought it up with the police.

I meant what I'd said to J.X.—Zag was no murderer. I didn't believe for one minute he'd killed anyone. Not deliberately. Not intentionally. Not in cold blood. But I'm a mystery writer—as well as a true-crime

TV devotee. I know that terrible things happen. I could imagine a scenario where Zag inadvertently got mixed up in a crime while trying to cover for someone else. I even suspected who that someone else might be.

And if that was the case, I wanted to help my old friend find a way out. Especially now that he was so ill.

J.X. opened his mouth, and I said, "I know, but this is real life. If he were going to kill anyone, it would have been that girlfriend of his. But no. He took her back *every single time*. And then she dumped him when he needed her most. No. I'm telling you. Zag was the kind of guy who lovingly carried spiders out of his house because he didn't want to squash them."

"You've convinced me," J.X. said. "But keep in mind what your beloved Agatha Christie said."

"'Good advice is always certain to be ignored, but that's no reason not to give it?'"

"No. 'Every murderer is probably somebody's old friend.'"

"The house on Hiawatha has been released as a crime scene," I informed J.X. over our meal. Candlelight, fine china, and my favorite person in the world sitting across from me. *That's* romance.

"That's good news."

"Rina says the Kaynors insist they won't go back there. They're still planning to sue."

He shrugged, refilling his wineglass. "Let 'em."

"Yeah, but I'm not thrilled about wasting all that money on a court case. Even assuming I win, I'm not sure the Kaynors can cover my court costs. I suspect they're having financial problems, which would be one reason they want to back out of the sale."

"Are you thinking of honoring their request to cancel the sale?"

"Hell no!"

He smiled faintly. "Then we'll deal with it when it happens. Right?"

"I suppose so." My motto has always been: *why wait till tomorrow when you can worry today?*

"I've got some news too," J.X. said. "But I don't want you to be too disappointed if it doesn't pan out."

"What news?"

"You asked the other night whether Emmaline had been interviewed after the incident with the clown. And I thought maybe I should double-check. Sometimes people are out, things get missed. It happens. It shouldn't, but it does."

"And?"

He exhaled a long breath—it always pained him when law enforcement appeared derelict in their duty. "She wasn't interviewed because she was already on her way out of town when she saw him."

I put my fork down. "Him? *The clown?*"

J.X. nodded. "She saw him sitting in a van in front of her house. She noticed him because—"

"There was a clown in a van outside her house."

"Well, yes, but also because he was using binoculars to scope out our place. She started to take down the license, but he got out with the balloon and went up to our door—and her taxi arrived. She missed all the excitement. She only got back today."

"So she didn't get the license-plate number?"

"No. But as she was getting into her cab, she noticed the van's license-plate frame had an advertisement for Intrepid Car Rentals."

"The van was a rental?"

"It looks that way."

"That's something."

"It is. It's a starting point. It's more than we had. If we can prove Jerry rented that van, we'll have him cold."

"He'd have to show ID to rent a vehicle. But his ID could have been fake."

"That's possible," J.X. said. "Which is why you shouldn't get your hopes up too much. But SFPD is showing photos of Jerry to every Intrepid franchise in the county. They're also showing photos of the clown."

"They're..."

J.X. nodded. "It's possible he went in wearing a costume. I think his visit here was spur-of-the-moment. Izzie had served him with the TRO late morning, and by late afternoon he was on our front porch. I think that restraining order pissed him off big-time, and I'm hoping that means he got careless."

"I hope you're right," I said. Jerry had been pretty careful so far.

Despite my concerns with lawsuits and stalkers and whether I still had what it took to give Miss Butterwith and Mr. Pinkerton the send-off they deserved, it was a good evening and a great meal—the last meal we would share for the next two weeks—and the haunted-house cake was a huge success right down to the last moist, gooey, chocolaty bite.

"This is *terrible*."

I had borrowed J.X.'s Kindle and downloaded Zag's latest book: *Arsenic and Angel Food*. I started reading while J.X. brushed his teeth, but when he left the bathroom, I put down the device.

"I think I'm going to pack tomorrow," he said. And then, "What's terrible?"

"Zag's latest book. It doesn't sound like him at all. I mean, the plot sounds like him, but the writing itself is not Zag."

"He had a stroke, after all. There's bound to be a change in tone. Wouldn't you think?"

"True. It does read like it was written by someone with brain damage."

J.X., in the process of pulling on a clean T-shirt, made a strangled sound.

I said, "I'm serious. This thing doesn't even make sense in parts."

"If he's really putting out thirteen books a year, something's going to suffer."

"Him, for one thing. And here I thought three books a year was a lot. I'm not surprised he had a stroke."

J.X. studied me. "Do you think he's hiring ghost writers?"

"Maybe. If so, he needs to shell out for better ghosts." I considered it and shook my head. "No. I don't. Zag took too much pride in his work. He *loved* writing."

"So?"

"I don't know." I sighed and clicked off the device, setting it on the bed stand. I slipped my glasses off, folded them, and set them atop the Kindle.

J.X. said, "You do realize, even if Zag has lost his mojo, it doesn't have anything to do with you and your writing."

I looked up in surprise. "I know that."

"Do you?"

"Yeah. Of course."

"Okay."

I folded my arms beneath my head, studying the Allan P. Friedlander painting over the fireplace. *A Good Year*. And so it had been, despite a few bumpy patches. "What were you saying about packing tomorrow?"

"That. If I have to leave later tomorrow, no big deal. I'd rather spend the evening with you."

I smiled. "Good choice."

He joined me in bed. "Are you for sure going out there to visit Zag tomorrow?"

"Yes."

"But you'll be back in town tomorrow evening?"

"Yep."

"And you'll go by Nina's for Gage's Halloween party?"

I took great pains not to sigh. "Yep. I promise I'll show up for the Halloween party."

"You don't have to actually take part—" He broke off at my look of consternation.

"*Take part?*" I echoed. "In a child's Halloween party?"

He swallowed a laugh. "But if you could just…kind of throw yourself into it. Be in the moment—"

I continued to gaze at him with horror.

"At least try to enjoy yourself," he finished, starting to laugh for real.

I shook my head. "Yes, I'll try to enjoy myself. Hopefully your ex will serve adult beverages in addition to the popcorn balls and caramel apples."

"She's not my ex."

"Oh, but she *is*," I said with an evil smile. He opened his mouth to protest, but I overrode him, "And I promise to take lots and lots of photos of Gage and the rest of his gang—and I do not use the word *gang* lightly. If ever a tyke was destined for a future as a criminal mastermind, it's that one."

J.X. ignored that. "It isn't about the photos, though. It's about—"

"Bonding with my soon-to-be nephew," I finished for him.

"I know you don't see it, but you're winning him over. I know Gage. He's secretly fond of you."

"That is one well-kept secret!"

J.X. looped an arm around my shoulders, hauling me over. "And you're more fond of him than you let on." He said it with the cheerful confidence of the totally deluded.

"Sure I am."

J.X. cocked a quizzical eyebrow.

I laughed. "Okay, he's maybe not as bad as I thought. And yes, on my honor, I will go by Nina's tomorrow night and do my best to do my duty to Gage and my country and obey the Scout Law."

"Were you a boy scout?" J.X. asked in surprise.

"For about a month. Until it was time to go camping."

He chuckled, drew me in, and a few very pleasant minutes passed in each other's arms.

"The thing about the wedding," J.X. said suddenly, interrupting the natural flow of events.

I groaned. I'd had a feeling he wasn't going to give up so easily. "It's one day out of the rest of our lives. If a big wedding really matters to you—"

"No," he said quickly. "No, it doesn't. I wanted a big wedding, an unforgettable wedding because—"

I turned my head to study him. "Any circumstances that involve us getting hitched would be unforgettable."

He said sheepishly, "I know. The thing is…I was feeling sort of… competitive. Because of David. I guess because of his coming back into your life."

You have to sit up to goggle appropriately. Lying down, you just look like you were run over by a cattle stampede, which is how I felt. I sat up—and goggled. "David's not back in my life. Not even close."

"Well, he kind of is. You're working together to find the Dickison kid."

"I wouldn't call that work. And I wouldn't call that together."

"Yeah. Well." He scratched his nose. "I just sort of…"

I stared at him.

"You *are* jealous," I said slowly.

At last I had discovered my superpower. I had the ability to turn hitherto cool, confident, clearheaded men into insecure, anxious paranoiacs.

He made a face. "Is it really a surprise? I lost the last contest between him and me."

"We had this conversation, right? I didn't dream that. We had this out. Going back to David was the biggest mistake of my life. Maybe you've forgotten that, but I'm not likely to."

He flicked his lashes up, looking uncharacteristically uncertain.

"*Honey,*" I said. "The idea of you jealous of David is…it's comical. You're worth ten of him. You're ten times the man he was. You're ten times the man he could ever hope to be."

J.X. smiled. "Now you're just trying to make me feel better."

"I *am* trying to make you feel better. Because I love you. And part of why I love you is that's all true, every word of it. He doesn't hold a candle to you."

J.X. laughed, looking more like his normal self. "A candle?"

"Or a flashlight. Or an LED emergency light. Pick your favorite light fixture. David is a dim bulb by comparison."

He snorted, but after a moment he smiled. "And you claim you're not romantic."

CHAPTER NINETEEN

Pandora Boxleitner's home looked like the domicile on the haunted-house cake.

True, the cake house had been made of dark chocolate, and this structure was the color of dirty linen. But the wide eaves and turrets, the decorative spindles, corbels, and brackets were straight from the same *Psycho* blueprint.

Nor was that due to any Halloween decor. No effort had been made at decorating the classic Victorian farmhouse for the holiday. The Boxleitners lived too far out in the countryside to be plagued by trick-or-treaters.

I parked beneath the shady trees and walked across the whispering yellow grass and up the squeaking steps to the wraparound porch.

I pressed the doorbell, but I couldn't hear any ring. The buzzer felt loose.

I rapped briskly on the wooden frame screen.

I waited.

Nothing happened.

That was odd. I'd verified the details of my visit with Pandora only the day before. But no, it wasn't odd. The old house was huge. If she wasn't in one of the front rooms, there was a good chance she hadn't heard me.

I knocked again more loudly.

Nothing.

Unease prickled the hair on the back of my neck. It was *so* quiet. Even the birds were silent on this hot, still afternoon. The heavy air had a buzzy feeling; you could feel the crackle of static electricity.

To my relief, I heard a bolt slide. The front door opened on squeaky hinges. A woman peered out of the gloomy interior.

"Mr. Holmes?" her voice was small and sweet. She blinked out at me through large, round glasses.

"Hi. Yes. Pandora?"

"Yes." She unlatched the screen and pushed it open. "Come in. I'm so glad you made it."

I had never actually met Pandora in person. All our communication had been over the phone and through email. She didn't look like I expected—not that I could see her clearly after the brilliant sunlight. I'd been picturing someone younger and more...sturdy. Caring for an invalid took energy and strength. This woman looked frail—and not a lot younger than me.

She was medium height, slight, despite the baggy clothing, with lank mouse-brown hair, those hideous glasses, and a very pale complexion.

Granted, maybe caring for her ailing relative had drained a lot of the vim and vigor out of Pandora.

We shook hands. Her grip was firm. She had long, coral square-tipped acrylic nails. The nails seemed out of character for this woman, though they matched the idea of her I'd formed fourteen years earlier.

"Uncle Zag has been looking forward to this so much."

"Me too. I was so sorry to hear he'd had another stroke."

Her smile was a white blur in the dark entrance hall. "This way. We have a hospital bed set up for him in the front parlor." She wore a loose white smock, blue leggings, and rubber-soled tennis shoes with a floral pattern. Her footsteps were almost soundless.

I could see framed photographs hanging on the wall, but the light was too dim to make out any faces.

I asked, "When did he have the stroke?"

"Hmm," she mused. "I think it's been just over three weeks now. She smiled at me sadly.

"Oh? So recently?"

"Yes. Yes, it was very recent. He'd been doing so well too. We sort of forgot he'd ever been ill."

"Well, yeah. I saw his backlist on Amazon. That was some staggering productivity."

She threw a look over her shoulder. "So that's how you tracked us down to Sunol? Through the Amazon site?"

"Yeah, it's right there on Zag's bio that he now lives in Sunol."

She sounded startled. "Is it?"

"Well, Sophie Snow's bio."

"*Oh.* Sophie. Right." She laughed. It was a light and girlish sound. The pastel laugh didn't quite match the orange fingernails. "You must be one of the few people around who remember Uncle Zag was Sophie Snow."

Was?

"I'm sure that's not true," I said.

She laughed again. "I'm sure it is. Publishing has changed a lot in fourteen years, as you must know. So many new faces, so many new books."

"True. I was surprised Zag decided to go into self-publishing. He was always so loyal to his agent and the people at Millbrook."

"Well, he really didn't have a choice. He wasn't able to write for so long. When he was finally able to come back, no one remembered him. No one cared about Sweetie MacFarland."

"Huh," I said noncommittally.

We had reached a double doorway leading into another room with pulled shades and drawn drapes. Pandora put her hand on my arm.

She said softly, "Try not to be shocked at the change in him. You won't be able to understand him, but he can definitely understand you."

"Okay."

"Stay as long as you like. You're the only visitor he's had in ages."

I studied her face. Despite the spectacles, the lank hair, the almost ghostly pallor, I couldn't get over the feeling that I'd met her before. Older, and a little heavier—the hair was completely different—but yet she was somehow familiar. Except, of course, I'd never met Pandora in person.

Maybe at some point I'd seen a photo of her?

"I will. Thank you."

She nodded brightly and led the way into the room, almost instantly vanishing in the shadows. I followed cautiously, resisting the temptation to put my hands out in front of me. It wasn't quite that dark, but it was close. And why *was* it so dark? All I could figure was Zag's eyes must be very sensitive to the light. But, Jesus, what a depressing atmosphere.

I could see there was a fireplace across from the doorway. A large clock hung on the chimney breast. I couldn't see the face, but I could hear its slow, solemn *tick*. Weirdly unrestful. Most of the furniture had been moved against the wall to make way for the hospital bed in the middle of the room. The bed was slightly raised, and the man under the blankets was facing our way, but it was hard to tell if his eyes were open. His head was swathed in bandages.

"Here's Christopher Holmes, Uncle Zag," Pandora fluted in her high, sweet voice.

He made an inarticulate sound and moved his right arm a fraction.

"Hey, Zag," I said in what was probably too cheerful a voice, but I can't pretend I wasn't shocked silly by all the bandages. Even with Pandora's warning ahead of time. It wasn't just his head; his left arm was in a sling, and his chest was swaddled too.

What the hell?

I went to Zag's bedside and took his hand, gazing down at what I could see of his face.

It certainly looked like Zag under all the gauze and surgical tape. Older, more grizzled, but pretty much as I remembered him. His eyes were green, which was right, and remarkably bright and alert.

He feebly squeezed my hand and mumbled something.

"I'll leave you two alone," Pandora said from right behind me, and I barely managed not to jump.

"Thank you," I said.

"Just yell if you need anything."

Zag grunted in what seemed to be approval.

Pandora left the room on her little silent-cat feet.

"I'm really sorry to hear you've been ill again," I said. "I wish I'd known you were living nearby. I'd have been to see you sooner."

He nodded and gave my hand another squeeze.

I drew a breath. "And I wanted to say how sorry I am that I never got around to seeing you the last time. I wish I had a good excuse. I always meant to, but things kept coming up, and then I...didn't."

He made a murmuring sound, kind of like, *Hey, don't worry about it.*

"I read your new book. I enjoyed it a lot."

That time he sounded like he was in pain, and I didn't blame him.

All the while I was talking, I was thinking. I'm no medical expert, but I did some reading up on cerebrovascular accidents when I had to bump off Sir Cecil Hogsbody in *Take Your Medicine, Miss Butterwith*. While it was conceivable that Zag had undergone brain surgery after his stroke, I couldn't think of any reason he'd be swathed in bandages like this. Even his head bandage seemed a bit extreme. Did he really need that strip across the bridge of his nose? What good was that supposed to be doing?

J.X. hadn't been completely unjust in his suspicions. It had occurred to me that once I was here on my mission of mercy, I might be able to get information out of Zag or at least a hint as to his thoughts on the situation at the Hiawatha property. *Blink once for yes, twice for no!* But it was immediately obvious that this would not be possible.

"This is a beautiful old house. Queen Anne, right? I've never been out this way before, though I've been living up north for the last four months. I miss LA, but I like it better than I thought I would."

Another grunt, another little squeeze.

"I haven't been writing. Wheaton & Woodhouse dropped my series. But Rachel managed to get me a new deal, so it looks like I'll be starting a new Miss Butterwith book this week."

Another little squeeze, another grunt.

"I've gotta say, I'm so impressed by the-the volume of work you've produced over the years. To have had such a serious setback and then manage to more than make up for it in creative output is outstanding. Amazing. I know you'll do it again."

Even for someone as talkative as myself, a one-way conversation with someone you don't know well is difficult. Also, the handholding was beginning to creep me out because with each passing minute I was more and more sure that Zag was not the man in the bed.

Where the idea came from, I don't know, but once it dawned, I couldn't shake it.

This was not Zag.

Then who the hell was he? I had no idea. Presumably Mr. Boxleitner? If there really was a Mr. Boxleitner? He did look like Zag, at least superficially, but clearly, he wasn't a double, or they wouldn't have hit on the idea of wrapping him in bandages.

I kept talking.

"You're really lucky to have such a caring family. Pandora seems like a lovely girl. A really good person."

"Zag" watched me with those oddly alert eyes.

By that point, I was babbling.

"My boyfriend's got the same type of family," I said with a silent apology to the Moriarity clan. "We're going to be getting married soon, I think, and then we're going to go to Italy on our honeymoon. I've never been, but it's supposed to be a great place. I think we might go swimming with dolphins or take a gondola for a spin."

Zag mumbled something. Probably along the lines of, *Will you please fuck off.*

"Anyway, it's been so great to see you. I don't want to tire you out on my first visit. I'd like to come back soon, if that's okay with you?"

He squeezed my hand.

"Great! Well, and who knows. Maybe by the time we get the wedding figured out, you'll be well enough to attend. You beat this thing once," I was still gabbling as I freed my clammy hand and began to make my way through the grayout, trying not to trip over any stray footstools or end tables. "I'll just say goodbye to Pandora. I've got to get back home before the trick-or-treaters show up tonight. Don't want the boyfriend to send the search party after me." My laugh sounded hollow to my own ears.

He turned his head to watch my retreat to the doorway.

I was hoping like hell that Pandora was busy in the cellar, digging a fresh grave or something, but nope. She was hovering right outside the doorway, listening to our—my—conversation. When she stepped out of the shadows, I jumped and made a sound more appropriate to a small rodent at the sight of a large cat.

"Oh! Hey. There you are!" I said with manic cheerfulness. "I should get going, but thanks for arranging this."

She smiled. Her eyes did not turn red. She did not grow fangs. But somehow that smile still gave the same effect.

Did she know that I knew? Had I given myself away at any point? I was very much afraid terrified recognition was written all over my face.

"Did you have a nice visit?" she asked in her candy-coated voice.

"Oh yes! Too short. But I kept it brief because I don't want to wear out my welcome."

She twinkled at me. "No fear of that!"

"He—Zag—seems in good spirits. Considering."

Considering that he was dead and had been buried in my backyard for fourteen years.

"He's always believed in the power of positive thought." She smiled again, and I knew then for sure why "Pandora" had seemed peculiarly familiar despite my having never met her.

Pandora was Felicity Dann. Zag's longtime off-and-on girlfriend.

Gone was the tousled blonde hair and sexy makeup and stylish, vaguely provocative clothing, but it was her all right.

How had I not instantly guessed? Hadn't I seen this exact same scenario played out in episodes of shows like *Your Worst Nightmare* and *Dateline* and *48 Hours?* No wonder Zag's books read like they were written by someone else. They had been. Not only was this woman a monster, she was a *terrible* writer.

There was a muffled *thump* from the parlor. Felicity didn't bat an eye. I pretended I hadn't heard it either, but my mouth went dry.

I pried loose a few more desperate words. "I'd like to come again, if that's all right?"

"Of course," she said. "So long as Uncle Zag is up for it."

All the while we were making our way down the lightless hall to the front door, I was on edge, expecting something to happen. Did she have a pistol hidden in that oversize smock? I wouldn't have been surprised. Had I been lured to the house for some nefarious purpose? It seemed unlikely, but this was a woman who was not short on imagination or daring.

I could feel perspiration soaking my underarms and back by the time we reached the screen door.

Pandora unlatched it. "Can I ask you something, Mr. Holmes?" she asked casually.

"Sure!" I gazed longingly past the porch to the silver gleam of my Lexus half hidden beneath the shade trees.

"What made you look Uncle Zag up after all this time?"

I saw the chasm open before me. Should I lie or tell the truth? Which was more dangerous? Surely if Felicity knew Zag's body had been discovered, she wouldn't have risked a visit from me. Or would she? What was that comment she'd made about my being one of the few people who could connect Zag to Sophie Snow? Was I loose end she could not afford?

I said, trying to match her offhand tone, "My agent got a new deal for my series, and I was feeling kind of nostalgic. I wondered how Zag was doing these days. We started out together, you know."

"Yes, I know." Behind the huge lenses, her eyes were gray. I remembered that now. They held mine in an unblinking stare.

"I looked him up online, and you know the rest."

She said lightly, "I think I do. Well, have a safe trip." She gave the screen door a small push, and I barreled through with a gasped, "Bye now!"

The whole way across the seemingly endless expanse of dead lawn, I expected to hear a shot, but the silence was unbroken except for the distant sound of farm machinery. The air was hot and stagnant. Dead.

One of these days I would learn to listen to J.X. Assuming I lived long enough.

My knees were wobbling as I finally reached my car. I jumped in, managed to get the key in the ignition after a couple of tries, and started the engine. To my almost tearful relief, the Lexus roared into life. I reversed in a wide, drunken arc, and headed back down the dirt road through the woods.

It was all I could do to not floor it. But they'd let me leave the house, so they must not realize I knew? Right?

I watched my rear view for any sign of pursuit. The woods seemed to swallow the house behind me. I fumbled for my phone. "Hey, Siri!"

Nothing.

"Hello? Siri? Hi, Siri!"

Siri was not speaking to me again. Why did she hate me? What had I ever done to her?

"Siri? Hello, Siri? Siri, hey!"

Stony silence. Had I forgotten our anniversary? What did she want from me?

"Siri, get me J.X.! Siri, for the love of God, *call J.X.!*

My phone suddenly spoke. "What can I help you with?"

"Siri, get me J.X. Hurry."

"I'm sorry. I didn't get that."

"CALL. J.X."

"I've never really thought about it," Siri said calmly.

"Huh? Siri—"

"Checking messages."

"What? NO. Siri. No. Bad girl! CALL J.X."

A male voice said, "Hey, this is Joey. I think you have the wrong number. I don't know anyone named Dicky. Sorry."

Click.

"Siri, please. Please—"

"Calling J.X.," Siri said as though all I'd ever had to do was ask.

The phone rang and rang. He would be on the road by now. Even so, he would have his cell handy. He always had his phone handy.

God. God. God. Please pick up.

I saw a flash of blue in the trees, then movement out of the corner of my eye. My head jerked up in time to see a 4WD tractor driven by a mummy—*a mummy*—crash through the wall of trees and lurch to a stop in front of me, completely blocking the road. I dropped the phone, swinging the steering wheel and braking hard, but there wasn't enough room or time to maneuver.

The passenger side of the Lexus plowed into the chassis of the tractor, the airbag exploded from the dashboard, and the day went black.

CHAPTER TWENTY

"I didn't agree to *kill* anyone!"

"Then what the hell did you crash into him for?"

"To stop him! You said to stop him if he seemed to figure it out."

"Exactly. Stop him in order to do *what*?"

"In order to…stop him."

"*Seriously*, Ray?"

My head was thumping painfully. I unstuck my eyelids, feeling for my sleep mask, but I wasn't wearing it. The room itself was dark. I cautiously lifted my head.

It smelled…weird. Musty. Dusty. Fusty. In the gloom I could just make out the shadowy shape of bedposts, a tall chest of drawers, and a dresser with a framed oblong mirror that offered the blurry image of myself peering around in bewilderment.

Where the hell was I?

A male voice, unfamiliar to me, seemed to be speaking from the corner of the room. "Look, Fliss, I agreed to help you with a scam. I never agreed to murder."

Murder?

I tried to sit up. It took a couple of attempts. I felt sick and dizzy and weak. I put a hand to my forehead and felt a lump the size of a small planet. Apparently, the sky really *was* falling.

I got my legs over the side of the lumpy mattress and stood up. I immediately felt nauseous and had to sit down again. My head pounded in sickening time to my heartbeats. I thought about lying down again and knew I could not give in to that desire.

"Then what's *your* suggestion?" That voice I knew. That voice belonged to Pandora Pearce. No, Pandora Boxleitner. No again. Felicity...something. I couldn't remember her last name. Zag's psycho girlfriend. Although, in fairness, I'd never pegged her for psycho. Just manipulative and completely self-centered.

"I don't know, but I'm not getting involved in something like that."

My heart plummeted. I recognized that particular note of protest. My voice took on the same note when I was arguing with J.X. about something I knew I would ultimately have to give in to.

J.X.

I felt around for my phone. It was not on me.

Neither was my wallet or keys or a handy-dandy pocketknife like the one Miss Butterwith always carried.

Felicity's distant, echoey voice was saying, "Do you think *I* like it? Of course I don't *want* to have to do that. But what's our option? He *knows.*"

"Maybe he *doesn't* know."

"He pretended not to know a body was discovered at my old house. Why would he do that? And even if he didn't know, how do we explain Uncle Zag running him off the road?"

"Maybe he didn't see," Ray said sulkily. "Maybe he won't remember."

"Ray, do you really want to take that chance? Do you really want to risk everything we've built?"

I had another try at standing up. Not fun. I swallowed down the sickness, managed to get to my feet and reel my way across the room to where the voices seemed to be coming from. There was an old-fashioned heating register at the bottom of the wall. It was acting as a conduit for the conversation taking place in another part of the house. I slid down the wall, kneeling next to the register so I could hear better.

"But is it that big a deal?" Ray protested. "You pretended your boyfriend was still alive. You wrote a bunch of books using his name. That's like a misdemeanor. You probably wouldn't even spend a year in jail. If we get charged with *murder*—"

Felicity shrieked, "I'm not going to jail!"

"I'm just sayin—"

"And we *won't* get caught."

Ray's answer was too quiet to make out. I closed my eyes. I was so *tired*. More than anything on earth, I wanted to go to sleep.

I might even have dozed off for a second or two. My eyelids jerked open as Ray yelled, "Really? With his goddamned boyfriend calling his cell every ten minutes?"

Felicity muttered something I couldn't hear. I knelt closer to the grate, then realized footsteps were coming down the hall toward my room. I pushed up and staggered back to the bed, lying down—collapsing, really—and pretending to still be out.

I heard a key in the lock, the door flew open, the overhead light went on.

"Wake up," Felicity snapped. She crossed to the bed and smacked me.

As bedside manners went, hers left something to be desired.

I winced, fluttered my eyelids, moaned, "Where am I?"

"See?" Ray's voice said from the doorway. "He doesn't remember."

"Oh, bullshit," Felicity returned, unimpressed. "He remembers all right. You're right where you deserve to be, Mr. Holmes. This is what you get for sticking your pointy nose in other people's business."

Pointy nose?

I opened my eyes, pushed up on my elbows, and said, "Hey, Ray? For the record, she didn't just steal her boyfriend's identity. She murdered him. You might want to take that into account before you agree to become her murder accomplice."

"Shut up!" She tried to slap me again, and I grabbed for her wrist. We tussled, and then Ray came to her defense.

When I came back to my senses, Felicity was saying, "He's lying. I told you exactly what happened. Zag was cleaning his pistol, and it went off."

"Zag never owned a pistol in his life," I said.

"How would you know?"

"And how would he accidentally shoot himself in the *back* of the head?" That was just a guess. I'd remembered the pillow in Zag's grave.

She turned to glare at me. "You just won't stop, will you?" And to Ray, "Do you see now what we're dealing with? We *have* to shut him up. He'll destroy us otherwise."

Ray peered over her head at me. He had removed the bandages. He did look a bit like Zag—brown hair, square and rather blunt features, green eyes—but not so much that I would have mistaken him for the real thing.

He said, "What about the boyfriend? The boyfriend knows he came here today."

"I've thought of that," Felicity said.

"She thinks of everything," I said. "That's not always a good thing."

Ray said, "Shut up, or I'll punch you again."

I didn't think it would be useful to be punched again, so I shut up.

Felicity thrust my phone in my face. "Call your boyfriend. Tell him you had a great visit with Zag, but you're tired and you've decided to stay in Sunol tonight. If you say anything else, *even one word more*, you're dead, and we'll figure out how to explain it later."

"What if I don't?"

She drew out a large butcher's knife—where the hell had she stowed *that* on her person?—and held it up. The overhead light glinted off the razor-sharp tip.

Ray recoiled. "Fliss!"

She ignored him. To me, she said, "You want to find out?"

No. I really didn't. I took the phone from her. I could see the long list of J.X.'s messages—he was never one to give up easily—and pressed to return the last call.

Like everybody else, I've always wanted to believe that should I ever end up in a situation like the current one, I'd come up with some clever last-minute plan for saving my life. But honestly? As the phone began to ring, nothing occurred to me. I couldn't think of a special secret code only he would understand to communicate my peril, so I decided to simply shout, *They're holding me prisoner, they killed Zag, and they're going to kill me. I love you.* Or as much of that as I could get out before they did, indeed, kill me.

That was my entire plan. I did not have a backup. So when J.X.'s message came on, I stumbled. It sounds sappy, but my last wish was to hear his voice, his live voice, one final time—even if he was most likely going to be yelling at me.

But that was not to be. I cleared my throat. Felicity raised the knife, and Ray drew his fist back as though to punch me. I said, "Hi, Julian, it's Christopher. I had a great visit with Zag, but I'm tired and I'm going to spend the night in Sunol." I hesitated.

"Hang up," Felicity whispered fiercely. "Hang up, or you're dead."

"I love you," I said huskily, and disconnected.

She snatched the phone out of my hand. "Good. Done." She said to Ray, "See how easy that was?"

Ray looked doubtful. "He said it like he was a robot. Like he was under duress."

She shrugged. "He's tired. That fits." She gazed at me thoughtfully. "It has to look like an accident. A car accident. Yeah, his car's already damaged, so that will work."

Ray's eyes met mine. He looked away. He muttered, "You know, once we do this, there's no going back."

"There's already no going back, Ray," Felicity said.

"Not for her. There is for you," I said.

Felicity swung on me. "Goddamn it. We need to tape his mouth shut. That's the first thing."

Surprisingly, Ray said, "Tape residue. We can't afford to leave any physical evidence that indicates he was held prisoner. No tape. No rope burns. Nothing like that. We don't know what shape the body will be in when they find it."

I recognized a fellow fan of true-crime TV. What a shame he wasn't using his powers of observation for good instead of evil.

Felicity said indifferently, "No problem. We'll burn the car after we crash it."

"No," Ray said. "Cars don't naturally burst into flame. Crime-scene investigators will detect accelerant. That would be a giveaway that the accident was staged."

Felicity huffed out an exasperated, "Fine. You're suddenly the expert? You tell me how you want to handle this."

"We have to think it through. We can't mess this up. We have one chance to get it right."

"We can't take all night, Ray. We need to get this handled."

Ray said stubbornly, "We're risking life sentences. I'm not doing anything until we've got every detail figured out."

"Jesus fucking Christ! Just stab him and we'll bury his body in the woods."

She tried to hand the knife to Ray, but he put his hands up. "Hell no, I'm not stabbing him. There's a good chance the blade will slip, and then my DNA is liable to show up."

"Are you being funny, Ray?"

Ray glared at her. He did not look like a guy who had ever been funny. He said, "No, I'm not being funny."

Felicity looked from me to Ray. Her chest rose and fell, but then she seemed to calm. "Okay. You know what? You're right. If a thing's worth doing, it's worth doing right. Let's go figure out the details." She nodded at me. "Knock him out again."

Ray shook his head. "The bruising on the body has to be consistent with—"

"ARE YOU KIDDING ME?" she shouted. "Then we're tying him up, and to hell with the goddamned rope burns."

Felicity charged out of the room, slamming the door behind her so hard, the mirror on the dressing table fell forward, knocking all the little glass bottles and knickknacks off the dresser top. Mirror and bottles smashed to bits, broken glass flying everywhere. The smell of old perfume and bath oil mingled with the general fug.

"That was an antique, Fliss!" Ray shouted, going to the window.

Her response was muffled but clearly profane.

I watched in astonishment as Ray yanked back the heavy yellow drapes and pushed the sill up. He stared at me. "You've got two minutes, and then I'll have to kill you."

He turned and left the room, closing the door. A moment later I heard the lock turn.

For one split second I gaped at the closed door—and then I jumped for the window.

It was pitch-black outside and as cold as the bottom of a well.

For some reason, I had expected it to still be daylight, so night— and bitter autumn chill—came as a shock. I tumbled out the window with more speed than grace, landed awkwardly in deep dry grass, and took off running for the distant tree line.

I knew the darkness worked in my favor, but that cover only stretched so far. It was a full moon, and the wide, empty field between the back of the farmhouse and the road back to the highway was as brightly lit as a film set.

I'd never make it. I could already hear Felicity shrieking in alarm behind me. I didn't dare look back. I veered and headed instead for a towering cornfield.

As I dived through the ten-foot wall of green stalks, the strange, sweet, earthy smell of popcorn and diesel rose up from the damp ground. I put my hands out, pushing my way through the forest of rustling stalks and drooping leaves, feeling the sting of little cuts against my palms, a burning itch against my face.

I plowed on for another yard or so, and then my legs gave out and I sank down on the still-warm earth. I couldn't do it. I couldn't go on. Adrenaline will only take you so far. I was battered, bruised, and probably concussed. I'd been punched in the face. Maybe more than once. I couldn't remember.

I was as terrified as I'd ever been in my life, and yet I couldn't find the energy to keep moving. I knelt there, heart thundering, lungs on fire, listening to the faraway sound of Felicity and Ray calling to each other. I couldn't quite hear the words, but the tone did not sound like, *Forget about him, let's go home.*

I let my arms give and lowered myself the rest of the way to the ground, resting my face in the cool, moldering whatever the hell that was.

Woody Allen had it right: "Life is full of misery, loneliness, and suffering—and it's all over much too soon."

I thought of J.X. He was going to be very sorry for thinking I'd blown off Gage and the Halloween festivities when he learned I was dead. I enjoyed that morose reflection for a time, and then Felicity said clearly—and from only a few feet away, "Get the tractor. He's got to be in here somewhere."

I froze.

Somewhere ahead of me, Ray replied, "He's trying to make his way back to the highway."

I lay absolutely motionless, not daring to breathe, and watched her tennis shoes pass a few inches in front of my face.

"Ray, I'm *telling* you, I *saw* him run into this field. I saw it with my own two eyes."

"You think I'm going to mow down this entire field on your say-so?"

"You will if you don't want to spend the next thirty years in jail."

Ray swore and came tromping toward me. As his boots came into view, I rolled aside. His footsteps faltered and then kept going. He pushed through the wall of stalks and vanished into the crinkling, whispering darkness.

Felicity muttered, "I know you're in here somewhere, you bastard."

I waited, breathing into my hand to muffle the sound. The pollen was making my sinuses itch, and I began to fear I would sneeze. Why the hell was she just standing there? What was she waiting for?

Oh, right.

She was waiting for me to move.

To make a sound.

I wrinkled my nose, squinched my eyes shut. Terrible, fraught seconds passed.

The urge to sneeze faded. I opened my eyes and found myself staring into the beady eyes of a big, fat rat.

My lips parted. The rat looked as horrified as I felt. It turned tail and ran right over Felicity's feet. Felicity let out a blood-curdling scream and crashed past me, running back toward the house.

At least, I thought it was toward the house. By now my sense of direction was completely befuddled.

I got to my knees and then, wearily, to my feet. I could still hear Felicity smashing through the stalks, screaming and swearing at the top of her lungs.

I could hear something else too. The sound of a tractor heading my way.

"Oh, come *on*," I protested. "*Really?*"

But yes, really. The roar of the tractor grew louder. Much louder. I could see its headlights filtering eerily through the stalks, beams of light shooting crookedly through a maze of peeling stalks, rough leaves, and silken tassels. Dust and pollen shot up like upside-down rain.

I began to run perpendicular to the tractor's line of travel, and at last came out on the far side—in time to see a station wagon heading slowly down the dirt road leading from the house to the main road.

What the hell now?

Ray was mowing down my hiding place, and Felicity was cutting me off from the main highway. How long could I play hide-and-seek out here?

And that's when the idea came to me. This was my chance. Maybe my only remaining chance. With the house empty, I could find a phone—maybe even my phone—and call for help.

In fact, I could hide *in the house*. I could hide in the very bedroom they'd held me prisoner. They would never think to look there.

Now, there were a lot of problems with this plan, but I didn't see them at the time. I was exhausted, sick, and desperate.

I stuck to the edge of the remaining cornfield and started back toward the house. Eventually the cornfield came to an end. I stumbled my way through a pumpkin patch—nearly going into cardiac arrest as a tall scarecrow loomed up before me—and dropped to my knees, gulping for breath.

From under the shaded brim of his floppy straw hat, the scarecrow gazed at me with implacable black-stitched eyes.

I wiped the tears from my eyes and vowed that if I managed to get out of this alive, I would marry J.X. and give up amateur sleuthing forever.

By this point, there was only a small square of cornfield left. I watched the remaining stalks fold under the giant tires of the tractor, and then pushed off my knees and sprinted toward the low-hanging porch.

I dragged myself up the stairs, pulled open the screen, reached for the front-door handle, and—found it locked.

For a moment I could only stare stupidly.

Now what?

Plan *B?* I didn't *have* a Plan *B.*

I turned, looking back toward the road, and spotted Felicity's returning headlights.

Belatedly, I noticed something else. The tractor had stopped. No one was sitting atop it. That was because Ray was walking toward the house. In fact, he was only a few yards away.

I turned and staggered down the porch, climbed over the railing, and dropped into a flower bed. Pansies and alyssum. They felt cool against my sweaty face, and the sweet honey smell of the alyssum was oddly comforting.

I heard the crunch of tires, the squeak of brakes, the slam of a car door.

"Anything?" Felicity demanded.

Ray answered, "No."

"He's here somewhere."

"If he made it to the highway—"

"He didn't make it to the highway. He might have made it into the woods. I don't think he even made it that far."

Maybe it would be okay. Maybe she wouldn't notice me. Maybe she wouldn't think to look this close to the house. Maybe…

"You don't think maybe this has gone far enough?" Ray said.

"Are you kidding me? Ray. If it was necessary to kill him before, it's *imperative* now."

I lifted my head. Listened closely.

Was that—?

Sirens.

Police sirens.

Were they—?

Yes. Headed this way. *Yes.* I could have cried with relief. And they say you can never find a cop when you need one.

"What the hell is that?" Ray said in a very different tone of voice.

"Ray, we don't have t—"

"Shut up," he snapped. "You hear that?"

The three of us listened to the fast-approaching wail.

"*Shit*," Felicity exclaimed. "How the hell—?"

"Get in the car," Ray told her.

Somehow I managed to stand. I came around the side of the porch in time to watch Ray and Felicity race to the station wagon.

Ray had just slid behind the wheel as a caravan of cop cars came pouring down the dirt road, red and blue strobe lights slicing through the night.

I wobbled my way to the bottom of the porch steps and sat down on the first step, watching dreamily as patrol cars filled the front yard. As a matter of fact, I wasn't sure I *wasn't* dreaming. The events of the night were all starting to feel very far away and removed.

The police got out of their cars and surrounded the station wagon with their weapons drawn. There was a lot of shouting and yelling, and then Felicity and Ray exited their vehicle with their hands up. They got down on the ground as directed.

After a time, I realized I recognized one of the voices. It was the loudest and angriest voice, and it kept saying, "Where the hell is he? He better be okay. If you did something to him, if you harmed a single fucking hair on his head—"

I pushed up from the step and called, "Hey, is this what you're looking for?"

I was vaguely aware that an army of guns swung in my direction, but I only saw the tall man in jeans and a leather jacket. He turned my way and said, "*Kit?*" in a funny, cracked voice.

I started toward him, and the next thing I knew, I was locked in J.X.'s arms and he was kissing me over and over.

"Jesus Christ, Kit," he said. His voice was shaking. "I thought— I was afraid— I thought—"

"Trick or treat!" I said, and closed my eyes.

CHAPTER TWENTY-ONE

"Admit it," I said. "You thought I bailed on an evening spent frolicking with Gage and the Great Pumpkin."

"No," J.X. said. He was sitting on the side of the bed next to me, watching me eat a late but very delicious breakfast. "You gave your word. You gave your word as a former boy scout."

I cocked a skeptical eyebrow, and he said, "Well, yes, it did go through my mind. Of course."

I grinned and reached for a second English muffin from my lavish breakfast tray. I slathered it with butter, spread a thick layer of raspberry jam, and crunched into it. I sighed my pleasure. It's a well-known fact that nearly being murdered entitles you to forty-eight hours of bad carbs, guilt-free.

J.X. watched me, smiling. "You're clearly feeling better."

"Mm-hm."

It was the morning after Pandora, a.k.a. Felicity, and her reluctant co-conspirator, Ray, had tried to do me in. The first day of November *and* the rest of my life.

In the end, I did spend the night locally, but in Fremont, not Sunol. Sunol doesn't have either a hotel or a motel, which Felicity would have done well to remember because that fact, combined with my desperate effort to tip J.X. off by using the names we never used with each other, had sent my betrothed jetting straight to the Alameda County Sheriff's Office.

It was not the first mistake Felicity had made. That had probably happened when she forced Zag at gunpoint to sign over his power of attorney to "Pandora Pearce," and then she'd witnessed that same transaction as Felicity Dann. Murdering Zag and burying him in his own backyard had not been smart either, but in her defense, she'd gotten away with it for nearly fifteen years.

Why had she taken such a ruthless and potentially self-destructive step? It turned out that Zag had finally gotten tired of Felicity's lying, cheating, and manipulating. He decided not to move in with her and not to sell his house to me after all. Felicity had not taken kindly to losing the money from that sale or access to Zag's very comfortable checking account and credit cards, and there was also the matter of a hefty insurance policy he had taken out in her favor several years previous.

Poor Zag. His big mistake had been to fall in love with the wrong person—and who hasn't made that one?

Anyway, it had taken J.X. a while to convince the sheriffs he was not trying to pull an elaborate Halloween prank, but as I've learned over the past year, he can be very persuasive when he chooses.

By the time I had finished receiving medical attention and giving my statement to law enforcement, it was long after midnight. Felicity and Ray were behind bars, and all the good little ghosts and goblins had retired for the night. J.X. had booked a room at the first hotel he could find with a vacancy—and room service—and we had promptly crashed.

"I'm disturbed to learn you too have a duplicitous streak," I commented, polishing off the last of my muffin.

"*Me?*" J.X. sounded amazed.

"Pretending you had left town when in fact you were heading to Nina's to spend the evening bobbing for apples and playing snap-dragon with Gage and the other little monsters."

"I'm not sure what snap-dragon is, but I didn't plan on spending the evening with only Gage," J.X. pointed out.

"True." I poured myself more coffee.

"The thing is, I had news regarding Jerry, and I wanted to tell you myself."

"What news?" I braced myself, ready to hear that Jerry had once more outfoxed the system. "Bad news?"

"No."

No? Then why did he look like that? So...guarded.

"Clearly not good."

"Mixed."

Just tell me."

"Jerry's bail has been revoked. He's back in jail."

"That's great! What happened?"

"A couple of things. He was identified as the man who rented an Intrepid van matching the description of the one Emmaline saw."

"That's terrific." Why did he think this was mixed news? It was fantastic news.

"And Happy Harold contacted me to let me know that Jerry has been working as a clown. He performs at kiddie birthday parties and visits sick children in the hospital."

Jerry wasn't completely evil? That did not give me the pleasure it should have.

"But he's back in jail now?" I asked.

J.X. nodded. He still looked grim around the edges.

"So what's the problem?"

He hesitated.

"Obviously there *is* a problem." I put down my coffee cup.

"Jerry was parked on our street when he was picked up."

"He was…" Even knowing the likelihood of the police keeping an eye on our place, he had come back. Frankly, that was unnerving.

"It gets worse."

I said faintly, "Does it?"

"When the van was searched, they found duct tape, rope, plastic cable ties, and…a couple of other items."

I made myself ask. "What other items?"

J.X. said without expression, "A Taser."

"A…Taser." I swallowed the unpleasant taste in my mouth. "He was planning to abduct me? Kill me?"

J.X. said with obvious reluctance, "We don't know for sure. It's possible."

"It seems more than possible! It's straight out of the *Misery* playbook!"

J.X. covered my hand on the bedspread. "Don't freak out about this, Kit. Jerry is not getting out on bail again, and when he comes up for trial, he's going to be convicted."

"Sure," I said.

"You've got to trust the system to do its job."

Right. The same system that let Jerry out on bail so he could stalk me dressed as a creepy clown and put in motion his plan to abduct and maybe kill me?

I didn't say that, though. I said, "Okay. I'll try."

He squeezed my hand. "Happy Ever After, right?"

"You bet," I said.

Although I tried to convince J.X. I could make my own way back to San Francisco and Cherry Lane, he insisted on driving me all the way home and making sure I was resting comfortably in bed before finally, reluctantly saying goodbye.

"This is going to be the longest two weeks of my life," he muttered, holding me tight.

Same for me, but I said briskly, "It'll pass before you know it. And when you come home, we'll start planning our wedding."

His eyes lit. "Really? You're ready for that?"

"Yes." I said it without hesitation. There's nothing like believing you won't survive the night to help you get your priorities in order.

His smile was brighter than the Tuscan sun or Etruscan gold or some such simile. It was bright and happy, and that made me happy. "Okay. I'm going to hold you to that."

"You can hold anything of mine you like."

He muttered, "I'm not going to be able to leave if you keep saying things like that."

I locked my hands on his shoulders and pushed him back. I said sternly, "If you're going, go."

"*If* I'm going—?"

"Go," I said, and meant it.

He went.

When the sound of his Honda died away down the street, I pushed back the bedclothes and went downstairs to the kitchen. I opened the freezer, took out a mini frozen pizza, heated it in the microwave and headed to my office.

I turned on my computer, opened Word, took a thoughtful bite of pizza, and sat for a moment staring at the blank page. This was always the hardest part.

I closed my eyes, placed my hands on the keyboard.

Ah. There we go—

The phone rang.

I groaned, glanced at the caller ID, and groaned again.

I picked up the phone. "Yes?" I snapped.

"You're not the only detective in the family," David said cheerfully.

"I never claimed to be a detective." And I sure as hell never would again. I added, "In fact, I claimed repeatedly *not* to be a detective. Furthermore, *we* are no longer a family."

"Be that as it may—"

"*Be that as it may?* What does that mean? What *it may* is we are divorced and no longer a family."

"I found Dicky."

"You…"

"Yep."

After a stunned moment, I said, "You're kidding."

"Nope." He was so smug, it was practically oozing through the handset.

"Where is he?" I demanded.

"Just as I thought. Living with his sister in Florida."

"So he's okay?" I mean, I had certainly hoped this was the case, but I was still sort of shocked to hear it.

"Yep."

"He's fine?"

"Seems to be."

"Then why the hell did he go into hiding?"

David said, "He didn't. He just left the state."

"But..."

"Yeah," David agreed. He sounded less smug. Almost glum. "I asked him about that. He said he'd realized almost immediately he'd made a mistake. That the fun part was the chase, the flirtation. He couldn't think of a way to tell me. So he just took off."

I couldn't think of anything to say. In the end, Dicky had done me a favor, but it didn't really change the fact that he'd also caused me a lot of pain and heartache. And David too, I supposed. Although David had probably got his just desserts. Even so, to my surprise, I felt a little sorry for my ex.

"That's..."

"It is. I agree. The little shit. Anyway, I thought you'd want to know. He's fine. He's been fine the whole time. He's working as a PA for Tansy Hoffmeyer."

"Tansy Hoffmeyer? The one who writes the Ice Fishing mysteries?"

"Right."

"He used to make fun of her books!"

David said dryly, "Well, we know now what *that* means."

Hm. Maybe he had a point.

"He said to tell you he was sorry about everything," David added.

I had to laugh. "That's some sincere apology if he couldn't be bothered to make it himself."

"I think he's uncomfortable with the whole situation."

"Ya think?"

"Oh, and congratulations on solving the mystery of the body in the backyard. You're still four cases ahead of me."

I said bitterly, "I can't take credit for this last one."

"According to Detective Dean, you can."

"Really?" I was sort of flattered to hear it.

"They're still holding Reggie Chow. Deliberately giving a false confession is a bigger deal than I thought. They're charging him with obstruction of justice."

"Why *did* he confess?" I asked.

"Just attention-seeking, per Dean. I always told you that kid was a menace."

"Yikes." A thought occurred. "You and Dean seem pretty chummy all at once."

"She told me she appreciated my insight and perspective on this case."

Say what?

I opened my mouth but could think of nothing to say to that.

"Hey, listen." David's tone grew elaborately casual. "I don't know how often you get back to the Southland, but if you'd like to get together the next time you're in town—"

I chuckled. "Sorry. That ship has sailed."

"Right, right," he said. "*But* if that ship should ever return to port—"

"Bon voyage, Captain Ahab," I said, and hung up.

I went back to staring at the blank page on my computer screen.

The cursor blinked, waiting patiently.

I smiled and began to type.

The December snow had turned to gray, slushy wet as Miss Butterwith, with her new black umbrella over her head and her old red galoshes over her outdoor shoes, closed the garden gate behind her and started off toward High Street...

AUTHOR'S NOTES

Keen-eyed readers will note that the street Kit and J.X. live on is now named Cherry Lane. This was the original intended name for their home address; however, somehow, when finalizing *The Boy with the Painful Tattoo,* I ended up changing the name back to the street that served as my inspiration.

Readers may also view with skepticism the devious machinations of our primary villain; regular viewers of the Investigation Discovery channel will be aware the most outlandish details were inspired by real events.

Did you enjoy this book? You might also enjoy

THE GHOST WORE YELLOW SOCKS

His romantic weekend in ruins, shy twentysomething artist Perry Foster learns that things can always get worse when he returns home from San Francisco to find a dead body in his bathtub. A dead body in a very ugly sportscoat— and matching socks.

The dead man is a stranger to Perry, but that's not much of a comfort; how did a strange dead man get in a locked flat at the isolated Alton Estate in the wilds of the "Northeast Kingdom" of Vermont?

Perry turns to help from "tall, dark, and hostile" former navy SEAL Nick Reno—but is Reno all that he seems?

THE GHOST WORE YELLOW SOCKS

CHAPTER ONE

There was a strange man in Perry's bathtub. He was wearing a sports coat—a rather ugly sports coat. And he was dead.

Perry, who had just spent the most painful and humiliating twenty-four hours of his life, and had driven over an hour from the airport in blinding rain to reach the relative peace and privacy of the chilly rooms he rented at the old Alston Estate, stood gaping.

His headache vanished. He forgot about being exhausted and starving and soaked to the skin. He forgot about wishing he was dead, because here was someone dead, and it wasn't pretty.

His fingers still rested on the light switch. He turned the overhead lights off. In the darkness, he heard rain rattling against the window; he heard his breathing, which sounded fast and scared; and from the living room he heard the soft chime of the clock he had bought at the thrift store on Bethlehem Road. Nine slow, silvery chimes. Nine o'clock.

Perry switched the light back on.

The dead man was still in his bathtub.

"It's not possible," Perry whispered.

Apparently this didn't convince the corpse, who continued to stare at him from beneath half-closed eyelids.

The dead man was a stranger; Perry was pretty sure of that. It—he—was middle-aged and he needed a shave. His face was sort of greenish-red, the cheeks sunken in as though his features were slipping. His legs stuck out over the side of the tub like a mannequin's. One shoe had a hole in the sole. His socks were yellow. Goldenrod, actually. They matched the ugly checked jacket.

The stranger was definitely dead. His chest wasn't moving at all; his mouth was ajar, but no sounds came out. Perry didn't have to touch him to know for sure he was dead, and besides that, nothing on earth would have made him touch the corpse.

He couldn't see any signs of violence. There didn't seem to be any blood. Nor water. The tub was dry and empty—except for the dead man. It didn't look like he had been strangled. Maybe he had died of natural causes?

Maybe he'd had a heart attack?

But what was he doing having a heart attack in Perry's locked apartment?

Perry's glance lit on the mirror over the sink, and he started, not immediately recognizing the pale-faced, hollow-eyed reflection as his own. His brown eyes were huge and black in his frightened face; his blond hair seemed to be standing on end.

Backing out of the bathroom, Perry closed the door. He stood there trying to work it out through the fog of weariness and bewilderment. Then, eyes still pinned on the closed door, he took another step backward and fell over his suitcase, which was still sitting in the center of the front room floor.

The fall jarred Perry's thoughts into so^r
action. Scrambling up, he bolted for the ap
scrabbled to undo the deadbolt.

He yanked open the door, but it banged shut
away by a ghostly hand, and he realized the chain w
shaking, he unfastened that too and slammed out of the

It seemed impossible that the hall should look just as
he had trudged upstairs five minutes earlier. Wall sconces ca
shadows down the mile of faded crimson carpet leading to the w
staircase.

The long lace draperies stirred in the window draughts. Nothing
else moved. The hall was empty, yet the disturbing feeling of being
watched persisted.

Perry listened to the sound of rain whispering against the windows,
as though the house were complaining about the damp, the wood rot, the
mustiness that permeated its aged bones. But it was the ominous silence
on the other side of his own door that seemed to flood out everything
else.

What was he waiting for? What did he expect to hear?

Despite his desperation to get downstairs to lights and people, he
felt peculiarly apprehensive about making the first move, about making
a sound, about doing anything to attract attention—the attention of
something that might wait unseen in the dim recesses of the long hall.

He had to force himself to take the first step. Then he barreled
down the hallway, narrowly missing the half-dead aspidistras in their
tall marble planters. Despite the reassurances of his rational mind, he
kept expecting an attack to launch itself from the cobwebbed corners.

Reaching the head of the stairs, he hung tightly to the banister
to catch his breath. His knees were jelly. Uneasily, he looked behind
himself. Nothing but the twitching draperies stirred the gloom. Perry

down the stairs. Fifteen steps to the next level; he took them two ____me.

Reaching the second floor, he hesitated. Ex-cop Rudy Stein lived this floor. An ex-cop ought to know what to do, right?

Mr. Watson had also lived on this floor, but Watson had died a week ago in Burlington. His rooms were locked, his belongings collecting dust waiting for a man who would never return.

Not that Perry believed in ghosts—exactly—or was too chicken to face another dark, drafty hallway, but after that moment's hesitation, he continued down the rest of the grand staircase until, at last, he reached the ground floor which served as the lobby of Mrs. MacQueen's boarding house.

Someone was just coming in the front door, pushing it closed against the sheets of rain. Overhead, the chandelier tinkled musically in the gust of the storm's breath, throwing eerie colored red shadows across the man's figure.

He wore a hooded olive parka, and for a moment, Perry didn't recognize him. In fact, he couldn't see any face at all in the cowl of the parka, and (his nerves shot to hell) he gasped, the soft sound carrying in the quiet hall.

Shoving the hood back, the man stared at Perry. Now Perry recognized him. He was new to Mrs. MacQueen's rooming house, an ex-marine or something. Tall, dark, and hostile.

Perry opened his mouth to inform the newcomer about the dead man upstairs, but the words wouldn't come. Maybe he was in shock. He felt kind of funny, detached, rather light-headed. He hoped he wasn't going to pass out. That would be too humiliating.

"What's with you?" the man said. He was frowning, but then he was always frowning, so there wasn't anything in that. He actually wasn't *that* tall—slightly above medium height—but he was muscular, solid. A human Rock of Gibraltar.

Finally Perry's vocal cords worked, but the man couldn't seem to make out his choked words. He took a step closer. His eyes were blue, marine blue, which seemed appropriate, Perry thought, still on that distant plane.

"What's the problem, kid?" the man asked brusquely. Obviously there was a problem.

Breathlessly, Perry tried to explain it. He pointed upward, his hand shaking, and he tried to get some words out between the gasps.

And now the corpse upstairs was the second problem, because the first problem was he couldn't breathe.

"Jesus Christ!" said the ex-marine, watching his struggle.

Perry lowered himself to the carpeted bottom step of the grand staircase and fished around for his inhaler.

* * * * *

Perfect ending to a perfect day, Nick Reno thought, watching the queer kid from across the hall sucking on an inhaler.

The divorce papers had arrived that afternoon, but what should have felt like relief felt like another failure. The job at the construction company hadn't panned out, either. It was the wrong time of year for construction—the wrong time of year for everything, it seemed. And now this. For the last few hours Nick had been hanging on to the idea of a stiff drink and some solitude, and what he got was this damn boy having hysterics.

"Kid, pull yourself together." What was his name? Something Foster. Nick had noticed it on the mailbox in the lobby.

The kid continued to huff and puff, his thin chest rising and falling with the struggle to breathe. Maybe he'd just missed an episode of his favorite soap opera. Maybe they had discontinued his favorite flavor at Starbucks. Who the hell knew? Queers.

Nick looked around the suspiciously silent lobby. Where were all the busybodies who normally littered the halls of Mrs. MacQueen's nuthouse?

"I could use some help here," he called out, whether to the Almighty or the closed doors, he wasn't sure. But after a moment he heard a chain slide. Deadbolts began scraping, latches cranking, turn knobs clicking. Old Miss Dembecki's door opened a crack.

The kid, who had turned a lovely shade of blue, lowered the inhaler long enough to wheeze, "There's a...dead man—" Suction resumed.

"There's a *what*?" Nick demanded. "Where?"

People were now creeping out of their rooms into the hall. Miss Dembecki, wired for sound in pink curlers, pulled a gingham nylon bathrobe around her skinny body. "What's happened?" she demanded querulously. "What did you do to him?"

"I didn't touch him." Nick glanced up as a floorboard creaked.

Suspended above them was a white moon of a face. Stein, the ex-cop, shone down on them. His mouth made an O as round as the rest of his perspiring face: round eyes, round mouth, squashed nose. "What's going on? Somebody in an accident?" His voice floated down.

Dourly, Nick eyed the kid. "I don't know."

"Perry, whatever's wrong?" quavered the old lady.

Perry. That figured, Nick thought grimly. A pansy name if there ever was one.

Across the hallway another door opened.

A cat wafted out of the Bridger woman's apartment and pussy-footed toward them, white plume tail waving gently. The kid made a panicked sound and pointed with his free hand.

Nick pivoted impatiently, but Ms. Bridger, six-feet-nothing, red-haired, and clad in an emerald kimono, was already scooping up the offending feline and shutting it back in the apartment.

Dembecki called, "Miss Bridger, perhaps you... Something's happened to Perry." She cast an accusing look in Nick's direction.

Nick began, "Look, lady—" then gave it up, stepping aside as Jane Bridger rustled up in her silk dressing gown. There was a dragon embroidered on the back of her gown. She was doused in Poison perfume. Nick recognized it as Marie's favorite, and his stomach knotted.

"Perry, sweetie," she cooed, joining the kid on the bottom step. "What's wrong?" To Nick she explained, "He has asthma."

"I noticed."

Foster lowered the inhaler once more and got out, "Dead man...in my...bathtub."

He was speaking to Nick as though somehow it was Nick's problem; maybe he thought Nick was the only one equipped to deal with a dead body scenario.

The door to the landlady's apartment opened at last, and Mrs. MacQueen billowed out in a cloud of cigarette smoke. "What's all the racket?" she rasped. "What are you people doing now?" A blast of canned TV laughter followed from her rooms.

"Perry's ill," Miss Dembecki quaked. "It's his asthma."

Bridger patted Foster's shoulder kindly. Her long fingernails were blood red against his white shirt. "Hang in there, sweetie. Take slow, deep breaths." Her robe slipped open to reveal the outline of breasts so perfect they had to be fake. Nick raised his eyes. If Stein leaned any further over the banister he was going to take a nosedive.

Two small dogs burst out of MacQueen's rooms, and nails slipping on the hardwood floor, scrabbled their way to Bridger's door, barking hysterically.

Fed up, Nick stepped back, treading on Miss Dembecki's slippered foot; he hadn't noticed her sidling up behind them. Now she yowled like an injured cat.

"Sorry," Nick exclaimed.

"Why can't you look where you're going?" moaned Miss Dembecki, hobbling to one of the overstuffed chairs by the fireplace. The fireplace was unlit. It had never been lit as far as Nick could tell. Maybe it was supposed to be decor. It just emphasized how unwelcoming the damn house was.

Foster gulped out more vehemently, "There's a dead man in my bathtub!"

Dead silence. Another burst of televised laughter. Someone tittered nervously.

"What does *that* mean?" demanded MacQueen finally. She reminded Nick of James Cagney in drag, sort of sounded like him too.

"It means somebody ought to go upstairs and check it out," Nick said.

The boy shot him a grateful look.

"Who, *me?*" MacQueen actually backed up in one of those you-won't-take-me-alive-copper moves.

"You own the place. You're the manager, aren't you?"

"But, that's...I mean...sure, but..." Her bug eyes traveled from face to face. She licked her colorless lips. The others were making sounds, wordless excuses, apologetic noises.

"Forget it," Nick said. "I'll go." It would be a relief to escape the freak show for a minute or two. "Where are your keys, kid?"

Foster said, "I didn't...lock the...door." He still sounded breathy, but he wasn't blue anymore. He kept a tight grip on the inhaler.

"It's the third floor. The tower room opposite yours," MacQueen informed Nick.

"Got it." Nick started up the stairs.

On the second floor, he passed Stein, who twitched him a meaningless smile but didn't speak.

Nick continued his climb to the third floor. It was dark and quiet up here; the scent of cats and the sound of TV didn't reach. Neither, half the time, did the heat. Lace curtains over the poorly sealed windows floated up like specters then flattened back against the wall. Not the best visibility: the long hallway was badly lit; a pair of half-dead plants on tall pedestals provided suitable cover for ambush.

A funny feeling prickled across the back of Nick's scalp. It was a feeling he had learned not to ignore during fourteen years in the service—though unexpected in a broken-down mansion in the middle of the Vermont woods.

He considered, and discarded, going back to his quarters and arming. He was pretty confident he could handle any garden-variety scumball who might have sneaked in.

Approaching the kid's apartment cautiously, Nick turned the doorknob.

The door swung open onto a large chilly room that smelled of rain and turpentine. It looked more like an art studio than someone's living quarters. The curtains had been removed to allow more light. A spattered drop cloth covered much of the floor. A canvas half-covered with inky pine trees rested on an easel near the window. Blank canvases were stacked against the wall; painting utensils covered what appeared to be the dining room table. There were paintings everywhere: on the walls, on the floor.

In the middle of the room was a suitcase.

So the kid had been gone overnight; that meant someone could conceivably have got into his rooms and…dropped dead.

Except the bathroom door was open, the light on. Nick had a clear view of the tub. It was empty.

Surprise.

Had he really expected to find a dead man in a bathtub?

Nah, but something had sure scared the shit out of little Perry. The few times Nick had passed him on the stairs he seemed quiet, polite, and reasonably sane.

Nick advanced down the hallway.

The bathroom was big, old-fashioned, the twin of his own. The tub was one of those claw-foot porcelain jobs, running hot and cold water through separate spouts, making it ideal for scalding your feet. There was a small, bullet-shaped window over the tub. For laughs Nick opened it, gazing down on distant muddy ground and tree tops sparkling wet in the house lights.

Nobody and no body.

There was a streak of brown on the inside of the tub. He knelt to check it out. Red clay? Paint? Rust? That smear could be a lot of things, and yet instinctively the hair rose on the nape of his neck. He scratched at it with his thumbnail, sniffed his thumb. Was he imagining that coppery, metallic smell?

No damn way.

He noticed black scuff marks on the tile. Like somebody's heels were dragged across the floor?

Nick's eyes narrowed thoughtfully. Rising, he made for the bedroom. Not much to see. A twin-size bed, a battered bureau. The only thing out of order was one brown shoe lying in front of the closet. He picked it up. Cheap leather. Size 14. There was a hole in the sole. Nick set the shoe on the window ledge, glancing at the bed. A stack of books sat on the night table. Library books. *I Like 'Em Tough, They Can't All Be Guilty, I Found Him Dead, Secrets of a Private Eye.* A bookshelf was packed with paperbacks flaunting equally lurid titles.

His mouth curved wryly. Okay, now things made sense.

Still, remembering the terror in those wide brown eyes, he opened the closet door. Oh boy. The kid even hung up his pajamas.

He glanced under the bed. Someone had raised their little boy right. No dust bunnies, no dead bodies.

Cursorily, Nick glanced through the other rooms and closets. No corpses. There was an asthma chart pinned to the refrigerator, which told its own sad little story, and a box of Froot Loops on top of the fridge, which Nick found grimly amusing.

As he shut the front door, the painted canvases lining the living room caught his attention. Nick didn't know anything about art, but he knew what he liked. He liked these. There was a sureness and maturity to these calm studies of covered bridges and autumn woods that one wouldn't expect. Chalk one up for the boy next door.

The landing on the second floor was deserted when Nick reached it. Stein had either got bored or fallen over the balcony. Same scenario in the front lobby. MacQueen had escaped back inside her apartment and turned up the TV volume. In fact, the only people left were Foster, who seemed to have recovered somewhat—the inhaler was no longer in sight—and the voluptuous Ms. Bridger, who stood before the unlit fireplace.

"All clear?" she inquired cheerfully. Her red hair and green dressing gown were like a shout in that drab room.

"Yeah." Nick remembered the streak of red clay on the tub and dismissed it.

"No way. That can't be!" Foster's thin face tightened. "Then they moved him," he said stubbornly.

"*They?* What, it's a conspiracy?"

Foster flushed. He had that baby-clear skin that advertised his emotions like a billboard.

"Sweetie, sweetie," cooed Bridger. "Couldn't it have been a bad dream?"

"Or too many detective stories?" Nick put in.

Foster was still sitting on the bottom step or the grand staircase. He glared up at Nick. "I wasn't asleep!" He turned that angry gaze toward the Bridger chick. "I got back from the airport, walked in, and there he was. I wasn't sleeping. I wasn't hallucinating."

"There's no dead body now."

Foster swallowed hard. "I think we should call the police."

Bridger looked in dismay to Nick. How was it Nick's problem? Let them call the police. Just leave him out of it.

"But, sweetie, Mr....uh. Mr.—"

"Reno," Nick supplied reluctantly.

"Mr. Reno has already checked. The police won't find anything now. Right? We don't want to cause trouble."

Nick glanced at her. Maybe a little hard around the edges, but still a surprisingly good-looking woman to be living out here in the middle of nowhere. What was it about the cops that worried her?

"The police have forensic people," Foster said stubbornly. "Trained people who have equipment that can find microscopic traces of blood or hair."

Nick thought of the bloody streak in the tub again. The possible scuff marks on the tile. "Listen, kid—"

"Perry. Perry Foster." Foster rose as though he had made up his mind.

"Whatever. Foster, the police are not going to send out their forensics team in the worst storm of the decade because of a crank call."

"I'm not a crank! There was a dead body. Someone put him in my *locked* apartment and took him away again. Someone in this house."

Bridger glanced nervously at MacQueen's closed door. She chewed her bottom lip and said, "Sweetie, let's the three of us go inside my apartment and think this through."

Nick opened his mouth, but Foster beat him to it. "I can't go in there," he said obstinately.

"I'll put the cats away."

"Their dander—"

"Oh, for cryin' out loud!" Nick exclaimed. "I don't care what you people do, just don't involve me."

The kid, Foster, gritted his jaw, but his eyes were glittering ominously as he stared at Nick. "Sure. Thanks for your help," he managed, politely.

Nick started to turn away. "The police might want to question you, Mr. Reno," Bridger warned. Her eyes shone like green glass.

Nick drew a deep breath and exhaled slowly. "Let's go inside and talk this over," he said very calmly.

* * * * *

The police arrived while they were having coffee. The coffee was laced with brandy, which, according to Nick, was a mistake, but clearly the whole night was a mistake as far as he was concerned. Calling the cops was the biggest mistake, and he had waxed loud and eloquently—but mostly just loud—on the topic.

Now he was brooding in silence, taking up half of Jane's horsehair sofa. The police, having heard Perry out, tramped upstairs to investigate. Nick Reno had been right. There was no forensics team, just two weary and wet deputy sheriffs in yellow slickers, looking mighty unamused.

Before the deputies headed upstairs, Nick filled them in about the mud smear on the tub and the scuff marks on the tile.

"How come you didn't mention those things before?" Perry accused when the door closed on the officers of the law. "Those are clues."

"Let the cops decide if they're clues or not," Nick returned.

"More brandy?" offered Jane. He held out his cup, and she topped off his coffee.

Perry stared down at his mug. He knew the other two were irritated with him for insisting on phoning the police; it was like they were operating in an alternate universe. Of course he had called the police. Any normal person would call the police.

So now the three of them sat waiting for the law to finish, drinking spiked coffee and eating decorated cookies hard enough to crack a tooth on. The brandy was getting to Jane; she was flirting with Nick.

Perry's gaze wandered around the room. There were two Christmas cards on a table. One was from an insurance company. The other was lying face down. Jane was not the Suzy Homemaker type. Her apartment was a mess. She must dress and undress walking from room to room, he decided, eyeing a silk blouse draped over a lamp shade. The tabletops were dusty, and there was cat hair on the overstuffed furniture. His chest tightened as he noticed it.

"How are you feeling now, sweetie?" Jane asked Perry, as though reading his expression.

"Fine." He shot a diffident look at Reno and then looked away. Nick Reno was staring at him like he was a dork.

"What happened while I was upstairs?" Reno questioned suddenly.

Jane shrugged and pulled at the shoulder of her slipping dressing gown. "Nothing."

"Mr. Center came out of his rooms," Perry offered.

"For about half a minute. He went straight back inside," Jane clarified. "Everyone did. Miss Dembecki went back in her apartment and locked the door. Ditto Mrs. Mac. It's not like anyone thought you would find anything." She patted Perry's hand apologetically, asking Nick, "Why? What did you expect?"

Nick Reno had the kind of face that gave nothing away. Instead of answering Jane directly, he asked, "How many people live here?"

"Seven, now that poor Mr. Watson is gone."

Nick's eyes narrowed reflectively. "That's the guy who died in the village? And Stein is the fatso on the second floor?"

"That's right. He works as a security guard at the mall most nights. It used to be Mr. Stein, Mr. Center, and Mr. Watson on the second floor. On this floor, it's been me, Miss Dembecki, Mrs. Mac, and Mr. Teagle since...well, it feels like forever. I'm sure you've met Mr. Teagle. He makes a point of meeting everyone." Her smile was sardonic. Mr. Teagle did not approve of Jane. "And way up on the third floor, it's just you and Perry in your twin towers."

Perry was trying to work out a timetable. There was no way anyone could have entered the house from the outside, or if already inside, use the main staircase without coming into view of the tenants crowded in the lobby. That meant that whoever had moved the body must have still been on the third floor during the time between Perry's flight and Nick's trip upstairs. Maybe the intruder had been in Perry's rooms when Perry found the body. Maybe he had been watching from behind the door the whole time.

It was an unsettling idea. "The body must be hidden somewhere on the third floor," Perry told them.

Jane quit tapping her carmine nails on her cup and stared.

"Where? My rooms?" Reno suggested dryly.

Perry's eyes narrowed, focusing on the notion. That *was* the most obvious explanation: there was no body because Reno had carted it off to his own rooms. He had been outside when Perry came downstairs. Could that mean anything?

Watching him add it up, Reno commented, "You've got a hell of an imagination, kid." And strangely enough, Perry was reassured.

"Maybe it went down the laundry chute. The corpse, I mean." Jane handed round the plate of wreath-shaped cement cookies.

Nick declined cookies with a shake of his head. "Describe this dead man to me," he ordered.

Perry thought hard. "He was about fifty, heavy-set. He needed a shave. His hair was reddish, like he dyed it. He was wearing a yellow and brown checked sports coat and mustard-colored socks. He had a hole in his left shoe."

Nick went on alert. "What kind of shoe?"

"A brown loafer."

"You're sure there was a hole in the left sole?"

Perry nodded, then gripped by sudden memory said, "He had bushy hair in his nostrils and a mole on his chin."

"More than I needed to know," Jane murmured.

A heavy hand pounded on the front door and she jumped. Perry faded to the color of one of the corpses in his tough guy novels. "It's the police," he got out.

"No kidding. We called them, remember?" Since the other two seemed paralyzed, Nick rose and opened the door to the deputies.

Tired and grim, the two officers of the law regarded them.

"I feel I gotta ask. Were you folks drinking this evening?" questioned the senior partner. In his rain slicker and hat, he strongly resembled the Gorton Fisherman—after hauling up an empty net.

"We had a snort for medicinal purposes," Jane volunteered over Perry's indignant protest. "We weren't together all evening, so I can't say beyond that." She stretched comfortably, and the deputies' gazes trained on her gaping neckline.

The Gorton Fisherman harrumphed. "There's nobody upstairs. No body."

"I told you that much," Nick said. "What about the blood?"

"Who says it was blood? Could have been…mud."

"You seen a lot of blood?" the second deputy sheriff queried. He was younger and seemed more pugnacious about being dragged out on a wild-goose chase.

"Enough."

Perry said, "What about the scuff marks?"

"Scuff marks don't mean diddly," said the deputy. "And I didn't see any mud." He glanced at his partner. "Did you see any mud?"

"Nope. That tub was clean as a whistle. Like someone just scrubbed it down."

"What does that tell you?" Jane put in.

The older man eyed her calmly. "That someone just scrubbed it down." His dark eyes rested for a moment on the brandy bottle in the midst of the coffee table clutter.

Perry insisted, "There was a dead man in my bathtub. He didn't get there by accident."

"Maybe he wasn't dead," the sheriff said. "Maybe he was a vagrant and he left after you found him."

There were so many holes in that theory, Perry didn't know where to start. He protested, "My apartment was locked. How could he have got in?"

"How would a dead man get in? A vagrant would have a better chance of breaking in than a dead man."

Inescapable logic. Still Perry persisted. "But he *was* dead. Someone brought him in and took him away again so you wouldn't believe me."

"It didn't take *that*," the deputy said. The older officer gave him a reproving look.

"Listen," Reno said. "I didn't believe in that dead body myself, but I saw a streak of something in that tub that sure as hell appeared to be blood to me. And there were black marks, probably scuff marks, on the floor tiles. Also, Foster said the dead man was wearing a shoe with a hole in the sole. I found that shoe. I left it on the windowsill."

"We didn't see any shoe with a hole in it."

"Did you check the bedroom?"

"Sure. We weren't looking for footwear specifically."

"Did you see the shoe on the windowsill?"

The deputies exchanged doubtful looks.

"I didn't see any shoe," said the Gorton Fisherman. "You want to check for yourself," he added, "be my guest."

"I'll take your word for it," Jane said. She smothered a yawn and said to no one in particular, "Gentlemen, I hate to be a party pooper, but I need my beauty sleep." She made a lazy shooing motion, and the minions of the law obediently retreated further into the hall.

"You're damn right I'll see for myself," Perry said, rising. But he couldn't help checking to see if Nick was along for the ride.

Nick was on board all right. He marched up the stairs, kid and cops trailing, and let himself into the Foster boy's apartment for the second time that evening.

Perry followed him in, staring around the rooms like he'd never seen them before. The night was taking on a hallucinatory quality.

Granted, he was somewhat sleep deprived. He stared at his suitcase in the middle of the floor. It seemed a lifetime ago that he had walked out of Marcel's wood-framed Victorian and caught the plane back to Vermont.

He trailed Nick into the bathroom. Sure enough, the tub was empty—and sparkling clean.

Nick ran his fingers along the rim. "Damp," he commented. Perry stared at him. The deputies crowding the doorway also stared at him.

Pushing through them, Nick headed toward the bedroom, zeroing in on the windowsill.

A shoe stood in plain sight on the ledge. It was black, small—maybe a size 9—in good shape.

A muscle clenched in Nick's jaw as he examined the loafer. "This isn't the shoe."

"See for yourself, buddy. It's the only shoe here."

Nick tossed the shoe to Perry, who caught it and swallowed. "This is my shoe," he said as though he feared his shoe was guilty of some misdemeanor.

"Yep, that's what we figured."

"I thought you didn't notice any shoes?" Reno retorted.

"We didn't notice any *suspicious* shoes."

"Shut up, Abe," the older deputy muttered.

Nick started to speak, then bit it back. This was a losing proposition. The cops had made up their minds about twenty minutes earlier; that was plain.

He glanced at the kid, and it was obvious that Foster knew it was all over, although he was gazing at Nick expectantly. Why? What did he imagine Nick could do about this? Even if Nick wanted to do something about it.

He stared back, and the kid looked away, gritting his jaw. His hands were shaking and he shoved them into his pockets.

The deputies took their leave.

"We'll say good night, folks. Keep safe." The senior officer, last out the door, tipped the brim of his rain-spattered hat.

Nick caught the door before it closed on their heels. He glanced back at Perry Foster. The kid was focused on the tub, framed in the bathroom doorway.

The underbreath comments of the deputies died away with the sound of their boots on the staircase.

Situation defused, Nick thought. Rack time at last. "I guess that's it," he said. "I guess I'll say good night too."

Foster's head jerked his way. "You're going?"

"Yeah." Nick was elaborately casual in response to the note he didn't want to hear in Foster's voice. "It's all clear here."

Foster was a frail-looking kid. He lived on his own and presumably held a job, so he couldn't be fourteen, though that's how old he looked. His wrists were thin, and bony knees poked out of the holes of his fashionably ripped Levi's. There were blue veins beneath the pale skin of his hands. Nick thought of the Froot Loops cereal and the asthma chart on the refrigerator.

Hell.

"Thanks," Foster managed huskily. "I know you probably think I'm psycho too, so I appreciate your helping me."

"I don't think you're psycho." Actually he had no idea if the kid was psycho or not. "I think you saw something. But whatever it was, it's gone now. It's over."

Nick thought of the shoe with the hole in it; he should have noticed right away it was too big for a pup the size of Foster. Someone had switched that shoe after Nick left. Someone had swabbed down the tub and the floor. Someone had balls of steel. But it was not Nick's problem. It was not his job to save the world. Not anymore.

"Yeah, well…" The kid managed one unconvincing smile. "Maybe I can get a hotel room in town." He picked up his suitcase. "I don't want to stay here tonight."

Nick's nod was curt. Great idea. Best idea yet. Except… A gust of wind shook the house. The lights flickered. From across the room, Reno heard Foster give a soft gasp. His eyes looked enormous. Like Bambi after his mom bought it in the woods.

It was a dark and lousy night. Not a night to be out driving if you didn't have to. The radio crackled with weather advisories. Anyway, what kind of bastard would send an asthmatic kid out in a rainstorm?

"Hell," he growled. "You can stay with me tonight."

There was that wash of color in the pointed face. "I don't want to be any trouble," Foster said hopefully.

Nick snorted.

ABOUT THE AUTHOR

Author of over sixty titles of classic Male/Male fiction featuring twisty mystery, kickass adventure, and unapologetic man-on-man romance, JOSH LANYON'S work has been translated into eleven languages. Her FBI thriller *Fair Game* was the first Male/Male title to be published by Harlequin Mondadori, then the largest romance publisher in Italy. *Stranger on the Shore* (Harper Collins Italia) was the first M/M title to be published in print. In 2016 *Fatal Shadows* placed #5 in Japan's annual Boy Love novel list (the first and only title by a foreign author to place on the list). The Adrien English series was awarded the All Time Favorite Couple by the Goodreads M/M Romance Group.

She is an Eppie Award winner, a four-time Lambda Literary Award finalist (twice for Gay Mystery), An Edgar nominee, and the first ever recipient of the Goodreads All Time Favorite M/M Author award.

Josh is married and lives in Southern California.

Find other Josh Lanyon titles at www.joshlanyon.com Follow Josh on Twitter, Facebook, Goodreads, Instagram and Tumblr.

For extras and exclusives, join Josh on Patreon.

ALSO BY JOSH LANYON

NOVELS

The ADRIEN ENGLISH Mysteries

Fatal Shadows • A Dangerous Thing • The Hell You Say

Death of a Pirate King • The Dark Tide

Stranger Things Have Happened • So This is Christmas

The HOLMES & MORIARITY Mysteries

Somebody Killed His Editor • All She Wrote

The Boy with the Painful Tattoo

The ALL'S FAIR Series

Fair Game • Fair Play • Fair Chance

The A SHOT IN THE DARK Series

This Rough Magic

The ART OF MURDER Series

The Mermaid Murders • The Monet Murders

OTHER NOVELS

The Ghost Wore Yellow Socks • Mexican Heat (with Laura Baumbach)

Strange Fortune • Come Unto These Yellow Sands • Stranger on the Shore

Winter Kill • Jefferson Blythe, Esquire • Murder in Pastel

The Curse of the Blue Scarab

ALSO BY JOSH LANYON

NOVELLAS

The DANGEROUS GROUND Series

Dangerous Ground • Old Poison • Blood Heat
Dead Run • Kick Start

The I SPY Series

I Spy Something Bloody • I Spy Something Wicked
I Spy Something Christmas

The IN A DARK WOOD Series

In a Dark Wood • The Parting Glass

The DARK HORSE Series

The Dark Horse • The White Knight

The DOYLE & SPAIN Series

Snowball in Hell)

The HAUNTED HEART Series

Haunted Heart Winter

The XOXO FILES Series

Mummie Dearest

OTHER NOVELLAS

Cards on the Table • The Dark Farewell • The Darkling Thrush
The Dickens with Love • Don't Look Back • A Ghost of a Chance
Lovers and Other Strangers • Out of the Blue • A Vintage Affair
Lone Star (in Men Under the Mistletoe) • Green Glass Beads (in Irregulars)

ALSO BY JOSH LANYON

MORE NOVELLAS

Blood Red Butterfly • *Everything I Know*
Baby, It's Cold (in Comfort and Joy) • *A Case of Christmas*
Murder Between the Pages

SHORT STORIES

A Limited Engagement • *The French Have a Word for It*
In Sunshine or In Shadow • *Until We Meet Once More*
Icecapade (in His for the Holidays) • *Perfect Day* • *Heart Trouble*
In Plain Sight • *Wedding Favors* • *Wizard's Moon*
Fade to Black • *Night Watch*

COLLECTIONS

Short Stories (Vol. 1) • *Sweet Spot (the Petit Morts)*
Merry Christmas, Darling (Holiday Codas)
Christmas Waltz (Holiday Codas 2) • *I Spy...Three Novellas*
Point Blank (Five Dangerous Ground Novellas)
Dark Horse, White Knight (Two Novellas)
Boy Meets Body, Volume One • *Boy Meets Body, Volume Two*

HEARTFELT THANKS
TO MY PATRONS:

Susan Sorrentino

Brian Dulaney

Sabine Biedenweg

Matthew DeHaan

Everett Kennedy Weedin, Jr.

Miki Prenevost

Alan Diego

Kaitlyn Abdou

Jayne Muir

Maite Suppes

Cheryll Athorp

Linda Eisel

Susan Rethoret

Steve Leonard

Scott McCluskey

Audra Rickman

Neele

Andrea Karg

Marilyn Blimes

Alexa Ebanks

Cassie Poe

Nancy Fields

David D Warner

Jessica L Ranallo

Catherine Morden

Beatriz Vargas

Katarzyna Borkowska

Debra Guyette

Jillee Elizabeth Sexton

Christina Rodriguez

Alaska Black

Jennifer Taulbee

Reanna Fesler

Joan Walters

Natalia Locatelli

Dianne Thies

Carlita Costello

Susan Reinhart

Johanna Ollila

Catherine

Frances Burgess

Wendy Oshea

Esha Bhatia

Jennifer Vranek

Cynthia Hemme

Karin Wollina

Chrystalla Thoma

Jacqueline Tan

Dianalee Rode

Kendra Chambers

Peg McMahon

Alison Butler

Carole Lake

Debra Woods

J.H.

EL Kinnison

Mary Barzyk

Karla Ruksys

Susan Wilson

Rachel C Owens

Michelle Kidwell

Susan Lee

Janet Sidelinger

Stephanie Bogart

Amy Schaffer

Andy Slayde

Ikue Kawahara

Siobhan Maura Bidgood

Marge Cee

Savannah Barlow

Sarah Toney

Julie Geagan-Chevez

Denise Dernorsek

Diana Teaman

Richard Hanley

Mai Yamamoto

James Kennington

Adell Phillis

Sandy Athey

Gretchen Kessler

Paul Budrow

Leigh Ann Wallace

Laura C.

JS

Jocelyn Harner

Danielle Buscetta

Marilyn J Ciruso

Anne-Marie McRoberts

Katia

Anonymous

Catherine Dair

Bobbi Lyons

Stacy

Nancy Schneider

Kelly

Michelle Ivey

captain_dh

Ha T Nguyen

Nicholas

Natasha Chesterbrook

Shelby P.

Juliet Beier

Tracy Goodin

Queenie J. Alexander

Elle P.

TRUE Ryndes

Ina Husemann

Christine Skolnick

Jackie Davey

Anne Ystenes

Rebecca Espinosa

Deborah Graham

Marilyn Abbott

Maureen Moss

Emilie

Ariel Morse

Alice Viviano

Christy Duckett

Karen Reck

Jamell Howell

Frauke Franz

Halcyone

Nancy Andrews

Kate Sobejko

Kat Kelley

Lucas A. O.

John Pollock

Cheryl A Keller

Michelle Vuko

Ekaterina Suryeva

Marie-Claude Emond

Abby Dain

Nicholas Tay

Theresa Harper

Katerina Petrova Black Stilinski

CJ K

Brigitte Wissner

Brittany MacDougall

Erica Lome

L.J. Thomson

Susan Woolard

Emily Frampton

Sekiei

Miwa Nakano

ËÉ°Ê°É

Beth W Geibe

Nikki

Anka Mauderer

Barbara Grossbaum

Susan Hoffman

Barbara Heath

Michelle Marquez

Phyllis Howell

Tina Good

KM McCormack

Connie Parrott

Sandra Fröschl

Daniel J. Coll

Holly

Liza Shahin

Sophie Wittlinger

Masselyn

Robin Kemball

Colette

Karla

Anne Stark

Melody Crone

Jennifer Janke

Elizabeth Andrews

Helen McMahon

Ashi

Brenda Snyder

AC

Sue Zheng

Ebony Cindric

R. Ruiter

Jennifer S. Swanson

Danielle Desjardins

Asako Saitou

Kay

Katelyn Sweigart

Heather Hill

Jojo

Sue Brown

JD Jones

Maile V.

Brigette Burton

Shay Rizon

Rio

Sara Stanton

Madeline Menzer

Vicki Hood

Patricia Mason

Nancy Collins

Tamara Webb

Denise Kyazze

K Miller

Tara Raimondo

Stacie Stanley

RJS

Adrian Stuart

Kelsey

Anika

Heike Schindler

Liu Yunjia

Robert Anthony

Indy

Maia Brown

Annery Marte-McNulty

Amandine Huntzinger

Tina Burgess

Deb R.

Ashley P

Cristie L.

Lisa Baker

Brian Howard

Joanne Perry

Molly Moody

Amanda Lagarde

Suong Doan

Brooke Hudson

Hanh Nguyen

Glee

Daniela

Kelly Gibbons

Rizo Pilko

Patricia Mangahis

Tish Lopez

Liz Madrox

Anne Hoffman

MtSnow

Nicole Zeller

Rae S.

Wanderlust14

Mike Martinez

Lynne Clifford

Lisa

Nicole Gordon

Mandy

Emlyn Eisenach

Anke Lüpges

Jordan Sophia Lombard

Gillian

TJ Edwards

Kristin Tomic

Wardy

Sherrylynn

Natasha Snow

Don M

Eveline Lo

Cris Niccolini

Kate Ellis

Sue-Ellen Gower

Queenie C.

Clary

Gnine

Monique Ford

EirinElli

Jo Ann Cerula

Geraldine Austin

Susan McCormick

Molly Basney

Jennifer Ronca

Jessica Riskedahl

Kaori Ueki

Sarah Wh

Karen Koijane

Pierre Houle

Tracy Timmons-Gray

Jessica L Avila

Jocelyn Bissett

Alice Brewer
Jennie Goloboy
Stephanie Gomez
Leahjberg
A.R. Foitswagle
Hanna högberg
A Moncy
Natalia Levine
Ali Pearcy
Kenneth E Mierow
Mary Grimm

Claire Serafin
Jeremiah Chen
Clare McHale
Miriam Nightengale
Susan McKenna
Michelle Thorla
Patricia Hurckes
Catherine Yuen
Susanne Birk
Andrea Whiteside
Anastasia Tsakiroglou
Nicole
Heather York
Liz Cowan
Bekah Andrews
A Coll
Eria
Sheena
L S Serna
Kamineo
Stephan Patterson
Freja K.
Harshini
Diana Quilty
Jenna Vance

Amber Pippin
A. L. Lester
Kerrilee
Theresa L Daniels
TZ
Eileen O'Brien Kernan
Linda Mrowka
Jacqueline
Elise Ivey
Patricia Davisson
Whitney Wilkening
Rosa Nieto
AmePourtant
Brynne Lagaao
Philipp Schmidt
Martine Drouet
Jules Wildt
Sara Bond
Susan Cox
Sowmya B
Annie Tate
Maria MacSmith
Virginia Modugno
Penelope Oulton
Marina
Juli-Anna Dobson
Stephani Kuperschmid
Carmen
Rohini Karve
Julie Salverian
Cathy Weber
Nancy Canu
Amy Jarvis
Sarah Guest
Richelle McDaniel
Britta Ventura
Trio

Jennifer Keirans

Elizabeth Hayes

Laura E

Artemis K.

Marianne Ciaudo

Philippa Howe

Joan De Leon

Rebecca Barr

Carolyn Zoe Brouthers

W DEC

Sarah G.

Teal

Kari Gregg

Annika B√°hrmann

Anu

Katherine Smith

Anne

Jessica DuLong

Mody Bossy

Kimberly Good

Vanessa

Malus

Dalia Cao

Adrian Bisson

Terzak

Stara Herron

Ami Savitri

Veroluc

JD Ruskin

Justene Adamec

Joanne Goh Ai Chin

Nadine Bretz

Rena Freefall

Clare London

Jacob Magnusson

Jennifer Collyer

Kevin Burton Smith

Marina Gonchar

Bambi White

Alienor Drasen

Made in the USA
Columbia, SC
07 March 2021